Call Down the Moon

by

Mary Gillgannon

The Soulmate Series

Call Down the Moon

Cover Art by *Angela Anderson*

The Wild Rose Press, Inc.
PO Box 708
Adams Basin, NY 14410-0708
Visit us at www.thewildrosepress.com

Publishing History
First Faery Rose Edition, 2014
Print ISBN 978-1-62830-664-4
Digital ISBN 978-1-62830-665-1

The Soulmate Series
Published in the United States of America

"It always amazes me how busy everyone is all the time," she went on. "Doesn't anyone ever relax and enjoy the simple pleasures of life? Like taking a walk at sunset, like we just did."

"That is true," he responded. "The simple things, being with the people you care about, that is what matters."

I love you, Allison. You are all that matters. He willed her to believe it. To feel what was in his heart. As soon as he kissed her, she would remember what they'd shared. Both in this life and in the past. At least he hoped so.

She turned down Mark's street. This was it. Everything depended on this.

Would he kiss her? Allison wondered. Should she let him?

Of course she should. She'd had a bit of a freak out, but it was over now. Whatever had happened at the reservoir wasn't real. Or anything to worry about. This was real. This man beside her. She'd made love with him a bunch of times already. Been as close to him as she'd ever been to anyone. During all those experiences, she'd never felt frightened or uneasy. Indeed, the opposite was true. Sex had never felt so right, so much like it was meant to be.

If she was having a past life experience, well then that was exactly what it was. A *past* life. It didn't have anything to do with the here and now.

Dedication

To Patrick, my Irish hero for all time

Chapter One

Ninth Century Ireland

The Nine Sisters danced upon the hillside. Light from the Seed Moon revealed their long flowing hair—raven black, blood red, gold and silver. It shone on their nakedness, young and old flesh shaped into the flowing lines of the Earth Goddess herself. Their bodies gleamed as they writhed and whirled, calling on the Ancient Ones.

Aisling stood in the center of the circle of women. Whorls of black and crimson marked her breasts and belly, while serpent shapes encircled her arms and ankles. Her skin felt heavy, as if the patterns covering her had substance, as if they were not merely dyes from earth and plants. Her body tingled and her nipples felt hard. Her lower belly and thighs burned with a heat that defied the cool night air.

Aisling took a deep breath. Her night. Her initiation. Although she had watched the Sisters dance many times before, she had never been part of the circle. She feared the gods would not speak to her. Even more, she feared they would pronounce for her some future she could not endure.

The dance grew more frantic. The women wove in and out, a ribbon of pulsing flesh. They formed circles within the circle. Three sets of three, the sacred number.

The whirling dancers bound Aisling in place in the center of the magic. The tension built. The night air crackled with energy, fierce as lightning. Their voices rang out in eerie exhortation and they ended the dance with arms stretched to the sky, long hair streaming down their backs.

A few heartbeats passed. Then they approached Aisling and guided her to the fire on the other side of the hill. As she reached it, Aisling turned and saw her companions' sweat-slicked faces, lit by the orange gold flames. They looked weary, empty. Maebbina, the oldest, took Aisling's arm firmly and guided her to a caldron near the fire. "Look," she said. "Look in the scrying bowl."

Aisling bent over the cauldron, heart hammering. She stared at the oily surface shining in the firelight. At first, she saw nothing. Nothing but blackness, the reflection of firelight, and her own face. She knew a sharp disappointment, mingled with relief. The magic didn't work. Everything was real and ordinary. She stiffened as something in the orb of liquid began to swell and grow. There was another light there, softer, grayer. Silver instead of the gold of the fire. It was filled with shapes. The sheen of armor and flash of weapons caught her eye. "Warriors," she murmured.

The women near her whispered with excitement. Aisling watched as the shapes in the cauldron grew nearer, filling her vision. The warriors were all around her. She could hear the clank and rattle of their weapons, smell the scent of them. Dust and sweat, and man. Their long hair flowed over their shoulders. Their hands stood ready on their weapons. Their hot breath covered her.

One of them grasped her wrist and fixed her with a piercing look, his eyes like the glowing green depths of a shadowed forest pool. "Aisling, my love," he whispered.

****

Denver 2012

"Guess what? I got my first magazine assignment! Isn't that great?" Allison Hunter sank down in a chair across from her best friend Megan in the crowded outdoor café. She dug in her bag for a hairband, then pulled her shoulder-length blonde locks up into a ponytail and secured it. "It's so hot. I feel like I'm melting."

"We'll get you a nice cold daiquiri to cool you off." Megan signaled for a waiter and then leaned over the table. "Now, tell me about this writing job."

"It's for *The Highpoint*. I know it's only a small regional magazine, but it's a beginning. And it sounds like a lot more fun than the technical writing I've been doing."

"That's fabulous. I knew free-lancing would work out for you."

Allison nodded. "The thing is, I may need some help, at least on the local angle. The article is supposed to be about the Wiccan/neo-pagan scene in Denver." She smiled coaxingly at her friend. "You mentioned once you were into that sort of thing."

Megan quirked an eyebrow, then sat back in her chair as the waiter brought Allison's daiquiri. "Go ahead, fire away. What do you want to know? What they believe? Who they are? How they practice the craft?"

"You're serious about this, aren't you?" Allison

asked, a little surprised.

Megan shrugged. "For work, I have to project a professional image or the agency's clients would never take me seriously. But when I take down my hair and put on a long flowing dress, I turn into a veritable pagan goddess."

"When did you get involved in Wicca?" Allison asked.

"High school. I was kind of wild then. Got into the whole Goth thing. You should have seen me in knee-high boots and a long black cape. At one time, I even dyed my hair black."

"I bet that was something." Allison raised her eyebrows in mock horror and motioned to Megan's dark red hair and ultra-pale skin. "You absolutely *don't* have the coloring for black hair."

Megan grinned. "Didn't you do anything crazy as a teenager?"

"Not me. I was a good girl. I never had the nerve to dabble in anything like that."

"A pity," Megan said. "You'll probably end up doing it later. Have a mid-life crisis and leave your husband and kids to go to a Buddhist ashram or something. I'm firmly convinced everyone has to indulge the mad, impulsive part of themselves or it stays inside them and festers. It has to come out sooner or later. If not in this life, then in the next one."

"Is that part of Wicca—believing in reincarnation?"

"Not necessarily, but since we're all connected to the great circle of life and a person's spirit never dies, it makes a lot of sense to me."

Allison took a swallow of her drink. "This is heavy

stuff. How am I supposed to condense all these intense spiritual ideas down into a fun, hip article?"

"They probably want sensational crap, stories about animal sacrifice and devil worship." Megan's mouth twisted. "So many people misunderstand the Wicca movement. It's only nature worship. What's so bad about believing we're all connected to the earth and its energy?"

"It sounds innocent enough to me. But you know how people are about religion. People have died over this sort of thing."

Megan nodded grimly. "That's true, all too true." She was silent for a time, then said, "I don't think I'm the person you should be talking to about this. I know a much better source."

"Who?"

"This guy I know."

Allison groaned.

"No, no, hear me out," Megan continued. "His name's Connar, and I swear, he's knows everything there is to know about the craft, at least the Celtic aspects. And he looks the part as well, like an Irish prince out of the legends." She leaned near, hazel eyes sparkling. "Long dark hair. Piercing green eyes. Tall. Great body. I could easily see him wielding a sword, slaying a dragon or something."

"You seem quite taken with him."

Megan sat back in her chair and shook her head. "Strictly one-sided, I'm afraid. He's always polite, but I never feel any sparks coming from him."

"Maybe he's gay," Allison suggested.

"No, he doesn't set off my 'gaydar' at all. I think it's more likely he got hurt by some bitch who didn't appreciate him and now he's playing it cool when it comes to women."

"Well, I'm not doing an article on lovelorn singles. If I were, I could find plenty of material in my own life." Allison repressed a sigh. "Are you sure you couldn't tell me what I need to know so I could skip interviewing this Connar guy?"

Megan smiled one of her little Cheshire cat smiles. "If this is your first article, you need the best source possible. And Connar knows absolutely everything about Wicca. All the myths and lore and philosophy, spells and incantations. He's like a walking New Age encyclopedia."

Allison narrowed her eyes at her friend. "I smell a set-up here. But if you won't help me, I guess I don't have a choice. So, where do I find Connar, the Irish prince? If I'm going to make my deadline, I've got start on this story right away."

"He runs a Wicca craft store on East Colfax."

"Oh, East Colfax. Great neighborhood."

"I'm sure the rent is cheap and he doesn't have to worry about being harassed. The hookers and winos aren't going to care about anyone's religious affiliation. And there *are* some decent establishments in the area— small theaters, art and poster shops and the like. You need to get out more, Allison. You're turning into a hermit, spending all your time in your apartment with your cat."

"Benjamin's good company."

"Right. But he's only a cat. I'm sure there are some needs of yours he can't fulfill." Megan raised her brows suggestively.

"I'm trying to get my career going. I don't need the

complication of a guy in my life."

"You mean you're afraid to even consider the possibility."

"Can you blame me? Justin burned me bad." Allison insides twisted. She'd never forget the shock and humiliation of coming home and finding her fiancé in bed with their cute teen-age neighbor. It had torn her up, broken her heart. And the worst of it was that she'd moved to Denver because Justin had wanted to, uprooted her whole life for the sneaky, manipulative bastard. Just thinking about it made her feel sick.

"You can't let one guy sour you on the whole sex. So what if Justin was a total jerk. There's other fish in the sea."

Allison shook her head. "I'm afraid I don't have very good karma with men—to use one of your New Age terms. I try to get interested in the nice, stable, reliable types, but they never make it happen for me. No, stupid me, I'm attracted to the exciting, dangerous ones, the bad boys." She rolled her eyes. "Which is why I've decided to avoid the whole dating scene for a while."

"It could get awfully lonely."

Allison leaned across the table, her voice intent. "I've made up my mind about this. Even if I do meet a guy I really like, I'm going to play it cool for a long time. I'm not going to fall for that 'sexual chemistry' crap ever again. It's only hormones, after all."

Megan gave a throaty laugh. "Ah, what wonderful schemes we come up with to change our lives. I wonder if it even matters. Maybe it's all predestined anyway. Maybe there's someone out there for each of us. A perfect soul mate waiting for us to enter their life."

Allison reached across the table and scooted Megan's half-full glass away from her. "That's enough margaritas for you, honey. They're starting to affect your brain!"

****

It was broad daylight, but Allison still felt a little uneasy venturing into the East Colfax neighborhood alone. She saw a homeless guy sleeping it off near the rundown Wendy's, and a gay couple strolling down the street arm-in-arm, their shaved heads a perfect match. She was acutely aware of how boringly normal she must look. That was her, a blonde, blue-eyed W.A.S.P. from America's heartland. She hated being such a cliché, and she knew it put some people off. They thought she must be insipid and dull, a mindless Barbie doll. Even Megan had taken awhile to warm up to her when Allison worked as a temp at the ad agency when she first moved to Denver.

"I thought you were so 'white-bread' when I met you," Megan had said. "I was surprised to discover you have a sense of humor and a brain."

Allison suspected she and Megan had bonded because of her romantic situation. As soon as Megan found out she was a *woman done wrong*, Megan had made it her personal mission to see that Allison got her life back together. Bless her for that. What would she have done without someone to turn to, someone willing to take her out and get her drunk and then let her cry her eyes out?

But she was done moping. From now on, she was going to concentrate on her career. Be practical. Sensible. Careful. Ditch all those stupid notions about love making the world go round.

She passed another unconscious wino. This guy was so utterly still and unmoving, she worried he was dead. She shuddered as she passed him and then immediately spotted her goal. The Magic Cauldron. An ordinary-looking storefront with a sign featuring a black cauldron with a Celtic symbol on the side. Relieved to have reached her destination, she hurried to the entrance and pushed open the door. A bell chimed as she entered.

****

She is here. My beloved Aisling.

Connar MacDonal's whole being came alive as the woman entered the shop. He'd been aware of her since she'd left her car, and had felt her coming closer and closer. He'd feared she would walk right past, and he'd have to follow her and make up some excuse to engage her in conversation. But, unbelievably, she had entered the shop. As if she were here to see him, as if she knew, as he did, that she was his soulmate, the core of his heart, the woman he had traveled a thousand years through time to hold in his arms.

Of course, she didn't know who he was. Siobhan had warned him Aisling wouldn't have any memory of her past life. How could she? All those years her spirit had lingered in the Otherworld, waiting to be reborn. Everything she once had been and felt and known would have faded from her mind. Even their love. And yet, as she approached him, he couldn't help hoping against hope that somehow she would remember.

She moved down the aisle of the shop, glancing around, as if looking for something. He held his breath, unable to speak or move. His whole body vibrated, thrilling to her nearness. She approached the counter, smiling. "You must be Connar," she said. "I didn't see you standing there when I first came in."

She knew his name! He was speechless with wonder. Maybe Siobhan was wrong! Maybe…

"I'm Allison Hunter," she continued. "My friend Megan told me about you. Said you were exactly who I needed to talk to."

Their gazes met. He waited for her to respond, to recognize him, to feel the love, the connection, the unbelievably intense bond they had once shared. Nothing happened. If anything, she seemed to withdraw.

He felt as if he had been struck a blow, but he forced himself to focus on her words. She'd said Megan had sent her. Megan? He wracked his brain and finally recalled a woman with wavy red hair and a mischievous smile. She'd come into the shop a few times, and he'd talked to her at the pagan gathering in the mountains last summer. He'd discussed Celtic mysticism with her, but he was always careful about how much he said. If anyone ever expressed amazement at his knowledge of past practices, he always joked that he must have learned it in a past life.

Abruptly, he realized he hadn't responded to Aisling's greeting. Her smile was beginning to look forced. In another moment, she might leave. He cleared his throat, struggling to assume the persona he'd taken on in this era. "Yes, I'm Connar. I'm sorry. I didn't mean to look at you strangely, but you remind me so strongly of someone I knew in the past."

"Oh. I've experienced that a few times myself." The smile was back, but she was still nervous, fidgeting with the strap of her purse. She looked around the shop, then back at him. "The reason I'm here is because I'm a free-lance writer doing an article on Wicca and the pagan movement in Denver. Megan said you'd be able to tell me a lot."

She looked so sweet and tentative. It took all his will not to rush from behind the counter and pull her into his arms. Although he knew he should offer her his hand, he didn't dare. If he touched her, he would explode.

She glanced again at the crowded shelves of the store. "You have an interesting selection of merchandise."

He took a deep breath. "We try to cater to a variety of Wiccan practices."

She turned to look at him, blue eyes expectant. "Do you own the shop? Mister...?"

"Connar MacDonal Dunsheana is my full name, but you can call me Connar." He waited for a flicker of memory in her eyes. When there was none, his heart sank. Then, remembering her question, he added, "Yes, I do own the shop."

"Are you originally from Ireland? You have a bit of accent, but it's not the typical brogue."

He nodded, thinking a person couldn't be much more "originally from Ireland" than he was. Time travel was an imperfect form of magic, and Siobhan had only been able to guess at the year in which Aisling would return. He'd arrived in Denver two years ago and spent the time since acquiring the language and adapting to modern life. The growing pagan subculture had been a real blessing. Much of their beliefs and practices came directly from his own time, so it was easy for him to blend in. He used the gold jewelry he'd brought from the past to finance the shop, then sat back to wait. Siobhan had promised Aisling would someday appear in his life, and that the spell she'd worked in the ninth century would eventually bring them together, though it would be up to him to make her fall in love with him a second time.

Something he'd better keep in mind. He couldn't keep getting caught up in his own thoughts and letting the conversation lapse. Affecting a heavy brogue, he said, "Aye, I'm a Gael through and through. But I was but a wee thing when I left the blessed isle, so my native tongue has gotten a bit rusty, it has."

When she laughed at his jest, the sound was like exquisite music. How he'd missed that beautiful laugh. Their eyes met once more, and she looked away nervously. Pulling a cell phone out of her purse, she said. "Do you mind if I ask you a few questions?"

"Of course not. Ask me anything you'd like."

She nodded. After attaching a small mike to her phone, she set it on the counter. "Tell me about the store. Your merchandise."

He answered some basic questions, then moved from behind the counter and began to talk about the objects lining the shelves—spell books, wands, candles, crystals, jewelry, robes and cloaks. He explained the things, their uses and some of the beliefs involved, all the while thinking how naïve people of this era were in expecting these crude, mass-produced objects to be able to conjure the sublime and magical.

She held her phone close as he talked, her expression curious and interested. He told himself that for now he should simply enjoy her presence, savor her beauty, the sound of her voice, the scent of her skin, which he could detect despite the subtle perfume she wore. It was wonderful to be near her, even if it didn't satisfy his deeper yearnings.

When they reached the shelves where the cauldrons were kept, she said, "About the logo for your shop—what does it mean?"

"It's a symbol of transformation and plenty...like the cornucopia, the Greek symbol of abundance. In many traditional tales, one thing goes into a cauldron and another comes out. In other stories an enchanted cauldron provides an inexhaustible source of food."

"Why did you use it as a logo for your shop?"

"It seemed like a benign and positive image. A lot of pagan symbols either have negative connotations, or they were adopted by early Christians and have come to mean something else."

She nodded, glancing around the shop. While her gaze was directed away from him, he drank in the extraordinary details of her beauty. The way she pursed her full lips in concentration, the delicate line of her cheek and jaw, the whorl of her dainty, shell-like ear, visible beneath her upswept dark golden hair. Every minute aspect of her thrilled him. To think he'd once thought her lost forever.

"Well," she said, "That about covers the merchandise. But I want to know more about your rituals and beliefs. So much of society sees Wicca as dark and creepy, some sort of devil worship. I know that's not true..." She gave him a quick, sympathetic look. "But you know how people are, afraid of the unknown. If you could describe more about what you believe in, how you interpret things like life and death, the big issues."

She gazed up at him, looking so beautiful he could hardly bear it. It seemed like a perfect opportunity to explain. To tell her life and death were *not* absolute. To reveal what they shared in her past life, and how he had traveled across time to be with her.

But he remembered Siobhan's warning. "Don't expect too much of her. Although she possesses Aisling's soul, she's lived a whole different life. Her world is nothing like the one you knew her in. If you tell her too soon, you may frighten her. She could close off her spirit from you and never let you near. You could lose her all over again."

The thought terrified him. Siobhan was right. He had to go slowly. Let things between them develop naturally. He needed to make her fall in love with him—in this century. It was the only safe course of action. He couldn't be impatient and risk ruining everything. But how to proceed? He needed to spend more time with her. But not here. He needed a more relaxed, intimate setting. A date—that was the first step in getting to know a woman in this time period.

He smiled at her. "My beliefs are complicated. It might take a while to explain them. Maybe we could get together for dinner and talk more then."

He held his breath as she considered this. A slight frown marred her brow and a shadow darkened her blue-gray eyes. This wasn't the open, trusting Aisling he remembered—the woman who approached him so fearlessly the first time they had met. This Aisling was much more cautious and wary. She reminded him of a wild doe. One wrong move and she might go bounding away forever.

"Well," she said, "I suppose we could do that. But I

have to finish the article this weekend."

"We could get together tonight." His heart pounded.

"Tonight?"

He nodded.

"So we can talk about your beliefs? Right?"

"Or whatever else you'd like to talk about."

He watched her flush, her fair skin taking on the hue of a wild rose as she realized he was asking her out, rather than simply setting up another time for her to interview him.

Careful. Don't go too fast.

"I guess so," she answered. "Maybe we could meet somewhere."

Why was she so reluctant? She was obviously attracted to him. It showed in the way she held her body, the way she glanced at him when she thought he wasn't looking. Besides, it was impossible she didn't desire him. She was Aisling, his soulmate.

"What time would you like to meet?"

"Ummm. Seven?"

"Fine. You name the place."

"I go to Lo Do a lot. Parking can be a problem, but there are lots of fun places to eat."

"Wherever you'd like."

She smiled tentatively. "I always have trouble deciding on a restaurant. Maybe we could meet at the Tattered Cover Bookstore and go from there. It's a big place, so why don't we say we'll meet in…the history section."

Her eyes met his. The shock of remembered passion shot through him. He couldn't help himself. He had to touch her.

15

"It's a date," he said, extending his hand. He grasped her delicate flesh, and the past came rushing back in exquisite agony. The feel of her. Soft skin. Slender, cool fingers. How could he ever let her go?

"Until tonight." With all his will, he forced himself to release her.

"Until tonight," she murmured faintly. Then she quickly slipped down the aisle and out the door. He immediately went to the glass window of the shop and watched her walk down the street. She stopped once, turned around, and looked back at the shop. Her manner suggested she was confused. Or, maybe afraid.

"By Anu, the Great Mother Goddess," he whispered. "Please don't let her fear me. Give me a chance to love her, to make her remember."

Sighing, he returned to the counter. Taking out his keys from the drawer below the register, he went to the door and locked it, feeling like a sleepwalker. Somehow, he had to prepare himself for tonight, for the unbearable experience of being in her presence and having to observe the rules of twenty-first century social interaction. How long before he could touch her again? How long until he could hold her in his arms? How long before he could join his body with hers?

He was trembling. Somehow, he had to get a grip on himself. He took several long, deep breaths. Then he went into the back room of the shop. Walking past shelves of merchandise, he reached his sanctuary. There was a low table there, covered with candles. He lit them all, and then sat down on the carpeted area in front of the table. Rowan, the petite college student who helped him in the shop, probably thought he performed rituals here. But it was much simpler than that. He'd set up this place as a retreat, an escape from the oppressiveness of the modern world.

He closed his eyes and banished the concrete and steel realm surrounding him. Conjured up the familiar green, glowing landscape. Timeless rolling hills spread out before him. Trees. Rocks. Mist. Earth. The Goddess's body. Her spirit filling him and soothing him. The scent of growing things, of rain and sun. Home. The place where his heart lived. Where he would take Aisling someday, once he had her back.

The memories filled his mind…

He urged the two roan mares to a faster pace. The wooden wheels of the chariot bounced over the rutted ground and the horses' enameled harnesses jangled loudly. The herdsman had told him the Nine Sisters dwelled in a cave four valleys away. He glanced down at his foster brother, lying unconscious in the bottom of the chariot. Despite the cool spring air, Fergal's skin was flushed. The bones in his wasted face looked as though they might poke through the skin.

Connar quickly looked away. The herdsman said the Nine Sisters could do magic and had abilities far beyond any normal healers. He prayed it was true.

He guided the chariot down a ridge into a narrow valley dotted with clumps of hazel. As the ground grew soft and marshy, Connar halted the team. They could go no further without foundering the vehicle. As a soft rain began to fall, he drew his woolen bratt over his head and rearranged the sheepskins and furs to keep the dampness off his foster brother. As he bent near, he caught the rank odor of putrefied flesh and struggled to ignore the despairing thought that filled his mind: Why am I bothering? He's going to die.

Straightening, he clutched at the side of the chariot. He's come this far and defied both his father's and Fergal's wishes. He would not give up. He would find the Nine Sisters and they would save his foster brother.

He glanced again at the unconscious man. "Fool," he muttered. "If only you hadn't gone charging into that thicket. I told you to wait until the boar broke into the open. I told you even a trophy animal wasn't worth risking your life over."

He gritted his teeth as he endured the horror of it all over again: Fergal's defiant dash into the thicket. His scream of fear and pain. The horrifying sight of him lying on the ground, his leg torn open to the bone.

He shook off the image. There was no point reliving the past.

Perhaps he should set out on foot and search for the cave that way. But the shepherds had warned him the healing women shunned men, especially warriors, and were unlikely to show themselves. Maybe he should leave Fergal here and hope the healing women would find him. But what if they didn't? Fergal would end up as carrion for the wolves. He couldn't risk it.

Leaning against the side of the chariot, he tried to decide what to do. When he looked up again, a mist was moving slowly into the valley. It floated along the ground, like a cat slinking through the grass, then wafted upwards and curled arm-like tendrils around him, veiling everything in soft whiteness. The wreaths of vapor grew denser, until he could scarcely see his hand in front of him. A prickling sensation started along his spine as he recalled the shepherd saying the Sisters used a mist to guard their secret cave. Did that mean he was close?

He walked a few paces, trying to see something beyond the whiteness. One of the horses neighed. The sound seemed to come from far away. A shiver stole over him. He slowly made his way back to the vehicle and sank down next to Fergal. The Nine Sisters must know he was here. Would they come to his aid? Or leave him here, helpless and lost? He might end up trapped in this enchanted realm forever.

Somehow, despite his fear, he slept. When he woke, he was disoriented. He shook his head, then realized the mist was gone and two women stood waiting a few paces away. They were young and comely. Hardly the aged crones he'd expected. One of the women had black hair, the other, dark golden tresses the color of mead. Both were tall and fine-boned, graceful as roe deer.

The fair-haired one approached him. He had never seen such perfection in a woman. Her features seemed carved from ivory. Her eyes as deep blue as the twilight sky. Her mouth, the pink hue glimpsed in the depths of an abalone shell. She spoke. "Your companion sinks deeper and deeper into realm of death. You must bring him now, before it's too late."

Recalling the reason he'd come, Connar knelt down and hoisted Fergal onto his shoulders. The women walked away and he struggled to follow. After a few steps, he turned and looked back. The mist had risen again, and he could no longer see the chariot. The realization unsettled him, but he told himself he must trust the Sisters. Surely no one as lovely as the fair-haired woman could mean him ill.

They led him deeper into the valley, through a

narrow defile. He followed them into an ancient oak grove. Massive trees stood like sentinels all around. He sensed them watching him, their shuddering leaves whispering of his approach.

The oaks gave way to ash and rowan, then scrub and bramble. Among the ferns and moss a small stream sang and trilled among the rocks. The weight upon his shoulders seemed to lighten. The path grew boggy and the air dense. The dark reek of decay came to his nostrils and the lovely stream gave way to fetid marsh. In the silent pools, he seemed to see faces. Eyes and noses, gaping mouths. Spirits, he thought. The agonized countenances of those who met their deaths here.

A deep dread overtook him, and he looked around frantically for the women. Ahead in the green-tinged gloom, the fair-haired woman turned and gestured. He took a deep breath and moved toward her. The pathway was still treacherous, but gradually the ground became solid. The two women led him to an opening in the hillside, with a massive carved stone lintel.

A shudder passed down his body and stories from childhood crowded his thoughts. Of babies stolen by fairies and traded for changelings. Of men who fell in love with beautiful ban sidhe and disappeared forever. He froze in place, wondering if his soul was already lost.

The beautiful fair-haired Sister beckoned once more, her expression tender and full of concern. He started toward the cave opening, bending low with his burden as he followed her in.

Chapter Two

Allison paused on the sidewalk outside The Magic Cauldron and let out a deep breath. "Pull yourself together," she told herself sternly. "You promised you wouldn't do this. Ignore your hormones. Use your brain. Stay rational."

She started walking again, firmly putting one foot ahead of the other. She would not think about how the mere touch of Connar's hand had sent chills of excitement down her body, or about how gorgeous he was. She'd barely even met the guy. He could easily be some sort of weirdo. He owned a Wicca store, after all.

Her attempts to dampen her body's reaction didn't seem be working. She still felt weak and quivery.

When Megan said Connar was good-looking, she wasn't kidding. Long, thick, glossy dark hair. Sculpted features. Beautiful, long-lashed green eyes. And, amazingly, his looks didn't seem fake. He had the broad-shouldered muscular build that came from doing physical work, not lifting weights in a gym. And the faint bronze sheen to his skin looked like a real tan, not the perfect coloration that came from a salon. She'd also noticed a faint scar on his neck. It must be three inches long. If he were seriously into his looks, he would have covered it up or had it zapped with a laser. Maybe he was just a regular guy after all.

Yeah, right. And, he had some swamp land in

Florida he'd be willing to sell her for cheap. She had to be rational about this. This guy was too good to be true. There was bound to be a catch. Tonight, she'd figure out what it was.

A date. Damn. She'd sworn she wouldn't do this. But she did need to talk to him some more to get the information for her article. It wasn't a date; it was business meeting. Megan said Connar had never shown the slightest interest in her or any other women she knew. Clearly, his suggestion they get together had no hidden romantic sub-text. He was merely being friendly, trying to help her out with her article.

But her body didn't believe that. Her body was responding as if Connar had pulled her into his arms and kissed her breathless.

Oh, my!

She unlocked her car and got in, then took out her cell phone and dialed Megan.

"Hey, it's Allison."

"Hi. Did you change your mind about going out with me tonight? There's a new club near the 16th Street Mall and I thought we could—"

"Actually, I have plans. Connar asked me to meet him so we could talk some more about Wicca."

"Really?" Megan purred.

"It's not what you think. He's just being nice."

"Uh-huh."

"Well, I'm sure that's what it is. You said he doesn't seem that interested in women."

"So." Megan's voice was coy. "If you think it's only a business meeting, why are you calling me? To ask my permission?"

"Well, no. I guess I thought I should find out more

about him before we get together. Just to be safe, you know."

"Where are you meeting?"

"I suggested the Tattered Cover. We can decide where to go from there."

"A bookstore?"

"It seemed neutral and safe."

"Why are you so worried about this guy?" Megan asked. "I swear he's not a crazed serial killer. I know him well enough to be certain of that."

"Well, of course, he's not. I didn't mean that. I guess, I..." Allison took a deep breath. "The thing is I already like him too much. And I promised myself I wouldn't get involved with anyone for a while."

"Ah, so you really don't think it's a business meeting after all."

"I don't know. I mean, my instincts tell me...but since when can I trust my instincts?" Allison laughed weakly.

"Stop sweating it. Have fun. See what happens. Even if it is a date, who cares? Go with the flow."

Megan made it sound so simple. And maybe it was. After all, she wasn't even sure Connar was actually interested in her. She'd probably blown the whole thing out of proportion. "You're right. A date means nothing these days. No commitment. No expectations. And besides, I truly do need more information for my article. Like you said, he's a regular walking encyclopedia on this Wicca stuff."

"Sounds like a plan, girl. Hey, Allison, I have to go. I've still got work to do here at the office. But be sure and call me tomorrow and let me know how it went."

"Okay." Allison let out a deep breath. "Tomorrow. Then we can laugh about what an idiot I was to even think I had a problem."

She clicked the phone shut, started the car and eased onto the street. As usual, the traffic was crazy. At this rate, she'd get home about two this afternoon. She'd have time to go over her notes for her article for a few hours, maybe even write the intro. Then she'd get ready. Another worry loomed. What was she going to wear?

****

Allison carefully climbed the stairs to the upper level of the Tattered Cover Bookstore in her new high-heeled sandals. Her pulse was racing, her mouth dry. She couldn't remember the last time she'd been this nervous. What was it about this guy?

She reached the second floor and approached the history section. A quick glance revealed it was empty. She let out a sigh. Maybe he wouldn't show. That would be just her luck.

She paced around for a while, trying to relax and warm up. The place was well air-conditioned, and she was freezing in her sundress. What a stupid thing to wear. She should have chosen something sensible and business-like. Why hadn't she? Because in a part of her mind, she wanted this to be a date.

I want him to be attracted to me.

She shook her head at her own foolishness. It hadn't even been a month and here she was, breaking all the rules she'd set up for herself.

Her nerves were jangling. Somehow she had to get a hold of herself. She went over to the Irish section and began to browse. A book on the archaeology of the island caught her eye. She picked it up and began to flip through it. Fascinating stuff. All those tombs and standing stones. What had motivated those people to build such amazing monuments? Probably some kind of religious belief system. Was it the same one that inspired Wicca?

She put down the book and took out her phone. It was after six. He wasn't going to show. Something had come up. Something—or someone—more interesting than her.

She exhaled sharply, feeling a mixture of disappointment and relief. It was better this way, really it was. Fate was saving her from herself. The gods had looked down on her and said, this girl is headed for disaster. We've got to help her. Keep her from making another idiotic mistake.

Then she thought about her article. She needed a lot more material. If Connar didn't show, what was she going to do?

****

Connar paused outside the bookstore and forced himself to take deep, even breaths. How was he going to manage this? To be so close to her, and yet force himself to behave as if they were strangers? To restrain himself from touching her when every particle of his being screamed to be joined with her? It would be agony, torture. And yet, he had to exercise control. He didn't want to frighten her or make her uneasy. She might be his soulmate, but she didn't know it yet.

And he couldn't tell her. Not for a while. She'd never believe him. With a line like that, she'd think he was crazy, maybe dangerous. A stalker. He had to be very careful. Try to act normal.

But what was normal in this situation? If things went well at dinner, was he allowed to invite her back to his place? Dare he expect more than a kiss good night? Ah, to touch her, caress her, hold her in his arms. To make love to her. Surely once they were joined, she would have some memory of what they'd meant to each other in another lifetime.

How did most men go about these things? He knew there were books on this situation—how to pick up women and get them into bed. Maybe he should have done some research. But a part of him hadn't truly believed this day would ever come. Siobhan had promised he would see Aisling again, but when he'd arrived in the right time period and there had been no sign of her for months, he'd begun to have doubts. By now, over two years later, he'd almost given up hope.

"Excuse me." A young man motioned to indicate Connar was blocking the entrance to the store.

"Sorry," Connar murmured. As he stepped aside and watched the man enter, he considered following him and asking for advice.

This is my first date with her. What do I do?

The man would find his question very odd. And he didn't have time to wait for the answer. He was already late. Taking another deep breath, he opened the door and went in.

"My apologies for being late."

Allison got up from the chair as Connar walked up. "Oh, that's all right," she responded. "Traffic can be terrible." Damn, he was good-looking. The simple, collarless white shirt he wore set off his coloring and dramatic features to perfection. The black jeans, cinched at the waist with a leather belt with a Celtic style buckle, showed off his long legs and narrow hips. Yum.

She motioned to the book she'd been using to distract herself. "I can always find ways to entertain myself in a bookstore."

"Are you interested in Ireland?"

"Well, a lot of this is modern history, which doesn't do much for me."

"You like ancient times better?" Connar's expression brightened. It made him look even more incredible. His eyes were the shade of the moss that grew around the trees back home. Vivid, intense green. Unreal.

"Yeah, I guess. Life must have been simpler back then."

"Life is never simple." A look of sadness crossed his face. Allison was startled. Clearly, this man had experienced real disappointment and pain. The idea was reassuring. It made him seem human and vulnerable. Maybe he wasn't some god-like paragon after all.

"Where would you prefer to eat?" he asked.

"Maybe somewhere with outdoor dining, since it's such a nice night. I don't know the names of the restaurants around here, but we can walk around and see if we can find a place that looks interesting and isn't too crowded."

Connar smiled. "That would be ideal. I'm not familiar with this area either." He motioned. "After you."

She started for the stairs, walking carefully.

"I don't know how you walk in those shoes," he said.

She turned, laughing, and was startled by how

close he was. "It's a challenge." She kept walking. Her heart was beating much too fast. All she could think of was how big he was. How male.

Downstairs, he held the door as they went out.

"You're an old-fashioned gentleman, I see," she teased.

"Does that displease you?" he asked quickly.

"No. I think it's nice." She tried to smile reassuringly.

He appeared nervous. Around her? It couldn't be. She had to be the least intimidating person on the planet.

The sidewalk was crowded. Connar walked a little ahead of her, making his way easily. He had this amazing physical presence. People moved aside for him, impressed by his height and athletic build. She liked the way he took charge. He made her feel safe, protected.

Oh, no. It was starting all over again. She could feel her insides turning to mush.

Don't do it, Allison!

Slow down. Take a deep breath. Think of something else besides how hot this guy is.

She should be focusing on what questions she was going to ask him about Wicca.

He stopped on a street corner and turned to face her. Her heart seemed to leap into her throat. There was something about the way he looked at her. Electric. Intense. Almost as potent as if he were touching her. "Every place seems busy," he said.

"Ah…" She struggled to make her brain function. "We could put our name on a list."

"What if there is no place to sit?" A slight smile

quirked his sensual mouth and he looked down at her feet. "Those shoes might get a little uncomfortable."

She laughed, feeling breathless. For a moment, his gaze lingered on her bare legs. Oh, yes. The ten minutes of standing around waiting for the self-tanner to dry had definitely been worth it.

"We could find some food and take it with us," he suggested. "Go to my place."

"Sure." This was ridiculous. She'd deliberately suggested Lo Do so there would be a lot of people around. Now she was going to his turf. Had she lost her mind? It seemed she had. "How far away do you live?"

"Not far away. East of downtown."

"Maybe we should drive separately."

"I'm afraid I don't have a car."

She stared at him. She'd been thinking of him as a normal guy, but obviously he wasn't. He ran a Wicca store, for heaven's sake. Of course he was into alternative lifestyles.

Or was it that he couldn't afford a car? Maybe had trouble getting insurance? Of course, that was the catch. He was gorgeous, but poor. Again, she felt a sense of relief. He wasn't perfect after all.

He shrugged. "I like to walk. The store and my house aren't far apart. It can be unpleasant when the weather's bad, but I am used to being outside."

She nodded, still wondering how anyone could survive in Denver—the city of wide open spaces—without a car. "What about when you go out? Or, go to the mountains? You look like someone who craves fresh air and being outdoors."

He smiled. "That's why I don't have a car. I don't like to be inside a vehicle. "

She could believe that. This guy didn't belong in the realm of freeways and traffic jams. "We could take my car," she said brightly.

He nodded. "I'll buy you some gas."

Well, that was nice. She wondered what his apartment would be like. Some disgusting bachelor pad? No, that didn't fit him. There was a kind of elegance about this man. Maybe it was because he moved so gracefully. As if he was keenly aware of his own body. Like an animal. Or an athlete. "How do you stay in shape? You look like you must work out. Do you run, or go to the gym, or both?"

"I swordfight."

"Swordfight?"

He nodded. "I belong to a local SCA chapter and we do re-enactments. Mostly in the summer, but we must practice all year." The image of Connar in a Samurai warrior costume filled her mind. As she stared at him, he continued, "SCA stands for Society for Creative Anachronism. They dress up in medieval and dark-age clothing and pretend to live like people did in that time period."

"Like those guys who dress up like knights at the Renaissance Faire in Larkspur?"

"Aye...I mean, yes."

That was a lot easier to picture. Connar would look awesome in armor. "Do you joust on horseback?"

He shook his head. "I re-enact Dark Age battles. People of that time didn't fight on horseback. Although we—they did use horse-drawn chariots."

"You don't see a lot of those around, do you?"

"No." He looked wistful.

"Why the Dark Ages?" she asked. "It sounds

awfully obscure."

"That's the time where I feel most comfortable. Don't you ever have a sense of an era where you belong?"

"I guess not. Although maybe I just haven't encountered the right time period." She grinned at him, then realized he was serious, his expression unbelievably intent. It gave her a strange feeling.

"Here we are." She led the way to her silver Honda and clicked open the locks. As she slid into the driver's seat, she wondered if the way she drove would bother him. She knew she drove cautiously, especially for Denver.

Wow, he was big. Her car wasn't tiny, but he seemed way too large to fit comfortably in the passenger seat. It was those shoulders. Wielding a sword must really build up the upper body. He was built like a Greek statue.

What was wrong with her? Chemistry was one thing, but this guy made her practically swoon with desire. It was embarrassing. And dangerous. Already she was throwing caution to the winds. Going to a man's apartment, a man she'd met only a few hours ago.

Had she lost her mind?

"Take a left here," he said. "It's easier to take the side streets rather than going back to the freeway."

They should be talking, getting to know each other. She still had all those questions she needed to ask him about Wicca. But somehow driving took all her concentration. A part of her mind—the primitive part— was keenly focused on the man next to her. Having his body in such achingly close proximity to hers seemed to disrupt her thought processes altogether.

Megan always joked that men acted so stupid because having their blood concentrated in their penises so much of the time caused their brains to starve. But now Allison felt much the same. Her whole body was tingly and tender. There was no doubt a good share of her blood was somewhere else besides her brain.

Get a grip, she admonished herself.

"How long have you lived in Denver?"

At last, he'd said something. Maybe a little inane small talk would calm her. "A couple of years. I'm originally from the Midwest. I decided to come out here after college."

"What did your family think of that?"

"They were a little freaked, but they wanted me to be happy." In fact, they were totally against it. Not moving to Denver, but moving there with Justin. They'd never approved of him. It still grated on her that they'd been right. Which was probably why she'd stayed in Denver after the break-up. No reason to go crawling home like a complete loser.

"Sounds like your family cares about you," he said.

"Well, I guess so." She turned to Connar. "What about you?"

"My family? I haven't seen them in a while."

"And how long have you lived in Denver?"

"Almost three years."

"What brought you here?"

"I guess you could say I came here…searching for something."

Their eyes met. There was such hunger and longing in his expression, she nearly drove into a parked car on the side of the narrow street.

No. That look wasn't directed at me. It couldn't be. I barely know this man. He must be thinking about some other woman. Someone he lost a long time ago.

Was it possible he was on the rebound as well? Hard to believe someone who looked like him could be unlucky in love. Maybe that would help them keep things cool. If they'd both been hurt, then they'd both be careful and keep their distance.

Distance. Cool. Yeah, that was what she needed to aim for.

"Turn here," he said. "It's about two blocks ahead."

"Wow, you do live close to downtown." She glanced up and down the street. Old, old brick houses, an original Denver neighborhood. Most of them were well kept, but Allison couldn't tell if it was an expensive neighborhood or not. Certainly, she could never rent a place here. Too many shadows and alleyways where predators could hide. That was the trouble with being a woman in the city—you couldn't go for picturesque. Strip malls and housing projects might be soulless, but they were usually safe.

He motioned. "That's it. But you'll have to drive around back. Finding parking on the street is impossible."

"Another reason not to have a car," she quipped.

There was plenty of parking in back. The house had a small fenced-in backyard, guarded by a huge hairy, cream-colored dog. The animal rushed the fence as they pulled up, looking excited to see them.

"This is Mahon," Connar said.

"An Irish wolfhound," she said as she got out of the car. "I recognize the breed."

Connar opened the gate and the dog jumped up and put its huge paws on his chest to greet him. The animal had to be the size of a small pony! Allison eyed the five-foot fence dubiously. "Couldn't he jump the fence?" she asked.

"Of course, but why would he want to? The fence is meant to keep people from bothering him." Connar grasped the dog's collar and led him over to Allison. Mahon wagged his tail, his dark eyes bright, his expression friendly and happy. She petted him, noticing his coarse, thick fur.

"A beautiful animal, but he must be a lot of trouble to own. Dogs this size need a lot of exercise, I'll bet."

"I take him to the park every day. But you're right. It would be better for him if he lived on a farm or ranch. Still, I think he's content living here."

"Yes, he seems to be."

"And he likes you," Connar added.

"Dogs usually like me," she said. It was true. She didn't think it was so much a testament to her character as the fact that she was so non-threatening.

"I know." Connar gave her that look again. Soulful. Hungry. Was he doing this deliberately? Some sort of pick-up technique? A calculated means of trying to get her into bed?

Well, it was working. When he looked at her like that, her insides seemed to dissolve and her blood flowed south.

Stop it! I promised myself I wouldn't get in over my head!

****

Connor struggled to figure out what Allison was thinking. This woman was so much harder to read than the Aisling he'd known in the past he thought as he led her to the house. One moment she seemed open and relaxed, the next, she tensed up. He had to remember that even though she was Aisling, in this embodiment she'd experienced much different things. He might feel as if he knew her, but he actually didn't. She'd lived a whole lifetime—twenty-some years—before he found her. He knew almost nothing about what had happened to her, although he did have the sense she had been hurt by someone. He suspected it was a man who hurt her, which made him nearly witless with fury.

If he ever found out anyone had been cruel to her, he'd want to kill them. How dare they? His precious Aisling! But he couldn't act on such emotions. Siobhan had warned he shouldn't interfere too much in this world. It would disrupt the pattern, she'd said.

As Connar let her in the back way, Allison turned and asked, "You don't lock your doors?"

"Not the back door, at least not when Mahon's in the yard. I figure he's a good deterrent."

"I suppose so." She'd expected an entryway leading to an apartment door, but the back hall had steps going right into Connar's kitchen. "You rent the main floor?" she asked.

"The whole house is mine."

She digested this for a moment. That he owned property definitely moved him up the food chain. Which was not necessarily a good thing. She'd been thinking of him as a free spirit, an irresponsible, carefree guy. Someone she could never have a future with. But the fact he owned the house implied he was responsible adult. Not a flake. Not a loser. He was back to being perfect again. Which meant she was totally sunk.

The kitchen was fairly ordinary, but the living room was not. Beautiful antiques everywhere. Luxurious patterned burgundy carpet underfoot. Huge, expensive-looking furniture in brown velvet. The house—which must date back to nearly the Victorian era—had been beautifully restored, complete with carved moldings and a marble fireplace. "This is gorgeous," she said. "Did you do the work yourself?"

"No, I'm afraid I'm not good with tools." He shrugged. "Never learned when I was young."

Well, that was a relief. He wasn't a master builder, along with being a virtual Adonis. "What about all these antiques? Did you pick them out?"

"No. I had a friend help. Told him what I wanted and he put it all together."

He? This friend must be gay. Could Connar be…? For the briefest of moments, she wondered if that was the catch. Then she dismissed the thought. If ever there was a guy who was straight, it was Connar. And the furnishings were decidedly masculine. Rich dark colors. Sensual. Enticing. As if she hadn't fallen hard enough already.

"Would you like a drink?" he asked. "I have some wine. And beer."

Just what she needed. One drink and she'd be ready to rip off her clothes and follow him into the bedroom. Hell, she was ready to do that anyway! "Maybe we should eat first. What do you want to do about dinner? We were going to pick up something. But I guess we both forgot about it."

"We could call and order something."

His gaze said that what he wanted to eat was *her.*

Allison shifted her lower body as the breathless heat swept over her. This was too incredible. How could this man make her feel like this? She could imagine him laying her right down on the beautiful carpet and…

All at once, he broke eye contact. "There are many restaurants near here, but I don't know if any of them deliver. What would you like? Chinese? Vietnamese? Pizza?"

"A pizza would be fine." Food. A nice safe subject. Thank God he had some restraint. She surely didn't possess any.

Connar started toward a side door. "I'll get my phone. What kind of pizza do you like?"

"My favorite is pepperoni with green peppers and mushroom. If that's okay with you?"

He nodded and left the room. Allison let out her breath in a sigh. Wouldn't you know? At the very time in her life when she'd decided to swear off men for good, she had to meet Mr. Dream Man. Maybe it was some kind of test. If she passed it, she'd be rewarded with…what? What could be better than giving into her urges and going to bed with the most incredible-looking, sexiest man she'd ever met? She pondered the question while she waited for Connar to return.

And couldn't think of a good answer to save her life.

****

When Connar returned to the living room, he was struck by how uneasy Allison looked. He told himself that to her he was a stranger. It was only reasonable for her to be wary and cautious. But that didn't change how difficult it was for him to restrain himself. He didn't want to make polite small talk. He already *knew* her.

Her essence, her deepest spiritual self. The rest of it didn't matter.

But he had to be considerate, to put her at ease. "They said the pizza should be here in forty-five minutes. Would you like a drink while we wait?"

"Maybe some wine."

He went into the kitchen and pulled a dusty bottle from the wine rack, then dug in the drawer for a corkscrew. His hands shook as he inserted the corkscrew and worked it down. He couldn't believe this moment had come. Aisling was here. After all these centuries. It was...magic. He took a deep breath. She was the whole center of his world, his reason for existence. He had to make certain everything went perfectly.

Pulling out the cork, he poured each of them a glass of wine and took the glasses into the living room. She was sitting on the couch, looking so beautiful it made his chest hurt. He handed her a glass and sat down beside her. Not too close. He didn't want to distress her. But if he didn't touch her soon, he would lose his wits.

She took a sip of the wine. The tip of her tongue poked out in an unconscious gesture as she tasted it. Connar sucked in his breath. He couldn't endure much more. He was overwhelmed with desire. It was torment to be so close to her. To watch the rise and fall of her breasts beneath the tight fabric of her dress. To observe the pulse of life in her slim neck. To feast his eyes on the silken perfection of her skin. Every nuance, every detail of her body aroused him.

"It's good wine," she said. "I mean, I'm hardly a connoisseur, but it's very mellow." She looked at him, a shy flash of blue eyes. His mind went blank as he focused on her lips. Full and ripe, and moist from the wine.

He put down his own glass and cleared his throat, struggling for control. "Yes, it's good wine. I've been saving it."

"Saving it? For me?" Her voice was breathless, soft and light. Her pupils were huge, the black centers consuming the blue irises.

"Yes, for you." He took her glass of wine and carefully set it on the table to his right. Then, he reached out and put his hand on her neck. She didn't move, merely stared at him, lips slightly parted. He leaned forward to kiss her.

Chapter Three

Mmmm, he tasted good. Like heaven, absolute heaven. Male. Alive. Hot. And somehow familiar.

With most guys, the first kiss was a little awkward, as you both figured out how to slant heads, avoid noses, overcome the newness. There was nothing like that with Connar. Everything flowed. The pressure of his mouth was perfect. Everything matched up, as if they were two halves of a whole. The faint roughness of a five o'clock shadow around his mouth was unbearably arousing. His lips firm, yet soft. And so skillful.

His hand cupped her face, tenderly. The pressure of the kiss deepened. Flesh against flesh. Wetness against wetness. Shimmering pleasure. The caress of his fingers against her skin. Hard and warm. Her whole body dissolved. Became weightless. She was a glittering, gleaming being of desire floating on a wave of sensation.

He broke away. Took a breath as if he were drowning. She knew the feeling. His gaze met hers and she was startled by what she saw there. Not merely need and desire, but longing, almost desperation. The green of his eyes had turned stormy and wild. She felt herself fall into the roiling sea of his gaze.

He let out a sigh and then leaned over to kiss her neck. His lips teased, stroked, and played along her collarbone, the hollow of her neck, her jaw. She shivered with the sensation, and he used the movement to pull her onto his lap. Surrounded by his hard, muscular warmth, cradled against his chest, she felt the strength of him, the male power. Never had she felt so safe, so cherished.

He nibbled the lobe of her ear, and then used his tongue to trace upward. She let out a gasp. How had he known how sensitive she was there? His tongue probed the whispery darkness inside her ear, and she moaned. She was melting, dissolving in his arms.

He reclaimed her mouth, tongue kissing her. *Oh, God!* She reached out, grabbing his back, seeking his solid strength for support. His kisses became deeper, hungrier. She writhed and rubbed herself against him. The rhythm of his tongue thrusting inside her mouth drove her mad. She felt on the verge of climax.

His hands cupped her breasts, and she realized she needed to be naked. She gently pushed him away and reached up and undid the strap of her halter dress. Pushed down the top, exposing her upper body.

"Very beautiful," he murmured. He caressed her nipples, slowly and tenderly. Streaks of fire burst inside her. His big hands were so gentle, sublime. She felt his power, the strength of his fingers. And yet, he caressed her as if she was as rare and delicate as a butterfly.

This was unreal. Like something out of a movie. He knew exactly how to touch her. His skin. His smell. His taste. They seemed to flow out of her dreams. As if all of this was a memory. A perfect, magical memory.

She couldn't stop. She wanted all of it.

She slipped out of his arms. Bent down to take off her shoes. Struggled to undo the zipper at the back of her dress. When it wouldn't give, she let out a sigh.

She looked at him. His expression was rapt. Worshipful. It stunned her. And also made her uneasy. She wanted to ask him to help her undress, but she didn't quite have the nerve. *Please.* She sent him the mental message. *Make love to me.*

Gazing at Allison, Connar realized she wanted more. But he didn't trust himself to give it to her. His own need was too great, too intense. He was so hard. On the verge of exploding. And he didn't want it to be like that for her. Rushed and desperate. He'd promised himself he would take it slow the first few times. Pleasure her.

But how to hold back? She looked so exquisite. So perfect. Her breasts. Soft, creamy mounds. Sweet pink nipples. He could spend a day tasting them. Feeling the liquid warmth of her breasts in his hands. Inhaling the intoxicating female perfume that wafted from the gentle hollow between them. Sucking the hard little nipples like piquant, delicious berries.

He lowered his head and mouthed one of the plump jewels. She clutched at his hair and moaned. She looked fevered. Her fair skin was flushed. Her eyes bright and glistening. Her mouth, rosy and swollen from his kisses. He kissed her more, felt her slender form shudder in his arms.

"Connar," she moaned.

He knew what she wanted. The question was, did he trust himself to explore such shattering delights?

He pulled the skirt of her dress up over her hips. She wore some sheer, tiny undergarment. He could see the dark blond curls right through the material, the faint outlines of her cleft. His whole being seemed to go up in flames. Taking a deep breath, he grasped the strip of fabric and ripped it off. She moaned again and spread her thighs.

This isn't me. I would never do this. This is some fantasy, a dream. I'm going to wake up soon. I know it.

He was touching her, and everything he did was exactly what she wanted. He seemed to know her body better than she did. The ideal pressure. The exact rhythm. She was melting. Turning to pure, molten liquid. Hot wetness everywhere. She was shameless, too far gone even to think about being embarrassed. He'd pushed her past the point of reason or control.

He got on his knees. His strong hands held her thighs. She caught one dazzling glimpse of his beautiful face before she closed her eyes.

Then his mouth was on her. Sucking. Tasting. Devouring her. She screamed, shattering.

The aching heat built again. He slid his tongue inside her. Filling her. But not nearly enough. She wanted…The thought was lost as his tongue stroked some secret spot she had not known existed. Another blinding climax.

When she could almost think again, he was back on the couch beside her, holding her in his arms. She felt safe, adored.

Gradually, the mist of ecstasy cleared from her brain and she realized this man had just given her the most spectacularly wonderful orgasms she'd ever experienced. It seemed only fair to reciprocate.

Her gaze raked his body. Massive shoulders. Slim waist. Narrow hips. The obvious ridge of flesh thrusting against the black fabric of his jeans. She'd never felt like this about a man before. She wanted to get him naked, to stroke and pleasure him as he had her. To explore his beautiful body. She reached out, but before she could touch him, he grasped her hand in both of his and brought it to his chest.

She stared at him. "You don't want me to—"

"Maybe we should wait. The pizza hasn't arrived yet." His voice sounded choked, and all her instincts told her he was all but out of his mind with arousal. His response surprised her, but then, this man was full of surprises. If he wanted to stop for a while, she wouldn't complain. It would give her time to collect herself. It was unnerving to be so out of control.

She smoothed down her skirt, arranged the bodice of her dress, and retied the halter straps. "Where's your bathroom?" she asked.

"That way." He pointed to a doorway. "On your left."

In the bathroom, she flipped on the light and leaned again the vanity. It felt like she was still climaxing, little twinges of pleasure continuing to surge through her. Her reflection stared back at her from the mirror. Her hair was a mess, tumbled around her face. Her eyes looked wild and unfocused. "What the hell?" she whispered. "What did he do to you?"

****

Connar closed his eyes. He'd experienced one of the most magical, transcendent moments of his life and yet, he was still dissatisfied. The incredible intimacy they'd shared hadn't made Aisling remember anything. She still saw him as a stranger.

He'd been so certain she would recall something, experience some glimpse of the past. No matter what Siobhan said, he'd been convinced that when he kissed Aisling, loved her and held her in his arms, she would look into his eyes and *know* him. Her soulmate. The other half of her being.

He realized he was being unfair, asking too much of her. But still, he couldn't control his disappointment. What if she never remembered? What if she was locked into this world and time and would never belong to him? What if things between them could never be as they once were?

His mind went back to the past...

He was in the cave. The Sisters surrounded Fergal, who lay unmoving on a sheepskin pallet. The women chanted, although they used no words Connar recognized. Their voices made a strange droning sound. One of them, an older woman with brown skin, brown hair, and brown eyes, moved her hands over Fergal, not touching him, but making strange motions over his body. Despite himself, Connar was afraid. He had come here because he needed their magic, but the spell they seemed to be weaving over Fergal unnerved him. The more they chanted, the more panicked he became. He should not have come. Not only was it too late for Fergal, but his own soul might be in danger.

And then he sensed her. The beautiful one. She had not joined the circle but stood to one side of the cave. Their gazes met and held, and he knew a breathless wonder. No woman had ever looked at him as she did. As if she saw him for what he really was, not a warrior or a prince, but a man with an intangible essence, his spirit. She did not speak and yet he seemed to hear her voice. She did not reach out to touch him and yet he felt her flesh, the blood in her veins, her heart beating. A kind of soundless music floated around him. This was magic and yet it was more. Magic lasted only for a time, and this was endless, stretching into infinity.

Connar shook off the memory. He couldn't keep yearning for the Aisling he had lost. He had another chance. With this Aisling. In this time. He must focus on that.

Hearing a sound, he opened his eyes. Allison came toward him, smiling. For a moment, he thought she'd remembered something. "My purse," she said. She bent to retrieve it from the floor. Straightening, she smiled at him again. A sweet smile. Full of warmth. And yet, she wasn't smiling at *him*—her beloved—but another man. A man she'd just met.

As she returned to the bathroom, Connar repressed a groan. What would it take to make her remember? If their bodies were joined, his flesh deep inside hers— would that do it? But if it didn't…The idea filled him with misery. What if he loved her all night and she still had no inkling of what they'd once shared? What if, in the morning, she walked out the door acting as if all that had connected was their flesh? Their spirits would remain separate. The gaping hole in his heart would never be filled.

"Please, my beloved," he whispered. "Please remember. Please." He closed his eyes, concentrating, willing her to recall something. Some tiny fragment of the past. Anything.

****

Allison brushed her hair and struggled with her conflicting thoughts and feelings. Connar was incredible, a fantastic lover. That was amazing enough. But there was something else. When she went back to get her purse, he'd given her such a piercing, yearning look. The kind of look a man gave a woman he was in

46

love with. Not lust, *love*. To say things were moving much too fast was a serious understatement.

She'd promised herself she wouldn't get involved with anyone for a while. It was only common sense. The most basic kind of self-protection. And Connar's attitude was too strange. He didn't even know her. How could he be in love with her?

He couldn't. Which meant it had to be an act. A scary thought occurred to her. What if he was deliberately manipulating her, trying to control her somehow? Maybe it was some kind of spell. He did run a store that carried all the accoutrements necessary to do magic. No. That was ridiculous. Connar seemed like a sweet, normal guy. He had a dog, for heaven's sake.

She let out a deep sigh. This wasn't getting her anywhere. What was she going to do? She really wanted to go to bed with Connar. For the experience, if nothing else. To have one incredible night with the most gorgeous man on the planet, who also happened to be a sensitive, skilled lover. But if she did that, she would probably pay dearly for her pleasure. She'd end up falling for him. And then, if things didn't work out…well…it didn't bear thinking about.

On the other hand, after what they'd done together, it would be tacky to go out there and tell him she had to leave. She'd given him every reason to think she intended to spend the night. How was she going to get out of this?

She turned to get her purse and take out her compact. As she did, the floor seemed to shift beneath her feet. Reaching out to steady herself on the vanity counter, she gasped.

The bathroom had vanished. She stood on a cliff

overlooking the ocean. The wind whipped her hair and the smell of sea spray filled her senses. She was intensely and immediately afraid. Far below, the incoming waves lashed against the rocks, the water foaming furiously.

As she backed away from the cliff, dread built inside her. She'd always been afraid of heights. From behind her, she heard shouting, angry cries barely audible over the wind. As she turned around, her fear changed to terror. A group of people were coming toward her. They carried burning brands, and they had long hair and were dressed in outlandish garments, as if they were extras from some medieval movie. And they advanced toward her as if they meant to drive her off the cliff.

She turned and looked down at the rocks once again. Sheer panic paralyzed her. She was going to die!

Then, as suddenly as the scene appeared, it vanished, and she was back in Connar's bathroom. She blinked, wondering if she were going crazy. In the mirror, she saw the reflection of her white, terrified face. She clutched again at the vanity counter, sagging in relief.

After a moment, she staggered over to the toilet and sat down. Whatever had happened, it had seemed real. Incredibly real. *What's happening to you? What?*

If she'd ever done drugs, she'd have thought she was having a flashback. But she'd never dabbled in illegal substances.

She tried to breathe deeply and evenly. In. Out. In. Out. What if Connar had drugged her? Put something in her wine? But why? She'd been totally willing. It made no sense. But one thing was certain, her raging desire had been thoroughly quenched. She felt sick to her stomach. So shaky she could hardly stand.

She looked around the bathroom, tastefully decorated in shades of beige and cream. Everything appeared perfectly normal. But it hadn't been so normal just a moment ago.

She relived the horror of the sheer drop off the cliffs. The horror of those angry people coming after her. They meant to kill her.

Please! No!

She had to get out of there.

****

"I have to go now. I'm not feeling well."

Connar got abruptly to his feet as Allison came out of the bathroom. Dread rippled through him. "You're leaving?"

"I'm sorry," she said. "Maybe it was the wine. I mean, the wine was great, but I shouldn't drink without eating. I guess my blood sugar got too low. It made me nauseated."

He stared at her. Her skin was ashen. "I'm sorry," he said. "I didn't know. I didn't realize one glass would bother you."

She tried to smile, but failed miserably. "It's one of those things. It's not your fault."

She started toward the kitchen. He followed. "Are you able to drive? Why don't you stay here awhile? Until you feel better."

"I'll be fine. The worst is over." She turned to look at him. He swore he saw fear in her eyes. Fear? Of him? What had happened? Had he come on too strong? Scared her away? But she'd been so responsive only a little while ago.

"Can I call you? I enjoyed tonight this...being together. You were...beautiful." Couldn't she tell he'd never do anything to hurt her? That he'd rather die himself than see her suffer?

"Thank you. I'm afraid I have to go. I'll...uhh...call you later...at the shop."

She slipped out the back door. He watched her cross the yard. She stopped to pat Mahon, then continued on to her car.

His gut twisted with pain. He couldn't believe this was happening. He'd just found her and now she was leaving him. The promise to call meant nothing. The expression on her face as she left made it clear. She never wanted to see him again.

Connar leaned his head against the door and let out a long, low howl of pain. When the worst of the agony receded, he looked down to see Mahon beside him, whimpering, his dark eyes a mirror of his master's despair.

****

Allison sat in her car, trying to regain her composure. The whole evening seemed like a dream. One incredible, wild dream. In the space of a few hours, she'd experienced ecstasy and abject terror. She still suffered from the lingering aftereffects. Her private parts throbbed with exquisite satiation while the rest of her felt trembling and weak. Like she'd been running for her life. Which, on some psychological level, was exactly what she'd experienced.

What an extraordinary hallucination. She'd been actually able to smell the ocean. Feel the wind and sea spray against her skin. Nothing could do that except very powerful drugs.

And yet, it made no sense that Connar would have drugged her. It seemed totally out of character for him. Not that she really knew him. They'd just met. And everyone said Ted Bundy seemed like a nice, charming normal guy most of the time. Maybe Connar also had a dark side. A real dark side.

No, she couldn't believe that. There had to be some other explanation. Maybe the wine had gone bad, and some chemical in it had caused her to have some sort of out-of-body experience.

Or maybe she was losing her mind. At this moment, it seemed entirely possible. One thing was certain. She needed to talk to Megan about this. Calm, sensible Megan. She'd come up with a logical explanation.

****

As soon as she got home and safely to her apartment, Allison called Megan.

"Hello?" Megan answered sleepily.

"Hi. It's Allison. I need to talk to you."

"Now? I mean, it's late...or maybe it's early." Megan groaned.

"I'm sorry. I wouldn't bother you, but I'm desperate."

"What's wrong?' Megan sounded fully awake now. "Are you okay?"

"Yes. No. I mean, it's not life threatening. But I wouldn't exactly say I was okay." What would her friend think when she found out she was losing her mind?

"Well, spit it out, honey."

"It's about Connar...but not really. It's about what happened at his house."

"Connar? Oh, yeah, you had a date with him tonight. How'd that go?"

How did she explain this? "I...um...the date was fine, but, you see, this weird thing happened to me afterwards. After we...that is..."

"For heaven's sake, Allison. You're not making any sense. Start from the beginning. Tell me what happened."

Allison took a deep breath. "We met at the Tattered Cover, but all the restaurants around there were so crowded that we decided to go back to his place. I know it wasn't very smart. But I told myself you knew him, so it was okay."

"All right. All right. Then what happened?"

"Well, he offered me a glass of wine. I didn't want it at first because I hadn't eaten, but then he asked me again and I was hoping it would relax me. And...maybe that's where things went wrong. It could have been the wine. I can't imagine that he would drug me. He doesn't seem the type." Her stomach twisted. Could her instincts have misled her that badly?

"Of course he's not the type. What in the world would make you think such a thing?"

"Because after we made out, I decided to freshen up a bit. I went to the bathroom and while I was there I had this..." She took a deep breath. "...hallucination."

"Hallucination?"

"Well, that's the best word I can come up with. It wasn't like I was seeing things or dreaming or anything. I was *there*. All of the sudden Connar's bathroom was gone and I was in another world."

"What kind of world?"

Allison forced herself to recall details. "Well,

maybe medieval Ireland, Scotland, or something. The people were dressed like right out of *Braveheart*. Homemade fabrics. Leather garments. Long hair and beards. Swords and other bizarre weapons. I felt like I'd wandered onto a movie set. Except these people didn't seem to know it was a movie. They were coming after me. They had burning torches and weapons, and everything. I knew they were going to kill me. The only option I had was to jump off the cliff and die that way instead." She shuddered at the thought.

"And then what happened?"

She fought to get a grip on her nerves. "Then, just as suddenly, I was standing in Connar's bathroom and everything was normal again."

Dead silence.

"Megan, are you there?"

"Yeah. I'm just digesting all of this."

"I know. It's incredible." Allison ran her fingers through her hair in agitation. "I keep trying to come up with a rational explanation. The only thing I could think of was the wine. Either Connar put something in it, or it must have been tainted somehow. Have you ever heard of ergot? It comes from moldy grain and can give people serious hallucinations. Whole towns have been afflicted, even in historic times. They also think ergot poisoning might be responsible for some of the supposedly supernatural incidents that used to get women burned as witches."

"So, did you eat some moldy bread at Connar's?"

"Well, no. It's only an idea. But it sure sounds better than thinking he gave me some sort of date rape drug."

"Connar wouldn't do that."

"That's what I keep telling myself. Besides, it wasn't as if he needed to give me anything to make me compliant."

"Oh, and why is that?" Megan asked silkily.

"Because…if you must know, I was very taken with him. I mean we really clicked. All my talk about not giving in to sexual chemistry, that went right out the window."

"He's that good, is he?"

"Well, yeah. I mean, we didn't…but we probably would have…if I hadn't gotten scared out of my wits in his bathroom."

"By a hallucination." Megan's voice dripped disbelief.

Allison sighed. "I'm afraid so."

There was a long pause. Then Megan said, "You mentioned Ireland. What made you think it was Ireland?"

"It was very green and everything was misty and the cliffs were high and desolate and it somehow looked like pictures I'd seen of Ireland."

"Mmmm."

"Mmmm—what does that mean?"

"I was wondering. Maybe you picked up on some aura of Connar's from the past. He has amazing spiritual energy. Maybe he was envisioning this scene in his mind—something from a past life—and you internalized it and made it real."

"That's crazy! And what do you mean, a past life?"

"We've all been other people in other times. Some of us even have memories of those lives."

Taken aback, Allison paused, then blurted out, "Now you sound like Shirley MacLaine. I can't deal with all this woo woo stuff. Past lives? It's just too weird!"

"Do you have a better explanation?" Megan asked.

"No, but…"

"Listen, Allison, maybe you should come to my group tomorrow night. There are a couple of women who've done quite a bit of research on this sort of thing."

"Your group?"

"Actually it's called a coven. But I don't want to scare you off. They're very nice women. Perfectly normal. If you met them in any other circumstances, you'd never guess they weren't Episcopalian or something."

"Megan, I don't know…"

"It'll be okay. Pretend it's research for your article."

Allison gasped. "Oh, gosh! My article. I completely forgot about it!"

"Hmmm. Do you mean to tell me you were so busy exploring your sexual chemistry with Connar that you blew off the research you needed to do for your piece on Wicca? My, my, girl. It's starting to sound like you're smitten."

"Well, I'm *something,* that's for sure." Allison sighed. "I should let you go so we can both get some sleep. Maybe things will look different in the morning. I sure hope so."

"All right. I'll call you in the morning. *Late* morning. We can talk more then."

"Thanks. I'll wait to hear from you." Allison hung up the phone and lay back on the bed. Benjamin crawled up next to her and settled on her chest. As she stroked his sleek black fur, he began to purr. The pressure of his warm body made her realize if things had gone differently, she might be lying in bed with Connar right now. A wave of longing swept through her. It wasn't simply that Connar was gorgeous. Or even that he was the best lover she'd ever known. It was that being with him just felt so right. Like they belonged together.

Which was ridiculous. She hardly knew him. It was her hormones talking again. She was doing exactly what she'd said she wouldn't do, getting involved with someone on the basis of physical attraction and primal urges rather than thinking it out rationally.

Boy, she was conflicted. Torn in two by opposing forces. Maybe that was why she experienced the strange episode in Connar's bathroom. It was some sort of psychotic break, a reaction to the stress of trying to reconcile her body's incredible response with her recent decision to take things slowly.

Oh, yeah, she was ready for the loony bin all right. But what a way to go. She touched her mouth, remembering the splendor of Connar's kisses. If she ever let herself conjure up the most perfect, wonderful lover in the world, he would be exactly like Connar. Exactly.

Chapter Four

Megan's group—Allison tried not to think of it as a coven—was meeting at one of the member's homes north of downtown. Like all the houses in old Denver, this one was brick, a modest one-story. A flowerbed full of stunning roses bloomed in front. Allison rang the doorbell and was let in by a middle-aged woman with a lightly-lined face and shoulder-length white hair. "Hi, I'm Andrea. You must be Allison."

Allison extended her hand, disarmed by the woman's warm smile. "Glad to meet you."

"Come in and meet everyone, Allison." Andrea led her into a high-ceilinged living room with hardwood floors and sparse furnishings. Eight women of various ages were gathered in the room, visiting and drinking wine. Andrea took Allison around and introduced her to each of them in turn.

There was Rose, probably in her sixties, with short cropped gray hair and weathered skin. Barbara, Maggie, and Ginny looked to be in their thirties. Barbara had long platinum blond hair and glamorous make-up while Maggie and Ginny appeared to be more practical sorts. Maggie's brown hair was pulled back into a pony-tail. Ginny wore hers in a short bob. The three women Megan was conversing with were much younger. Sophia had short dark hair and wore no make-up. Gothed-out Misty looked to be barely out of her teens.

Stacy was plump, cute and freckled, and late twenties.

All the women greeted Allison warmly. Andrea brought her a glass of wine and everyone returned to visiting. "See, we're perfectly normal women," Megan said as Allison joined her group.

"Of course we are," Ginny said, grinning.

"Speak for yourself," responded Misty. "I abhor normal."

Megan laughed. "I did, too, at your age."

"Not me," said Stacy. "I was totally bland and boring in high school. I shudder when I think how I dressed and acted back then."

"Me, too," agreed Allison. "I like to think I've moved far beyond the stupidity of my youth…all of it." She rolled her eyes.

"Allison's still getting over an ugly break-up," said Megan. "Caught her long-time boyfriend cheating on her."

"Bastard! Do you want us to put a curse on him and teach him a lesson?" asked Misty, dark eyes gleaming.

"You do that sort of thing?" asked Allison, uneasy.

"She's kidding," said Megan. "We don't curse people. We're white witches."

"That's true," said Stacy. "One of our main precepts as a group is, 'Do no harm.'"

"But we could suggest the Goddess send your boyfriend a learning experience of some sort," Misty said with a wicked smile.

"Yes, tell me about the Goddess," said Allison. She glanced at her friend. "I hope Megan explained the main reason I'm here is that I'm researching an article on the neo-pagan movement in Denver."

"Oh, I see." Misty narrowed her kohl-rimmed eyes. "You're not here to participate, but to *study* us."

Allison shot Megan a panicked glance. Megan quickly interjected, "Actually, I told them you needed some information on past lives and how those experiences might manifest in the present."

"You told them about my...my hallucination?" Allison wondered which was worse. Having these women think she was some kind of snoopy journalist, or that she was nuts?

"I didn't tell them exactly what happened," said Megan. "Only that you had a strange experience, and it seemed to be connected to Connar. Most of them know Connar."

"Oh, indeed we know Connar," said Stacy. "He's about the most swoon-worthy guy in the whole Denver pagan scene." She gave Allison an accessing look. "So he actually asked you out...on a date?"

Allison felt herself blushing. "Not a date, exactly. More like an interview. We were going to discuss his beliefs."

"Oh, it was a date," said Megan, waggling her brows.

Allison blushed harder.

"Well, if Connar thinks she's okay, then I guess it's cool she's here," said Misty. She nodded to Allison. "Although if you've been talking to him, you should have all you need. Connar knows everything there is to know about craft and mystical belief."

"Trouble is, they didn't exactly *talk* during their time together." Megan teased. Sobering, she added, "In fact, making out is what triggered the hallucination...or flashback, or whatever you want to call it."

Allison glared at her friend, wishing she'd shut up. She'd rather not have the intimate details of her date with Connar discussed so openly. Having just met these women, she didn't want them to get the wrong idea. Sophia already seemed to be looking at her with disapproval. Why was she here? Allison wondered. Compared to the other women, she seemed so uptight, almost prim.

Rose joined the group gathered around Allison. "I couldn't help overhearing," she said. "Can you tell us more about this experience you had, Allison? Why do you think it's connected to a past life?"

"I don't actually think that," answered Allison. "Megan suggested it."

"What do *you* think it was?" Rose asked gently.

Allison felt more comfortable with Rose nearby. There was something warm and soothing about the older woman. And something familiar as well.

"I don't know," said Allison. "I initially thought Connar must have drugged me, but that doesn't seem reasonable. I mean, all of you know him." She glanced around at the group of women. "You don't think he'd do anything like that, do you?"

"Certainly not."

"Never."

"I can't imagine that."

"No, not Connar."

Their denials were swift and emphatic. All except for Sophia. "I don't know Connar," she said. "But people aren't always what they seem." She glanced around at the other women. "Perhaps Allison should be careful."

"Being careful is probably a good idea in any

relationship," said Rose.

"Especially with my track record." Allison rolled her eyes. But despite Sophia's warning, she felt a lot better about Connar. This was a bunch of pretty savvy women. If they thought Connar was a good guy, then he probably was.

Returning to the topic of her weird experience, she said, "The other thing I thought of was that maybe I got some tainted grain. You've heard of ergot?"

Several of the women nodded. "But you said you didn't eat any bread, right?" Megan reminded her.

"No, no bread. Nothing except a glass of wine. And I've never had one glass affect me like that."

"But what happened? Tell us," said Misty.

Allison nodded and began. Even describing the incident—the people chasing her, the rage and hatred in their eyes—she felt terrified all over again.

"Why did you think they were going to kill you?" asked Misty.

"It was the way they looked at me. I…somehow I knew they wanted me dead."

"It does sound like a memory," said Barbara.

"Where were you? Do you know what time or place you were in?" asked Rose.

"Ireland, I think. At least it looked like what I think Ireland looks like. I've never been there. As for the time period…well, it had to be centuries ago. These people weren't dressed in modern clothing, and they were carrying swords and sticks and burning brands." Allison couldn't quite repress a shudder.

"Connar's from Ireland," said Misty.

"That's what immediately got me thinking," said Megan. "I thought there might be some connection to him."

Several of the women nodded.

"So, you think it's something from his past projected on me?" asked Allison. In some ways, that would be a relief. She certainly didn't want it to be her own past life she was remembering.

"It's possible, I suppose," said Andrea. Their host hadn't said much up to now. She gazed at Allison thoughtfully. "Or, it could be your subconscious mind. The people chasing you could represent your unconscious fears."

"Like a psychic break?" asked Allison.

"You have been awfully stressed lately," Megan pointed out.

"I'm a psychologist in my 'other life'," said Andrea. "Before you leave, I'll give you my card. Call me if you want to talk."

Allison nodded. It would almost be a relief if what she'd experienced was simply a weird freak-out. Maybe drinking a glass of wine on an empty stomach had triggered it. If that was what happened, then what she'd experienced had nothing to do with Connar. Which meant she'd been pretty rude to him, running off like that. She'd have to call and apologize. With luck, he'd ask her out again. Just thinking about it made her heart beat faster and her insides feel all weak and gooey.

"Thanks, you guys," she told the women gathered around her. "I feel much better."

"Glad we could help," said Andrea.

"And now we should probably go outside and start the ceremony," Rose said. To Allison she added, "If we were truly being traditional, we'd probably wait until the Seed Moon was full. But we all have busy lives and have to find a time that works for everyone. We'd also probably wait for it to be dark. But the important thing is to make sure we celebrate the wheel of the seasons and honor the gods."

"About the gods," Allison began. "Can you tell me more about the deities you worship?"

"Let me pass you off to Barbara, while I get ready for the ceremony," said Rose. "She'll be able to tell you all about the different faces of the Goddess and the other forces we honor."

Barbara fell in step beside Allison as they went outside. Although the impeccably dressed woman with her soft southern drawl seemed an unlikely witch, Allison discovered Barbara was very knowledgeable. Rather than disrupt the informal mood by recording her comments, Allison pulled out a pen and small journal and took rapid notes, interrupting occasionally to confirm a spelling. By the time Rose announced it was time to begin the ceremony, Allison had several pages listing the names and attributes of various pagan deities.

After putting the journal away in her bag and stowing it near a chair on the small patio, Allison joined the rest of the women in Andrea's impressive yard. Roses, lilies, and dozens of other types of flowers bloomed in beds around the edges of an open area. Allison inhaled their sweet fragrance in the warmth of the summer evening.

Megan came to stand beside Allison. "I'll explain things as we go along."

Allison watched with interest as the women went through the various aspect of the ceremony. They cast the circle of protection, invited the women into the circle one by one, evoked the female and male deities, using the names Arianrhod and Lugh, and then performed a ritual thanking them for the sunshine and warmth of summer with an offering of bread and wine placed on the altar. Finally, Rose announced that, at Maggie's request, they were going do a banishing ritual to get rid of negative energy in their lives.

She passed around small pieces of paper and asked each of them to write down something they would like to banish from their lives. Then they each brought their papers forward and dropped them into a copper bowl, and Rose set the bits of paper on fire as she chanted a spell.

Allison had written down "weird hallucinations" on her paper. As it burned along with the other papers, she wondered if the spell would work. She had to admit there was something compelling and almost magical about the whole ceremony. Maybe it was being outside in the soft balmy air under a blue twilight sky. Or the pleasure of being with these warm, friendly women who had welcomed her so readily. Everything felt so comfortable, so right, almost as if she'd done this before.

Yeah, in one of my other lives, she thought, smiling to herself.

Next, Rose announced that having banished something negative from their lives, they were now going to evoke something they yearned for. She asked the women all to close their eyes and raise their hands to the heavens and think of something hopeful and happy they sought to welcome into the circle.

As soon as Allison closed her eyes, Connar's handsome face appeared in her mind, and she felt an intense rush of longing and desire.

Chapter Five

Sighing, Connar got of bed. There was no point trying to sleep. All he could think about was Aisling, or rather, Allison. He had to remember her name in this lifetime.

With a sense of resolution, he went to the bedroom closet. Hanging on the wall in the back was the sword. As he stared at it, his chest squeezed with pain and the terrible memory filled his mind. And yet, the sword was his talisman, his only hope.

He reached out a trembling hand, on the verge of touching the weapon. Then he groaned and turned away. He would not give up. Tomorrow he would call Megan at the ad agency where she worked and beg her to give him Allison's phone number. Somehow, he would convince her to see him again.

For the dozenth time, he tried to figure out what had happened to upset Allison so much. Had she remembered the last awful moments of her life as Aisling? He shuddered at the thought. If that was the only thing she recalled, then it would be a challenge to convince her to keep seeing him again. He'd have to explain everything, and it seemed far too soon to do that.

The only thing he could imagine was that Allison became upset because of how quickly things had progressed between them. She'd seemed skittish and wary from the beginning. He should have taken things more slowly. But it had all unfolded so naturally between them. From their first embrace, the rest had seemed inevitable. If he had another chance with her, he must control himself. He couldn't risk scaring her away for good.

He sighed again. How soon would Megan go in to work? The remaining hours of the night seemed like an eternity. There was only one possible way to distract himself.

He went into the living room, turned on some soft Celtic music, and seated himself on the floor by the fireplace. Gazing into the cold, empty hearth, he let the memories come.

****

Carrying Fergal, he followed the two women into the cave. In the first chamber, he caught a glimpse of symbols on the walls: coils and spirals, watching eyes. In the main living area, baskets, pots and weavings hung on the walls. Gathered there was a group of women, some old, some young. None looked as if they were related by blood.

"Welcome." An older woman approached him. Everything about her was brown—nut brown hair streaked with silver, tanned leathery skin, dark brown eyes. There was something about her that soothed him, something benevolent and familiar.

She nodded to Fergal. "A pity," she murmured. "He's so young."

Tears stung his eyes. Was he too late? "Is there no hope?" he asked hoarsely.

"Until a man ceases to breathe and his limbs grow rigid, there is always hope," the woman said. "Come.

Put him down by the fire. Let us look at him."

He laid Fergal on the sheepskin pallet the woman indicated. She moved her hands over the unconscious man, clucking softly. Another woman drew near. She also knelt next to the pallet and began to gesture over Fergal's prone form. Another woman came, and another.

In a short while, nine women had gathered around the pallet. They whispered, although he heard no words. They didn't touch Fergal, merely moved their hands over him.

A spell. An enchantment. Exactly what his foster brother had feared. What if they stole Fergal's spirit? Dread swelled inside Connar. He wanted to push the women aside, grab Fergal and rush out of the cave before it was too late.

Then he felt her. The woman who had guided him to the cave. She stood off to the side, not participating in whatever was happening to Fergal. Instead of watching the wounded man, she watched Connar.

As their gazes met and held, he knew a breathless wonder. She looked at him with such innocence, such unabashed curiosity. Like a child, a child in a woman's body. Her face and form stirred his manhood, but inside him, in his soul, he felt something else. He wanted to protect her. To hold her close and run his fingers over those silken, rosy cheeks. To kiss her eyelids and the tip of her nose.

She seemed so fragile to him, so utterly without guile. No woman had ever looked at him like this. As if she saw him for what he really was, not a warrior or a prince, but his intangible essence, his spirit.

It was unnerving. And yet, he could not look away.

The cave, Fergal, the other women—everything else had vanished, and there was only the two of them.

She didn't speak, and yet he seemed to hear her voice. She didn't reach to touch him, yet he felt her flesh, the blood in her veins, her heart beating. A kind of soundless music floated around him.

This was magic, and yet it was more. Magic lasted for only a time, and this was endless, stretching into infinity.

A sudden cry startled him, and the invisible thread connecting him to the woman snapped. His vision cleared and he realized Fergal had called out.

He hurried to the pallet. Fergal's face was contorted and red. He cried out again, a scream of agony. "What have you done to him?" Connar demanded.

He glared at the circle of women, on the verge of pushing them away from his foster brother. Then the brown one, the one who had greeted him, looked up and said, "It's painful to be born again. When he was in the spirit world, he was delivered from the trials of his body. But now that we have called him back to life, he suffers."

"I don't want him to suffer!"

The woman's expression grew puzzled. "I thought you wanted him to live. You can't have both things."

Connar took a sharp breath. His foster brother did look better. His pallor was gone and there seemed to be more substance to him. "Let me see his wound."

The brown woman nodded and drew aside the fur that had been draped over Fergal. Connar stared, scarce believing his eyes. The limb that only a short while before had been hugely swollen, black, and rigid, now looked like any man's leg. The muscles in the thigh were wasted, and there was some bruising around the stitches, but otherwise it appeared normal.

"I can't believe it," he murmured. "It's a miracle." He gazed incredulously at the women. "I thought you were healers. I thought you would dose him with herbs and medicine, or use a poultice to draw out the poison. But you didn't even touch him."

Connar took a step back. The fear that had afflicted him on the journey to the cave had returned, as intense as ever. These women were sorceresses. Or sidhe. He didn't know which was worse.

As the women moved away from the pallet, the one nearest Connar said, "Aren't you going to thank us? Even the poor shepherds offer us a fleece or some cheese. You're a man of wealth and power. Surely you can afford to give us something in payment."

"I-I..." he mumbled, utterly tongue-tied. What could he offer them? He reached for the torc at his neck. It was made of solid gold, with snarling wolf heads on each end. He held it out.

"What use would that be to us?" the brown woman said. "If you wish to reward us, give us something practical, something that aids our survival."

Connar glanced around the crowded cave. There were no men here to plant crops or hunt food. The women must make do with what they could forage from the area around the cave—roots and berries, nuts and seeds.

"I'm very grateful for what you have done for Fergal," he said. "And you are right. I am a prince, Connar mac Donal of the Deasanatcha. I will bring you food. Our grain is moldy and poor this time of year, but

I can offer you milk and cheese, honey, and fresh meat. Upon my honor as a warrior, I will kill a stag and bring you the whole carcass."

There was whispering among the woman, and a few of them stepped back, as if repelled. "We don't eat flesh," their leader explained. "But milk and cheese would be welcome. And even moldy grain would be greeted with gladness. Our own supplies are long gone."

Connar nodded. "I will bring you a whole cartload of foodstuffs." He looked around again. "But how will I find this place?"

A hint of mirth crinkled the skin around the brown woman's eyes. "You won't. Leave a cart in the valley, and we will unload it. You may return later to collect your vehicle."

Connar nodded in agreement.

"Now he must leave!" The dark-haired woman who had escorted him to the cave motioned angrily. "We've done our duty, and he has promised to do his. It's time for him to go!"

As if hearing her words, Fergal suddenly moaned. Connar knelt down by the pallet. "Fergal, what is it?" He looked up at the women. "Why doesn't he wake?"

"Do you think he would be pleased to find himself in this place?" The brown woman shook her head. "Those who don't believe in the Goddess are forbidden to come here. He will remain in a swoon until he returns to your world."

Realizing the implication of the woman's words, he asked, "What about me? Why was I allowed to come here? I don't know your Goddess. I'm a Christian."

The woman's brows quirked upwards. "Only those

who believe can make the journey through the mists. Perhaps you don't know your own heart."

"No!" the dark-haired woman cried. "His hands are filthy with blood! The Goddess would never speak to him!"

"Oh, Siobhan!" Another woman stepped forward and put her arms around the angry one. She had reddish hair and her skin was speckled with freckles like a seabird's egg. "Saaa, saaa. It's all right. If the Goddess allows him to come here, he can't be what you think."

The one called Siobhan continued to regard Connar with fury. Her gray eyes gleamed with hatred. "He's a man, a warrior. His purpose in life is to kill!"

Connar opened his mouth to argue with her, but the brown woman forestalled him. "Many of the Goddess's creatures kill for food," she said. "Wolves, badgers, foxes. She doesn't scorn them because of it."

"But that's not all he does," Connar's accuser continued, "That chariot he drove here, the weapons he carries, they're not meant for killing animals. They're meant for war. He slaughters his own kind for no other purpose than power and pride!"

The women all stared at Connar, seemingly appalled. He found it difficult to meet their gazes. War was something he had been trained for since boyhood, and he considered it a noble pursuit. But these women made him feel ashamed to be a warrior. "I've never killed a man," he said. "And if I did, it would be in defense of my home, my clan."

The women's disgust didn't ease. No! Don't let the beautiful one despise me! Connar looked around for the woman who had so beguiled him. Her expression appeared puzzled. Connar pleaded with her with his eyes, trying to make her understand he was not the monster the others thought him to be. Once again, the strange energy moved between them, and Connar felt as if they communicated, though neither spoke.

"No!" Siobhan broke away from the woman comforting her and rushed to the fair-haired one's side. "See how he looks at Aisling!" she said in a hysterical voice. "We must get him away from here. Now!"

The last word rose in a shriek. Connar's body tensed, an instinctive arousal to battle. But who was he supposed to fight? A group of helpless women? And yet, they undoubtedly had great powers. If they could bring Fergal back to life, they could surely cause his death with a curse. He regarded them warily, and then suddenly suppressed a laugh. It would be hard to say who was more terrified—him or them.

"I will leave," he said. "I don't want to distress you. Not when you've given me such a great gift."

The brown woman approached and put her hand on his arm. "You love him, don't you?" She inclined her head to Fergal.

Connar nodded.

She made a faint motion of satisfaction. "Fare thee well, prince and warrior. Grania will direct you back to the valley."

The red-haired, freckled woman moved beside him, and Connar knew a terrible stab of disappointment. He glanced desperately at the one called Aisling. How could he leave her, knowing he might never see her again?

"We must go," Grania said gently. "Your friend will rouse soon." Connar exhaled a sigh and went down on his knees to gather up his foster brother.

Chapter Six

Allison stared at her cell phone, trying to decide what to do. All her instincts told her Connar would never hurt her, and that belief had been reinforced by Megan and most of the women at the gathering. But she still had doubts. She'd done an internet search on him last night, and the results hadn't exactly reassured her, mostly because there *weren't* any results. She could find references to Connar owning The Magic Cauldron and having some involvement with a medieval reenactment group, but other than that, there was no evidence he existed. She told herself he probably came from such a small town in Ireland even the intrusive reach of the internet hadn't made it there yet. Still, it was strange.

Besides, she'd made a vow not to get involved with anyone for a long time. To play the field and have fun. It was clear things weren't going to be like that with Connar. Their relationship had turned serious almost immediately.

But maybe that meant he was *the one*…the person she was meant to be with…her soulmate. She choked out a laugh. What a bunch of romantic drivel! She'd thought Justin was the one, way back when. Look how wrong she'd been!

Still, she did owe Connar an apology. She'd rushed out of there like the hounds of hell were after her. And he hadn't done anything. Whatever she'd experienced wasn't his fault. She felt sure of that.

She breathed out a sigh. Here she was, back to where she'd started. She had to quit dithering. She had to...

The chime of her cell phone almost made her jump. Who? Oh, Megan.

"Hey."

"That was fast," Megan said immediately. "What are you doing, sitting there with your phone in your hand, trying to decide whether to call Connar?"

"Something like that."

"Well, I thought you should know, he called me at work. Guess he remembered the agency's name from when we met the first time. Pretty resourceful of the guy. Which means he's definitely smitten."

"Crap," muttered Allison.

"Why is him being smitten such a bad thing?"

'Cause it means he's as sharp and intelligent as I thought. That he's not like the usual losers who are too drunk to remember anything the next day, let alone months later.

"It only adds to my dilemma," she answered. "Anyway, what did he say—thanks for referring your psycho friend to me?"

"Of course not! He was worried about you. Afraid you were really ill."

She felt another twinge of embarrassment over her bizarre behavior. But what happened in the bathroom had been truly upsetting. "So, what did you tell him?"

"I told him you were a total lightweight and since you'd probably been too busy to eat much that day the wine had made you sick.'

Allison grimaced. "Gee, thanks. Now he probably thinks I'm an anorexic or something."

"Look, maybe you should just call him and explain things yourself. Wouldn't that make the most sense?"

"You're right," Allison agreed. "That's what I should do."

"Okay, then. You have his number, right?"

"Yeah."

"And by the way, what did you think of last night?"

"It was nice. All the women were great. Super supportive."

"And the ceremony?"

She wasn't about to tell Megan about her sense of having done something like that in the past. No point getting her started on the "past lives" thing again. "I'm sure there's something to the belief that whatever energy you send out comes back to you. If you decide to let go of negative thoughts, it probably helps. And by the same token, visualizing a goal probably helps you reach it. Self-fulfilling prophecy, you know."

"So, what was the negative thing you let go of?"

"My anger over Justin. I'm sure being mad over what he did isn't helping me move forward."

"And what did you visualize as the thing you desire?"

Allison was glad Megan couldn't see her blushing. "You know I want to be successful as a free lance writer. If the gods want to give me some help with that, I wouldn't turn it away." It wasn't all a lie. She did want that. It just wasn't the first thing that sprang into her mind. Visualizing writing success was a bit trickier than visualizing a hot guy.

"I guess I'd better let you go so you can call Connar."

"Well, yeah. But what about you, Megan? What did you let go of and what did you ask for?" She'd almost forgotten to inquire. Having all these issues was making her a bad friend.

To her surprise, Megan sighed. "I know I've always said my goal is to make a good living so I can enjoy myself and do what I want the rest of the time. But lately my job has begun to seem so meaningless. I've begun to feel like there's no purpose to my life."

"So, you asked for the gods to send you a meaningful job?"

"Not exactly. I left it more open than that. I'd just like to find what I'm supposed to do in this life."

"I think we all want that."

"'Course we do," Megan said in her usual cheerful tones. "Now, the minute I hang up, *you call Connar.*"

****

When his cellphone rang, Connar dashed into the bedroom and grabbed it. Maybe Megan was calling him back. Observing the unfamiliar number, he knew a keen disappointment.

"Hello," he answered glumly.

"Hey, Connar. This is Allison."

He sank down on the bed. Although he was almost speechless with relief and gratitude, he managed to answer, "Hello."

"I…uh…I wanted to apologize for the other night."

"Apologize?"

"Yes. The way I left…it was rather rude."

Don't sound too eager. Don't scare her off! "You were ill…upset. You weren't rude."

"I hardly said goodbye. Not my most gracious moment."

"I...I'm very glad you called." What else should he say? Should he ask her out again?

"Maybe—"

"I was thinking—"

They both spoke at once. Allison laughed nervously. "I thought we might try it again. Make it a real dinner date this time. Actually eat something." She laughed again.

"Yes. That would be nice." Nice? He sounded like a lackwit!

"We could talk more about the Wicca stuff....or not."

"Yes." Say something else! Don't make it so hard for her! "Where would like to meet this time? And when?"

"Umm...I thought...tonight's a weeknight, so most restaurants won't be as crowded."

Tonight! He'd hardly dare to hope to see her so soon! "Yes. That's true. Do you have a favorite place?"

Allison realized she really didn't. With Megan and her other girlfriends, it was almost always lunchtime when they went out to eat, and then it was a matter of finding someplace that wasn't too busy. With Justin, they'd always gone where he wanted to go. It was nice to have someone consider her wishes. Although she wasn't sure what to suggest.

"Do *you* have a favorite?" she asked hopefully.

****

She'd better take a sweater, Allison decided as she dressed that evening. Although it was another scorcher, the restaurant would probably be air-conditioned to death.

She'd worked on *The Highpoint* article much of the day, doing internet research to supplement what Connar had told her. But it had been hard to concentrate. Her body buzzed with excitement whenever she thought about seeing Connar that night. Before her first date with him she'd been nervous. Now some of the tension had eased and been replaced with a kind of lustful yearning. She could hardly wait to see him. To gaze at his fabulous face and supremely masculine body. To feel his firm, sensual lips on hers and have his arms around her.

Whew! Good thing they were meeting in a public place. No way was she going to let herself be alone with him...at least not until they'd spent some time getting to know each other a little better. His appeal was simply too potent.

She'd worn a dress again, partly because it was too hot for jeans and partly because Connar seemed to bring out her feminine side. And why was that? Was it because he was so super masculine? Or something else? Why were all her reactions to Connar so intense?

Better not think about it. She'd already done far too much obsessing. What the hell! It was only their second date!

She finished her makeup and brushed out her hair. Despite the heat, she'd decided to wear it down. After grabbing a sweater, she set out. As she was driving downtown—they'd decided on an Italian place on Sixteenth Street Mall—she wondered what sort of transportation Connar was using to get there. Did he call a cab? Take the bus? She couldn't imagine how he got along without a car. The only people in Denver she knew who didn't have cars were students too broke to afford one.

Given that he obviously had money, Connar's lack of a vehicle was either weird or admirable. He did seem like someone who would be concerned for the environment. Under the circumstances, she probably should have offered to pick him up. But that would put her at his house and pose the temptation of going inside and…No, she wouldn't think about that.

Since it was a weeknight, finding parking wasn't too tough. She walked quickly to the restaurant. He was waiting outside, looking like a vision of hotness. She let out her breath as she approached him. "Hi. Been waiting long?"

"Not long at all." *Only a lifetime*, Connor thought ruefully. She looked so beautiful, fresh and lovely as a summer's day. Amid their concrete, metal, and glass surroundings, she stood out like rare flower on a rocky, barren shore. A splendid sunset shining over stark mountaintop. Her flowered dress, her rose, ivory, and gold coloring—merely looking at her made his heart soar in his chest.

"Is everything okay?" she asked in a breathy voice.

"Of course," he answered, smiling at her. He had to stop staring. To get over his awe at finally being with her and try to act like a normal man of this time period. He must remember to attempt to fit in to her world. To talk and dress and act like someone who belonged in this time.

The hostess led them to a table and he helped her sit down.

"You're quite the old-fashioned gentleman," she said, her blue eyes sparkled teasingly.

He wasn't quite sure what that meant, but he nodded.

"Did you have any trouble getting here?"

"No. The bus stop is only a short distance away." He knew he should have learned to drive and purchased a car. But his first attempt at driving had been disastrous. A car was nothing like a chariot. He'd hated it so much, and despised feeling like a helpless clumsy youth. After that experience, he'd told himself he wasn't going to stay in this time period long—not long enough to make learning to drive necessary.

But seeing how uncomfortable she seemed with his lack of a vehicle, he cursed himself for failing to take on the challenge of driving. Apparently, for men of this era, the skill was important. But it wasn't that he couldn't *drive*. He could safely guide a chariot over the roughest ground. There had to be as much skill in that as in driving a motorized vehicle. Someday, when they went back to his own time, he would show Allison how competent he was in his own world.

"So, what did you do today?" she asked. "Work in the shop?"

"No. We're closed on Mondays. I took Mahon to the park and ordered some products on-line for the store."

"Is that how you stock it?"

He nodded. "I try to buy things made locally or in the British Isles. Unfortunately, China is often the best source, even for Celtic items. And you? What did you do today?"

"Worked on the article. Although now it's become *articles,* plural. The editor of the *The Highpoint* wants me to expand the story into a series."

"Are there any other questions I can answer for you?"

"I don't think so. I've done a lot of research on-line…not that I question anything you've told me, but simply to confirm spellings and that sort of thing. And last night, I went to this Wicca group Megan belongs to and observed one of their ceremonies."

"What did you think of it, the ceremony, I mean?" *Had seeing such a ceremony aroused any of her memories?*

"It was…interesting. I enjoyed meeting the other women. Some of them were exactly what you'd expect. Others didn't quite fit my idea of a pagan worshipper. There was one woman…seeing her you'd be certain she was simply a shallow trophy wife. But she was super nice and friendly. It just goes to show that you can't judge people by their appearance." She gave him a warm smile.

"That's true." It surprised him that being involved with a ritual with a group of women hadn't aroused any memories of her past life. Perhaps her spirit had been so traumatized by what happened at the very end that she'd buried her past life experiences deep within her subconscious. The familiar regret tore at him. If only he had realized how deep Fergal's animosity ran. If only he had been able to get Aisling away before everything went awry...

He took a deep breath and willed himself not to think about those things. When he looked up, Allison was watching him with a wary expression. "What's wrong? For a moment you looked...well...haunted."

"Nothing. I was only thinking about…about Ireland. I miss it sometimes."

81

"Do you go back and visit very often?"

"I haven't, but I could, I suppose. Purchase some things for the store." He'd vowed not to go back until he could take Aisling with him. But reuniting with his love was going to be more complicated than he'd expected. It might be months before this incarnation of Aisling was ready to return to *his* Ireland.

That thought reminded him they were supposed to be on a date, and they should be getting to know each other. Instead of brooding on the future, he must focus on the present.

He raised his gaze to Allison's. "Megan told me that before you started freelance writing, you used to work at the advertising agency with her."

She nodded. "That's what I did for my first year in Denver. I'm sure most people would think I was lucky to get the job, but I hated it. Copywriting can get boring when most of your clients are software and high tech companies. There were a few projects that were fun, restaurants and specialty stores, that kind of thing. But mostly it was deadly dull. Lots of meetings. Lots of hand-holding of executive types who didn't have a clue. Megan likes it all right, but she's more comfortable with people and willing to put up with more. It wasn't my dream job and at some point, the frustration caught up with me."

Her expression turned so sad and desolate, it nearly broke his heart. He waited, wondering if he dare probe. Then she shook her head, as if shaking off the dark mood and continued, "I'm very fortunate. I went to college on a scholarship and had some money saved up, mostly from an inheritance from my aunt. I have enough of a nest egg that I was able to quit the agency and try to make it as a writer." She met his gaze again and smiled wistfully. "But I probably wouldn't have done it if I didn't end up going through a bad break-up that made me reevaluate everything in my life."

How much should she tell him? Allison wondered. This was their second date...at best. Too soon to spill her guts. But there was something about Connar. He truly seemed to be listening. His amazing green eyes were focused on her with such tenderness and concern.

She'd never met a guy so empathetic.

"So, something happened?" he prompted.

Allison felt herself raise a cynical brow. What was with all the leading questions? Had this guy trained as a psychologist? She shrugged. "Classic scenario. Found out he was cheating on me. The rest of it was a total cliché, too. High school sweethearts move to the big city, and one of them discovers monogamy isn't what they want."

Connar nodded. "That must have been upsetting."

She shrugged again. "It was at the time. But after a while, I realized I was better off without that loser. He was the one who was holding me back. Always wanting me to be practical, to always have a plan. Once I broke free of him, I could finally start to pursue my dreams."

"And your dream is being a writer?"

This guy definitely knew how to get her talking. She nodded. "But that's enough about me. Why did *you* decide to move to Denver? Ireland's a long way from the Rocky Mountains." She watched him carefully. Despite the aura of intense sincerity that surrounded Connar, so far he'd been vague about his background.

He shifted in his seat, looking slightly uneasy. "It's hard to explain. I guess you could say I came here to pursue a dream of my own." He smiled that megawatt smile. "I had a dream about this place, and the dream made me realize that if I came here, I'd find what I was looking for. The thing that was missing from my life."

"And…ummm…have you…" She almost had trouble saying the words. "Found what you're looking for?" The expression in his eyes said that *she* was what he was looking for. That *she* was what was missing from his life.

He held her gaze for a moment. Then he said, "Not yet. I suppose it was a foolish notion anyway."

She let out her breath. She hadn't even known she was holding it. Okay. He was normal. Not a crazed stalker who'd fixated on her. He obviously liked her, but didn't believe she was the answer to his prayers. That was good. *Liking* her was good.

As Connar watched Allison's expression turn from near-panic to relaxed, he realized he'd narrowly avoided disaster. If he'd told her what she meant to him, that she was the sole reason he was in this place, in this time, she would have been horrified.

He wondered if he'd ever understand women of this era. Although, he did realize they had to be wary. In this time, women weren't surrounded by family and close acquaintances, and that made them vulnerable. They had to learn how to avoid the evil people, the serial killers, and other monsters that seemed to be part of this time.

Siobhan had warned him to take it slow. Her advice had been very helpful. Somehow, he would have to keep up the pretense for a while longer. To behave as if he was simply attracted to Allison and enjoyed her company, rather than seeing her as the center of his universe.

Do what you have to do, he told himself. *I'm so close. I've come so far.* Don't ruin it now.

Chapter Seven

"Do you have family back in Ireland?" Allison asked as the server brought their pasta.

He nodded. "Two brothers, although I haven't seen them in quite a while."

She was surprised he wasn't close to his family. But she wasn't going to dwell on it. She needed to stop psychoanalyzing this guy and simply enjoy his company. It was such a beautiful summer night, and he looked so handsome in the soft glow from the votive candle on the table. Her gaze drank in his strong jaw and well-muscled neck. Those amazing green eyes and sensual mouth. Mmmm. Maybe the wine she'd ordered was going to her head, but all she could think of was going back to his place and...

No. She wasn't going to do that. Making out would only lead to one thing, and it was too soon for that. Once she went to bed with him, she'd lose what little perspective she had. Better to suffer the torment of her current sexual frustration rather than get in over her head again. She reminded herself of her horrible experience in his bathroom. Maybe it was her subconscious warning her she was headed for disaster if she went to bed with Connar on the first date. Not that her subconscious had never been particularly helpful before.

The intensity of the experience still horrified her.

Having a psychotic break was something that happened to seriously unstable people, or people who did drugs that messed with their brains. Not normal boring women like herself.

She recalled the incident, trying to decide if it had been as intense as she remembered. As the images filled her mind, she no longer found them unnerving. The experience was like a weird video clip playing in her head, rather than a full-out hallucination. The passage of time was also helping put it into perspective. Maybe she wasn't crazy after all.

"Allison, would you like some dessert or coffee?"

She jerked herself back to awareness and realized the server was waiting by the table. "Uh, sorry," she mumbled. "That will be all." After the server left, she met Connar's gaze sheepishly. "Guess I got lost in my own thoughts. Sorry."

He smiled back. "It's fine. Everything's fine."

At this moment, she believed him. What could be better than this? A lovely date with the hottest guy she'd ever met. When she looked at him, she could almost imagine actual sparks flying between them. The attraction was that intense.

Connar pulled some cash out of his pocket and put it with the bill. "I suppose we should be going." His voice held the unspoken question. *What next?*

They delayed answering it by walking along the Mall, not talking much but people-watching and looking at shops. After a couple of blocks, Connar reached out and took her hand. Allison's whole body seemed to let out a sigh. When was the last time she walked around holding hands with a man? She'd probably been in junior high and the guy holding her hand had been a mere *boy*. No, she must have held hands with Justin at some point. She was just blocking it out, along with all the other things she was trying to forget.

Whenever it had happened, it hadn't been like this. She could feel the calluses on Connar's palm. The strength and power of his grip. And yet he was holding her hand gently, tenderly. Protectively. He made her feel small and delicate and feminine. Was that a bad thing? Did it mean he would try and control her as the relationship progressed? No way was she going to let that happen. From now on, she was her own woman!

****

What was she thinking? Connor wondered.

If only he had a better sense of this modern version of Aisling. He'd assumed when he found his love, things between them would be the same as they were back in his own time. But this Aisling/Allison was so independent. So strong. It made her even more appealing and interesting. He'd enjoyed talking to her, learning about her plans for the future. But he also worried that this Aisling didn't need him. The thought concerned him. She had her own goals and plans, and he wasn't sure how he would ever fit into them.

"My car's around the corner."

"Oh. Of course," he answered. Her words dismayed him. No! He wasn't ready for their time together to be over!

"I could give you a ride home," she suggested.

He perused her lovely features, trying to decide what to do. If they went to his place, would she be willing to come in? After what happened last time, he worried their night would end with her simply dropping him off. "But I don't want you to have to drive home by yourself," he protested. "Let me see you home. I'm sure I can catch a bus nearby. Or call a cab if necessary."

"But that's so out of your way. I don't want to put you out."

"I'll feel better if I know you've gotten home safely."

She looked bemused. He held his breath, wondering if he could sway her. Was she so independent that she resented him trying to take care of her?

Why not? Allison thought. Why not let him see me home? She didn't want the night to be over. Nor did she relish driving home alone in the dark. Of course, when they got to her place, she'd have to decide whether to invite him in. Despite her resolve not to let things go too far, she wanted more than just a goodnight kiss. Maybe they could make out a little before she went in. It sounded kind of silly, like they were a couple of high school kids. But staying in the car would allow them to take things a little further, but not too far. She'd done OK at remaining in control, up until now. Despite Connar's incredible allure, she hadn't let things get out of hand.

When they reached her car, and he let go of her hand, she experienced a sense of loss. Back to being grown ups.

On the drive to her apartment, they talked about the different neighborhoods of Denver. As they neared the area where she lived, Allison realized how much she hated it. "I don't know why I live here," she said. "It's so soulless. No trees. Just crappy apartment complexes, office buildings, fast food restaurants and a few stores, all national chains. Except for the view of the mountains to the west—when the air's clear anyway—this could be any city in the U.S."

"If you feel that way, why don't you move?" asked Connar.

She nodded. "I guess I could. I hadn't really thought about it until now. Justin chose this area, and after we split—well, in fact, I sort of threw him out." She couldn't quite suppress her grin. "After that I stayed here because it seemed safe." As she pulled into the parking lot of the apartment complex, she added, "It's open. Well lit. Relatively upscale. Not the kind of place where you'd expect a lot of crime."

"I suppose being a woman, you have to worry about that."

She nodded. Safe. Her background. Her whole life. Everything was about being safe. But she didn't want to live like that anymore. She wanted to live in a neighborhood that had character. Somewhere like Andrea lived. Or Connar. If she had to take a few risks to do that, it would be worth it.

As she turned off the car, she suddenly realized the well lit, openness of the area had an immediate disadvantage. The lack of privacy would make it awkward to do much more than kiss while parked here. She was going to have to invite him in.

For a few seconds, she wavered. This was exactly what she'd told herself she wasn't going to do. But then she looked at Connar and all her resolve vanished. "Do you...uh...want to come in?"

"Yes."

They left the car and walked to the building. The sparks of attraction that had been building between them all night seemed to burst into flame. All she could think of was that in a few seconds, there would be nothing to stop them from tearing off their clothes and pouncing on each other like animals. It made her feel breathless, almost dizzy with lust. Connar was right there beside her. So big. So handsome. So...mmmm...yummy!

Incredibly broad shoulders. Flat, hard stomach. Lean, sexy hips. Great butt. He was easily the hottest, best looking guy she'd ever dated. But it was more than that. Being with him felt so right. So perfect.

In the rational part of her mind, she fought the feelings building inside her. They weren't animals. And giving in to lust wasn't usually a good idea.

By the time they'd reached her apartment, she was feeling a little more in control.

Benjamin greeted her as soon as they walked in, and she spent some time fussing over him and introducing him to Connar.

"He seems to like you," she said, grinning as Benjamin purred ecstatically while rubbing his head against Connar's hand.

"I usually have good rapport with animals," Connar said.

And with women, I'll bet! Watching Connar pet Benjamin made her think how good it would feel to have him touch and stroke *her*. Pushing the thought away, she said, "Would you like some wine?"

"No thank you. Perhaps some water."

As least, he was behaving sensibly, even if she was out of control. She went into the kitchen and poured each of them some water from the pitcher in the fridge, then carried the glasses into the living room. He was sitting on the couch, not sprawled like most guys would be but sitting straight up, erect and alert. "Did you ever have military training?" she asked as she sat down beside him. "The reason I ask is because of the way you hold yourself." She sensed him tense a bit. What did that mean?

"I suppose that's because of all the training I've done for the re-enactments, the traditional sword fighting I do at events."

"Oh, yeah. You said that's how you stay in shape." As she said this, she saw him relax. For some reason, he'd been worried about her reaction. Maybe he worried she would think it was weird he belonged to a historical re-enactment group. But, no, he'd tensed up as soon as she mentioned his military bearing. Didn't he realize she'd meant it as a compliment?

It was cool to meet a guy who was so aware of his body and his immediate surroundings. It made her feel safe and protected, and she was finding she liked that. Although Justin had mostly called the shots in their relationship, when it came to her personal safety, she'd been on her own. Looking back, she could clearly see how dysfunctional their relationship had been.

"So, how often do you practice?" she asked.

"About once a week. I'd like to do more, but my sparring partner isn't available more often."

"I'd like to watch sometime."

Connar nodded, surprised. The Aisling/Allison of his time had been horrified by his skill with weaponry. Of course, she'd been taught by the Sisters to despise warriors. Her dislike of that aspect of him had probably contributed to his failure to protect her. The ever-present guilt stabbed at him. If he hadn't failed her in the past, he wouldn't have to be in this place, this time, trying to win her back.

At least things seemed to be going well. She appeared much more relaxed than last time. Maybe it was because she was in familiar surroundings.

When she sat down next to him, their bodies nearly touching, he wanted to pounce on her and immediately start making love. In need of distraction, he stood. "Your bathroom?"

"Down the hall." She gestured.

"Thank you." Heading in the direction she indicated, he took a deep breath. He had to get away from her for a while so he could regain control

Allison let out an involuntary shiver as Connar left her. Her body seemed to be aching and tingling with arousal, and they hadn't even kissed yet. She stood, restless, and started to pace. She could hardly wait until he got back. Hopefully, he'd be quick. She didn't want to think too much about what was happening, or to let her mind talk her out of this delicious, feverish state of expectation.

Minutes passed. What was he doing? Checking out her bathroom? It wasn't as neat as his had been. But she was a girl and it took a lot more work to look good. Maybe he was getting ready for sex. Getting out a condom. Undressing. What if he walked out of there naked?

The idea tantalized her. She thought about him sword fighting, imagining that glorious body of his in action. Maybe wearing a kilt. No, that was what they wore in Scotland, not Ireland. Maybe he could wear a tiny loincloth like Conan the Barbarian or something. Mmmm. That was a tantalizing image. Hurry up,

Connar!

When he came out fully-clothed, she knew a stab of frustration. Then he smiled at her, and she decided it didn't matter what he wore.

Still smiling, he approached. "You look so lovely tonight." He stopped next to her, put his hands on her arms and brought his mouth down to hers. She felt herself melt as their lips met. Swelling pleasure. The feel of his body against hers. His smell. His taste. Magic!

When the kiss ended, she was trembling. She gazed at him in wonder as he led her to the couch. Sitting down, he drew her next to him.

More deep, wondrous kisses. She was drowning. Going under. Then floating to the surface in a sea of shimmering delight.

The tension built inside her. The ache. The yearning. The need. She worried he would never go beyond kissing and she would die of sheer arousal. Finally, he began to fondle her breasts. Touching her taut, aching nipples through her clothing. It wasn't enough. She wanted to be naked.

She drew away and pulled down the top of her strapless dress and unhooked her bra. He stared at her breasts with a worshipful expression her 34B's had never come close to arousing before. He made her feel like a goddess. The most beautiful woman in the world.

She sighed as he gently cupped her breasts in his big hands. Then he leaned down to kiss them tenderly. His mouth against her nipples sent waves of pleasure through her body. Pleasure so intense it was almost painful. Or maybe that was simply the ache deep down inside her, the longing of her lower body to be touched and kissed and explored with the same reverence and attention.

The thought made her wriggle her hips, and he seemed to get the idea, skimming his hand down her body until he reached her thighs. She parted them in invitation and soon he was stroking upwards, pushing up her dress and caressing her thighs with slow, teasing movements that drew near her aching center, yet failed to ease her powerful need.

He kissed her as he tantalized her with his fingers, deep, hungry kisses that sent shock waves of pleasure through her body. She was ablaze. When he drew away, she thought she would die of loss. "Perhaps we should...go to the bedroom," he said.

She nodded, feeling almost too overwhelmed to speak. "Do you ...did you bring protection?" He looked baffled, as if he didn't have any idea what she meant. Well, damn. All along, he'd seemed like an old-fashioned sort of guy. She'd liked that a lot. Now she realized there was an inconvenient aspect to his anachronistic behavior. If he hadn't thought ahead to bringing protection, what were they going to do?

Having vowed not to get involved with anyone for at least six months, she hadn't given any thought to birth control. Her only hope was that Justin might have left some condoms somewhere in the apartment. "Uh...excuse me," she told Connar. "I'll be right back."

That's what she'd said last time...and then everything fell apart! As she left the room Connar felt a twinge of anxiety. Had he done something wrong? Failed her in some way? She'd talked about protection. She must mean...

He hadn't thought about that. In his time, people

seldom sought to prevent pregnancy. When he and Aisling made love in the past, the idea they might conceive would have filled them with joy.

But this was a different time. And this Aisling was much different from the one he'd known. This woman had all sorts of goals beyond being a mother. After spending so much time researching how people behaved in this era, he should have thought of this.

Crap! Where would he have put them? Allison slammed shut the drawer of the vanity in the bathroom, gritting her teeth in frustration. She and Justin hadn't had sex much before she found out about him and Kara and kicked him out. Had he used condoms with *her*? If so, there should be some around here somewhere. But where?

She went into the bedroom and began rummaging in the drawer of the nightstand on the far side of the bed. As far as she could remember, she hadn't gone through this drawer since Justin left. Ah, success! Beneath the Playboy magazine—yuck—she found a rather battered-looking condom package. She checked the expiration date. Still good, if barely.

She glanced at the door. Did she really want to do this? Now that she was thinking rationally again, she couldn't help wondering if going to bed with Connar was a good idea. And what was he going to think when she came back with a condom? If he hadn't thought to bring one, he probably wasn't expecting things to go this far this fast. He might be turned off by her obvious eagerness. He might think she jumped into bed with every guy on the second date.

In fact, nothing could be further from the truth. Her whole sexual experience was limited to Justin and a couple of guys in college. Since the break-up, she hadn't even kissed a guy!

"Allison?" Connar appeared in the doorway. "Are you...is everything all right?"

Seeing him, that gorgeous face, hunky body and the tender expression he always seem to have around her, all her doubts seemed to vanish. "Yes," she said. "Everything is fine."

She put the condom on the nightstand and went over to Connar. Now...back to that delicious foreplay.

As he took Allison in his arms and began to kiss her, some of Connar's tension eased. She still seemed willing. Willing and eager. It was hard to get used to this new Aisling. She wasn't demure or shy, but made it obvious she was deeply aroused and more than ready to make love with him. It was a surprise, but a delicious one. He gloried in the feel of her slender body so close to his. Her lovely, sweet mouth. The sublime taste and scent of her. Warm, lush woman. *His Aisling.*

His body urged him on. He broke off the kiss to finish unfastening the back of her dress so he could ease it over her hips. She stood before him clad only in a wispy pair of lavender panties and her sandals. He stared at her a moment, taking in the graceful curves of her body, the delightful contrast between her slim waist, delicate ribcage and the rounded opulence of her breasts. So finely made she was, and yet at the same time, so lush and womanly.

And her skin...silky smooth, ivory touched with pink and gold. Her nipples, a deep rose hue, reminded him of the rosy splendor of her intimate parts. He cupped her breasts in his hands, kneading the nipples softly until she gasped and reached for him. He wasn't certain what she wanted…until she pressed her hips against his straining erection and he realized she wanted them to be joined.

He wanted nothing else as much as that himself. But a part of him held back. He'd waited so long for this. Wanted it to be perfect. To savor every moment. Having barely had a chance to enjoy the sight of her beautiful nakedness, he wasn't quite ready for mindless passion to overtake them.

He kissed her tenderly, then put his hands on her hips and slid down her panties. Taking a step back, he drank in the sight of her, letting his gaze linger on the "v" of her thighs. Light brown maidenhair, although sparser than he recalled. Then he remembered that in this time, women waxed or shaved themselves there. A strange thing to do, and yet he supposed, with the skimpy clothing women now wore, they had no choice.

He raised his gaze to hers. "You're so beautiful."

She blushed faintly. "Thank you. I…I think you're beautiful, too." She reached out and started to unbutton his shirt. "In fact…I'd like to see more of *your* beauty."

As she began to undress him, amazement mingled with his deepening arousal. The old Aisling would never be so bold.

Standing there, feeling her delicate fingers on him, he thought he would burst into flames. It was so provocative, so delightful. As soon as his shirt was unbuttoned, she touched his chest.

"Mmmm," she murmured, a faint smile on her face.

He closed his eyes as she ran her hands over his body. When she stroked his nipples, he suppressed a groan.

"You could be a model," she whispered. "And pose for the cover of one of those racy romance novels. You have the perfect looks. The perfect body."

He gave in to the delicious sensations as she caressed his stomach. But when he felt her undoing his jeans, he reached up and grabbed her hands. He didn't know if he could bear that, to have nothing between his highly aroused flesh and her enticing fingers.

She laughed softly. "What's wrong?"

"Nothing," he breathed. "I...perhaps I should undress."

"Perhaps you should."

Allison felt a wave of amazement at her own boldness. She'd never acted like this with a man before. Connar brought out something in her...something daring and wanton. The anticipation of going to bed with him seemed to be going to her head. He made her feel as if she was in control, as if his beautiful body was hers to do with as she wished.

She watched as he sat down on the bed and pulled off his boots. Next, he stood and undid his black jeans and pulled them down, revealing plaid boxers underneath. He quickly stripped them off and stood there in all his naked glory.

Oh, my! She wanted to touch and fondle...and then, in very short order, have his very substantial erection inside her. But first, the condom.

She retrieved it from the night stand and opened the package. When he didn't reach out to take it, she decided to do something new for her and put it on him. He gasped as she touched him, then stood very still as she slid the thin sheathe over his heated flesh. Once it was on, she continued to fondle him until he grasped her wrists and drew her hands away. "I…I can't endure it."

She nodded, staring deep into his green eyes. Then he grabbed her and kissed her, hard passionate kisses that made her breathless. As his careful control vanished, her own restraint snapped. They were both suddenly frantic with desire. Before she knew it, they were on the bed and he was inside her, thrusting deeply.

Waves of sensation crashed through her. With a sob, she came…and came again. She climbed to another violent peak, then heard his muffled cry and felt him convulse against her.

They eased back down to earth. Even then he didn't release her, but held her tight against him, as if he couldn't bear to let her go. Ripples of pleasure and release still trickled through her. She felt stunned, overwhelmed.

This was what it was like when they talked about the earth moving!

How could it be like this? They'd only met a few days ago. How could she feel as if their souls had touched? As if they'd been joined not merely physically, but in some profoundly transcendent way?

Even more amazing was the sense he felt the same. After sex, guys usually withdrew. The old "roll over and go to sleep" thing. But this man continued to hold her, as if he couldn't bear to be apart from her.

Finally, with a kind of sigh, he drew away. She got up and went to tidy up. In the bathroom, she stared at herself in the mirror. She looked dazed. Out-of-it.

What was it about this guy…this wild Irish stud? Within hours of meeting him she'd had the most terrifying experience of her life. A few days later, making love with him, she'd experienced the most incredible, utterly sublime pleasure of her life.

Who was he? Where did he come from? Was any of this real?

Chapter Eight

Connar stared at the bedroom door. It was perfectly normal for Allison to leave and go to the bathroom. Still, he remained uneasy. It reminded him of when they were at his house and everything went awry.

He got out of the bed and dressed, telling himself that things were different between them now. They'd made love, and it had been astounding. And although she hadn't behaved exactly like the Aisling/Allison he remembered, he had no doubt the woman he'd held in his arms only moments before had enjoyed what they shared immensely.

Which brought him to the next dilemma. He paused in putting on his shoes, and contemplated the next step to reclaiming her in his life. Should he tell her who he was and what they'd shared in the past? All his instincts told him she was a long way from being ready for that. In his time, making love implied a connection, a commitment. But after observing people in this era, he now knew making love was something people did simply for pleasure, rather than having it mean anything. For all he knew, that was how Allison perceived what they'd shared. Although how she could be casual and unmoved by such a profound experience, he couldn't truly understand.

He'd felt as if their very souls had touched. As if time itself was meaningless. That was what he expected to feel with her, but even so, it had been extraordinarily powerful. If she experienced even a tiny bit of what he had, she must recognize the connection between them. She could no longer view him as a stranger, could she?

He glanced at the door again, wondering when she would return. He longed to see her. But he also feared her reaction to what they'd shared. What if she remained untouched, unmoved? What if she still saw him as a man she'd just met, a stranger? What if after tonight, he was forced to wait days before he could see her again?

That's probably what would happen, he thought with a sigh. By the standards of this time period, they were at the very beginning of their relationship. He couldn't expect things to move too quickly, despite the ecstasy they'd shared.

He must wait until she was ready. It didn't matter how long it took. What mattered was that eventually she would once again be his.

When she came out wearing a short silky robe, he knew exactly what to say. "I should go home. I need to be at the shop to open at nine tomorrow."

She nodded. "I should probably get some sleep myself. But I wanted to tell you…" When she hesitated, he wondered how she could seem so shy and demure now when she'd appeared so uninhibited earlier. Blushing, she said, "That was wonderful. The best I've ever experienced. Although I did kind of get carried away."

"We both did," he reassured her. "And it *was* wonderful."

No man should have a smile like that! It turned her all gooey inside and made all her thoughts scatter.

Allison walked him to the door. He leaned over and kissed her lightly on the mouth. "I'll call you tomorrow," she said.

He nodded and then gave her one of his deep soulful looks before leaving.

Afterwards, Allison turned off the lamp by the couch and sat there gazing into the darkness. Benjamin crawled up on her lap and began purring. "You liked him, didn't you? I like him, too. Damn but I like him!"

How was she ever going to go to sleep? Her whole body tingled, and she felt so alive and full of energy she was ready to turn a cartwheel or start dancing or something. Sex with Connar had been intensely satisfying, but also had the effect of making her want more of it. "The guy is like meth or something, Benjamin. I have sex with him once and I'm addicted. I just want more and more." She sighed, wishing she hadn't been so reasonable and practical and said okay when he mentioned leaving. "If I'd asked him to stay, I'll bet he would have," she mused.

She sighed again, remembering the feel of Connar inside her. The magic of his kisses. The way he smelled and tasted and…

"You've got to stop this," she told herself firmly. "Think of something else. Withdrawal is going to be a bitch, but you have to go through it sometime."

She moved Benjamin aside so she could get up. He climbed on her lap again as soon as she sat down at her desk in the second bedroom she used as an office. She spent some time going over the second of her series of articles. Then, finally feeling tired, she went to bed.

****

Connar lay in bed. As replete and satisfied as his

body felt, a vague discontent gnawed at him. He'd made love with Allison/Aisling. Their bodies had been joined in ecstasy. Yet it didn't feel as if their spirits had connected the way he'd hope. The Aisling of this world still remained somewhat a stranger. She was not truly *his*, and he wondered if she ever would be. Perhaps the kind of love they shared in his time was no longer possible in this one.

No, he didn't believe that. What they shared transcended time. If their love wasn't so incredibly powerful, he'd never have been able to trace Aisling to the future. He needed to be patient, to let things unfold naturally between them.

But a part of him remained uneasy. Something in this world was interfering with his connection to Aisling. Some darkness or fear caused her to keep her distance. What was it that made her panic the first time they'd shared loveplay at his house? The memory of her leaving, her eyes wild and full of terror, haunted him. In the past, it had been Fergal who destroyed things. What opponent did he face in this time period?

Fergal. Connar's thoughts drifted back to the past. If only he had been able to convince his foster brother that the Sisters had done nothing evil to him. But Fergal was so stubborn.

The memory came back to him:

"Connar? Where am I?"

Looking down at Fergal, Connor knew a rush of joy. His eyes were no longer fever-glazed, but alert and aware.

"You're on the way back to Dunsheauna," he responded. "And you're alive and well. Look at your leg. It's almost healed!"

Connar couldn't keep the exultation from his voice. He'd left the fortress on a near hopeless mission. Now, he returned in triumph. The only thing that would make him happier would be to have the fair-haired woman called Aisling at his side. But I will have her with me. I will. I could no more be parted from her than give up my own soul.

Abruptly, he knew a twinge of doubt. If only she weren't one of them, a follower of the Goddess, a devotee of the Old Ways.

Fergal, who had been laboring to sit up, finally forced his fever-weakened limbs to obey and gave a sudden cry. It was not a sound of relief, but of fear. "Christos save me! What has happened?"

"What's happened is that you're healed! The poison is gone. In a few days you will be hunting beside me once more."

"How?" Fergal clutched at his once ruined leg. "Where did you take me? I had such strange dreams. Of waves of light swirling around me. And women...their faces..." He shuddered.

"It was the Sisters, they healed you. It was magic."

Fergal stared at him, his eyes wide with horror. "You took me to them. How could you?"

"Would you rather I let you die? I had to do something!"

"And so, you ignored my wishes and took me to those evil, spell-chanting crones. Even though I forbid it!"

"And now you are strong and healthy again!"

Connar glared at his foster brother. What was wrong with Fergal? Had the fever damaged his wits? What man would curse those who had brought him back from the edge of death?

Fergal groaned, his features distorted with bitterness. "I tell you, I would rather have died. Those women...they did something to me. I can feel it."

"Aye! They saved your life! Look at yourself, at your leg, near healed already. There is nothing wrong with you, Fergal. Not a mark upon you. Of course, you feel addle-witted and weak. Anyone would after what you've endured. But it's no doing of the Sisters. They healed you! I saw it all. They didn't lay a finger on you, and yet your leg became whole and sound once more!"

Returning to the present, Connar exhaled a sigh. "You were such a fool. You never imagined how narrow-minded and stupid everyone would turn out to be."

****

Allison watched in amazement as Connar and the other man circled each other, swords raised. His opponent was a bulky man with long wavy, strawberry blond hair and a ruddy complexion. They were both dressed in old fashioned garments: loose woolen pants and tunics in a homespun plaid.

The fair-haired man lashed out with his huge sword. Connar whirled out of the way, then immediately struck with his weapon. As the sword slashed the man's shirt, she felt a wave of dread. They weren't using blunted weapons but deadly sharp blades!

The fight continued, with both combatants drawing blood. Her fear intensified. Connar looked as if he was tiring. She could see the sheen of sweat on his face. The fair-haired man lunged. His sword slashed Connar's right arm and Connar dropped his weapon. His opponent moved in to finish him off.

Allison tried to scream but no sound came out. Yet, the fair-haired man seemed to hear her. He left Connar slumped on the ground and approached her, his bloody blade raised. The look of utter hatred in his blue eyes almost made her heart stop. She stood frozen, unable to move. He drew near and—

Allison sat up in bed, gasping. Her heart was racing and she was perspiring profusely. She took deep breaths, trying to calm herself. Benjamin climbed on her lap, mewing as if he felt her distress. She petted him, hoping that soothing him would make her feel better as well. "It was only a dream," she murmured, "nothing more than a dream."

And yet… It had been so similar to her experience in Connar's bathroom. In both the hallucination and the dream, she'd been in fear of her life, and somehow Connar was involved.

But this was a dream, which meant it came from her subconscious. Maybe it simply represented her panic at the thought of becoming involved in a new relationship. But if that was the case, her subconscious was taking things too far. There were risks to getting involved—like ending up with a broken heart. But that didn't exactly equate with having some guy come at her with giant sword!

She let out a deep breath. Maybe the dream meant her subconscious was trying to warn her there was something dangerous about Connar, that he was a sociopath or a serial killer or something. But that made no sense. If he was a killer, he'd had plenty of opportunities to do her harm. He could have done her in the first night at his place. Besides, her instincts couldn't be that far off. No, she felt certain Connar was a good guy. Even Benjamin liked him, and Benjamin *never* liked men.

"This is ridiculous," she told herself. "It was a stupid dream. You have to stop obsessing about it and get some sleep."

She went to the bathroom and took some antihistamine, hoping it would make her drowsy, then returned to bed.

She finally fell asleep. If she dreamed, it was of nothing distressing enough to wake her. But in the morning, the memory of the nightmare still made her stomach clench. She decided to call Megan and get her take on it.

But when she reached her, Megan couldn't talk. "I'm about to go into a big meeting, Allie," she explained. "Call me tonight."

Allison put down the phone, feeling frustrated. "Maybe I should call Connar," she mused to herself. "Maybe he can think of an explanation."

As soon as he answered, all her doubts and worries seemed to vanish. They talked about their plans for the day and arranged to meet at his apartment that evening.

After breakfast, she tried to settle down to writing the second article in her series. As she reviewed details from the ceremony with Megan's group, she thought about Sophia's offer to give her more details on pagan ceremonies. Maybe she should call her. Talking about Wiccan stuff might jumpstart her creativity.

She grabbed her phone and punched in the number. A woman quickly answered, "Hello."

"Hi Sophia. It's me...Allison."

"Allison! That's wonderful. I was hoping you

would call."

"I wasn't sure I'd reach you. I thought you might be at work."

"I don't have a job. How can I help you? Are you still worried about Connar and what happened?"

"Ummm…not really." So not true. She hadn't been able to get the dream out of her mind. The unsettled feeling it aroused was part of the reason she was having so much trouble writing.

"About Connar, I think you should know…" Sophia hesitated. "He's a different sort of person. I would be wary of him."

"I thought you said at the gathering that you didn't know him."

"I don't. But whenever anyone talks about him, I get this feeling…I think you should be careful around him."

"Seriously?" This chick was taking the woo woo thing too far!

"I'm very sensitive to these things and something about him doesn't seem quite right."

Yeah, he's too perfect. Or maybe it's because he isn't interested in *you.* "I'll be careful, of course." Right. She'd already made love with him! That was hardly being careful.

Wanting to change the subject, she said, "Enough about Connar. What I need help with is the Wicca information."

She went down the list of things she wasn't clear about, jotting down Sophia's responses. As Sophia went on at length, Allison started to get over Sophia's aversion to Connar and focus on the article. "Wow, this is great stuff. You really know a lot about this."

"I've spent a great of time studying these practices."

"So, how did you get into Wicca?"

"I was born into it, you might say."

"Your parents were Wiccan?"

"Two of my aunts were."

"Oh? Do they ever come to the group?"

"No. They're dead."

"Dead? Both of them?"

"Yes. They died in an…accident."

Allison could hear the pain in Sophia's voice. "I'm sorry. I didn't mean to bring up unpleasant memories."

"It's all right," Sophia said. "It happened a long time ago."

Determined to change the subject to something more pleasant, Allison returned to asking questions about Wicca ceremonies. When she felt like she had enough material, she thanked Sophia and tried to end the call.

"I'd love to talk more," Sophia said. "Maybe we could meet for lunch."

"I'm afraid I'd better stay home and keep working on the articles."

"Perhaps dinner?"

"I have plans. But maybe next week we could get together. I'll call you." *No way am I telling you my date tonight is with Connar, and I'm keeping the next few days open for him!*

"Please do call me. And if you ever want to talk…about anything, I'm here."

"Thanks. I'll remember that."

As Allison ended the call, she couldn't help wondering about Sophia's persistence. She was probably trying to be supportive. *Too bad it makes me feel smothered.* And then there were all the negative things Sophia had said about Connar. Thinking about the other woman's concerns, Allison experienced a twinge of doubt. But the people who actually knew Connar seemed to think he was an okay guy. She wasn't going to worry too much about Sophia's gut reaction to Connar. For all she knew, Sophia was one of those women who mistrusted all men.

Feeling reassured, Allison got to work on the second article. She was almost finished when her phone rang. *Connar.* Tingling warmth seemed to spread down her body as she recognized his number.

"Hello, Connar," she answered in her most seductive voice.

"Ah, hello." He sounded a bit taken back by her breathy tone. "How are you today?"

"Wonderful. And you?"

"I am also wonderful."

"Yes, you are." She couldn't help giggling.

"I know we talked about getting together tonight."

Panic surged through her. Was he canceling?

"But I thought maybe rather than waiting until tonight, you might want to come watch this afternoon when I have my sword fighting practice session."

"Why sure. That would be great." Would it? After her dream last night, she wasn't so sure she wanted to be around swords!

"My sparring partner and I practice at his shop—he does customized welding. That's the only place we've found that's open enough. We've tried once or twice to practice in a park, but it tends to draw a crowd and once someone called the police. My partner...some people are uncomfortable with the way he looks."

"Why is that?"

"He's a biker, and when they see him with a sword, they tend to overreact."

"Ah," Allison responded. *A biker is fine. Just as long as he doesn't look like the guy in my dream.*

"If I give you the address, would you mind meeting us? Or do you want me to get a cab and come get you?"

If anything went wrong, she definitely wanted to have her car. "I'll come meet you. No problem."

"When you're ready, I'll give you directions."

Allison grabbed a piece of junk mail and a pen. "Ready," she said.

Chapter Nine

Not an area she'd want to visit alone after dark, Allison thought as she turned down the narrow street. It was in an industrial part of town with lots of warehouses, very run down. The gang graffiti she'd seen along the way didn't do much to reassure her. Rather than giving her a street number, Connar had described the shop—a wooden building with faded blue paint and an even more faded sign that read "Custom Metal Work."

When she found it, the place looked deserted, and she felt a tad uneasy as she got out and locked her car. She was trying to decide whether to knock on the narrow wooden door or see if it was unlocked, when Connar came out. He was wearing a long off-white shirt that looked like it was made of linen, loose plaid trousers and soft leather boots. She felt a touch of surprise that he wore medieval garb simply to practice. But there was no doubt it suited him. Yum!

His green eyes shone as he approached and she felt a thrill pass down her body. When he leaned over and kissed her lightly on the lips, the thrill turned into a full-out surge of lust. He took her hand. "Come in."

They entered a cavernous room. On the far side were the bulky shapes of several motorcycles and a vintage model car, but the rest of the space was empty. As she looked around, a door opened on the far side of the room and a man came out. His clothing was similar to Connar's, but he was even bigger. With his body-builder physique, long blond hair pulled back into a ponytail, and Fu Manchu mustache, he reminded Allison of a professional wrestler. She could see why people might find him threatening. But at least he didn't look like the guy in her dream.

Connar introduced the man as Mark. Mark nodded to Allison then shook her hand. She had the sudden thought that it might be cool to interview him for *The Highpoint*. There were a lot of biker types in the Denver area. Or she could do something on the medieval enactment group. Either way, he seemed like an intriguing guy.

Mark left to turn on the lights, which transformed the dimly-lit garage into a well-lit space. Connar led Allison to a bench. "You can watch from here." He gave her a boyish grin. "Wish me luck."

"I'll do better than that." She reached up to kiss him on the lips.

The two men retrieved their swords from a table at the far side of the room and walked to the middle of the open space. No wonder Connar had such a fabulous build. Wielding a sword that size would give anyone muscles.

He'd said the swords were special practice ones and not sharp, but they were obviously big and pointed and heavy, and could do some serious damage if they weren't careful. As they engaged in mock combat, Allison's heart began to race. She couldn't help remembering her dream and the fierce fair-haired monster who had wounded Connar and then attacked her.

But as the two men sparred, she began to relax. They moved with such grace, it was almost like a ballet. It was obvious they'd practiced together so much they knew each other's rhythms. They were very careful to keep their actual contact to glancing blows or quick "pricks" rather than more damaging strikes or thrusts. Their display was meant to give observers the idea of what sword combat would be like, without revealing the brutality of true battle.

But she'd seen the real thing in her dream and she knew it was terrifying. The memory of the fair-haired man slicing Connar's arm open filled her mind. She recalled the blood pouring down and Connar's sword falling to the ground. The next moment, it was happening right in front of her. She gasped as the workshop disappeared and she found herself in a grassy open area. The fair-haired man from her dream approached the bleeding Connar and stabbed him in the chest. Allison screamed.

The next thing she knew she was on the floor and Connar was looming over her, his face stark white, his eyes agonized. "Aisling," he whispered. "*Macushla.*"

Allison forced herself to breathe slowly and evenly. Gradually the world rearranged itself into some semblance of normal. Connar was crouched on the floor beside her, supporting her upper body. Mark stood nearby. She heard him say, "Should I call 911?"

"No!" she gasped. "I mean…I'm fine. I'm fine."

"You're sure?"

"Yes! Absolutely."

She felt like an utter fool. How was she going to explain what had happened? They'd think she was crazy.

She gently disengaged from Connar and sat up. "I'm okay."

"What happened?" asked Mark.

"I-I don't know. I guess I blacked out for a moment." She looked at Mark and then at Connar. She gave him a sheepish smile. "I'm afraid I did it again. Forgot to eat all day." She shrugged and tried to smile. "My stupid blood sugar."

Connar looked concerned. Mark just looked skeptical. No way did he buy her story. She thought about how she'd screamed. If they asked about that, it was going to be difficult to explain.

Connar helped her to her feet. "Mark, would you mind taking her home? I don't think she should drive."

"No! I'll be fine," Allison protested.

"Of course I'll drive her," Mark responded. To Allison he said, "Can't have you blacking out in traffic."

This was disastrous. She didn't want to go home. She'd planned a big night with Connar. She gave him a look of appeal. "All I need is something to eat. I'll be fine."

He nodded. "We could go to my place. Order something in."

"Whatever," said Mark.

"What about my car?" Allison asked.

Mark shrugged. "I can drive you there in your car and then have a buddy of mine pick me up."

He sounded a bit irritated with her. Allison couldn't exactly blame him. "I'm sorry to mess up your practice session, Mark. And make you go to all that trouble."

Mark shrugged again. "I'm going to change

117

clothes." He took off.

"I feel really bad about this," she told Connar. "I know you look forward to these practice sessions."

"It doesn't matter. All that matters is that you're all right." His expression was so tender, his green eyes intent. Allison could almost believe he cared more for her health than about cutting their practice short. She recalled his expression as he leaned over her. The look of absolute terror on his face. And what had he said? "Aisling" and then something else, something Irish.

It was probably normal that under stress he would revert to his native tongue. Aisling must be the Irish version of Allison. And it was sweet of him to be so worried for her.

She smiled at him, thinking that when they got to his place, she'd make it all up to him. "Do you want to change clothes, too?" She motioned in the direction Mark had gone.

Connar looked dubious. "Are you sure you'll be all right?"

"Of course. I'll be right here." She wanted to give him a kiss goodbye, but that seemed silly.

Connar nodded and went off to change.

****

She seemed well enough now, but what had happened to her? As Connar made his way to the back of the shop, he struggled to figure out what had occurred. He felt certain Allison's distress and her fainting must be connected to him. Perhaps she was remembering incidents from her past life. Maybe it was time to tell her who he was…and who she was.

But a part of him argued that she wasn't ready. It appeared the memories she had from her life as Aisling distressed her. He could only hope she didn't recall what he'd been forced to do to her at the very end. She definitely wasn't ready for that.

He met Mark coming out of his office. "So, what's going on with this chick?" Mark asked. "Is she anorexic or something?"

"Anorexic? What do you mean?"

"Well, she looks normal, but going without eating to the point that she freaks out and faints..." Mark shrugged. "Seems weird to me."

"I'm sure she's all right," Connar responded. "She ate heartily the other night."

Mark grinned. "Heartily. That's a weird way to put it. But you're always using those old-fashioned words. Guess it comes from growing up in Ireland."

"I'm certain it does." There were times when he longed to confide his background to Mark. But he wasn't certain how the other man would respond. Although they participated in historical reenactment events together, Connar didn't know Mark well enough to share his past.

"Too bad we had to cut short our practice," Mark said.

"I know. We'll have to try again later this week."

"Yeah. If you can tear yourself away from this Allison chick." Mark jerked his head in the direction of the bathroom. "She's pretty enough, but still...I'm not sure any woman is worth rearranging your life for."

If Mark only knew exactly how much "rearranging" he had done. "If you feel that way, it means you haven't found the right one."

Mark raised his brows, looking skeptical. "Maybe. But I doubt it."

"What type of woman would you be interested in?" Connar asked, curious.

"Someone kick-ass," Mark responded. "You know, a chick who can handle herself. There was a woman a few years ago who used to do jousting at the festivals. She beat more than a few guys. I haven't seen her in a while, so she probably got married and settled down." He made a face.

"We'll have to look for someone like that, the next time we do a reenactment."

"Don't worry about it. I'm content being a bachelor."

Connar wanted to tell him how being in love gave life meaning and fulfilled your spirit. But he knew that was something people had to find out for themselves.

Allison came out of the restroom. She looked fine now. He wondered again what had made her react so extremely.

As Mark drove them to Connar's house, Mark talked about the new sword he was having made. Connar watched Allison, wondering if she was upset enough to ask him to give up sword fighting. He felt a pang of loss at the thought of not having that link to his past, but he told himself any sacrifice he had to make to have Allison back in his life would be worth it.

****

What must Connar think of me now? The thought weighed on Allison as they drove to his house. She didn't want anything to ruin the chemistry they shared. Although for her, there wasn't much that could interfere with her body's reaction to his. Merely looking at him made her hot. Hopefully he felt the same way about her.

At Connar's house, Mark called a friend from his

cell phone and told Connar he would wait for his ride outside. As soon as she and Connar got into the house, Allison said, "I hope Mark's not too upset with me. I feel bad I ruined your practice session, and he had to go to the trouble of driving us here and getting a ride home."

"I'm certain all will be well with Mark," Connar replied.

"He doesn't seem like the type of guy you would choose for a friend," she pointed out. "Do the two of you do anything else together besides sword fighting?"

Connar shook his head.

"I thought as much. I mean, since his business involves cars and motorcycles, he must think it's strange you don't even have a vehicle."

"Mark has always been accepting of my circumstances. Now, about the pizza. Do you want the same thing you ordered last time—pepperoni with mushrooms and green peppers?"

He remembered her favorite toppings. Impressive. "That would be great," she answered.

Connar got out his cell phone. He apparently had a pizza place number in his contacts. What bachelor didn't? After he ordered, he asked Allison if she'd like something to drink. "Other than wine," he added, smiling.

"Maybe some milk or juice," she suggested.

She followed him into the kitchen, and he got her a glass of milk from a surprisingly well-stocked refrigerator. Observing that he had eggs and cheese, she decided she would make him breakfast in the morning. That is, if everything worked out the way she hoped. Once again, she felt a twinge of anxiety. *Please, don't let things get weird.* She truly wanted to make it up to him for messing up his sword practice with Mark.

"When is the next time you and Mark plan to put on a demonstration?" she asked.

"We're supposed to do one at the Renaissance Faire this weekend. Unless you'd rather I canceled. If you have other plans...or want to do something else."

He looked so intent and sincere. Was this man willing to give up something he enjoyed simply to please her? She felt touched and amazed.

"No, no. Not at all," she responded. "In fact, I'd love to go and watch you and Mark. I promise I won't faint or do anything weird." Could she really promise that? She still didn't know what had happened, what had triggered the hallucination.

He nodded, looking pleased, but also a little uncertain. He clearly didn't believe she had any control over her behavior. And who could blame him?

He told about their plans for the Faire and the times of the demonstrations. By then the doorbell rang. He paid for the pizza and brought the box into the dining room. The pizza smelled heavenly, and she *was* hungry. He brought out plates and napkins. Napkins? What a very unbachelor-like touch.

They scarfed down the pizza.

She was feeling much better when she finished. Now to satisfy some of her other appetites.

As Connar put the leftover pizza away, he told himself to go slow. But it was so difficult when she looked like that, with her cheeks slightly flushed and her lips plump and moist from eating. He thought this incarnation of Aisling was even more beautiful than the original. She'd had a better diet and used modern products to enhance her beauty. Plus, this Aisling seemed happier. She hadn't been controlled and dominated by other women all her life.

He recalled Aisling telling him she and Siobhan had been sent to the Nine Sisters when they reached puberty. Their mother had sent them to the sect because she feared they would end up married to some man who would beat and brutalize them as her husband had her.

Connar had been shocked to think a woman would believe her daughters could have a better life living in a cave with a bunch of strange women rather than marrying. Yet, he knew some men were cruel to their wives. A shameful thing and one that violated the ancient laws that honored women and respected their contribution to their tribes.

He couldn't understand it. To him, women were like the warmth of the hearth fire, magical and beautiful. Without them, life would be grim and comfortless.

"What are you thinking?" Allison was gazing at him with bemusement.

"What do you mean?"

"I mean, the way you're looking at me..." She lowered her gaze, looking embarrassed.

He responded with the first thing that popped into his head: "I was thinking about...how Irish you look."

She laughed. "I can't imagine that. I've always thought I was the epitome of the bland American blonde. Now Megan, she's the one who looks Irish."

"It depends on your clan. My tribe tended toward dark hair, with a few red-haired individuals. Anyway, it's not so much your coloring as your features that make you seem Irish."

"Your tribe?" She laughed again. "I think it's so cute how you talk about your background. No, no, I'm not laughing at you. I find your way of speaking so quaint."

If only he could tell her the truth. Let her know who she was and who he was. But something made him hold back. He had begun to realize he wanted to earn her love in *this* life, not depend on the connection between them in the past.

Glancing at her, his breath caught. There was such yearning in her gaze. It exactly echoed what he was feeling. He leaned over and kissed her gently on the lips. The mere touch of her flesh seemed to burn him, but oh, what a delightful fire!

"Love me," she whispered. "Please."

He nodded and drew her into his arms.

They kissed and kissed, until they were both out of breath and gasping. Then she drew away and stood. He watched in helpless expectation as she drew down the straps of her dress and wriggled out of it. Feeling nearly on fire with need, he got up to remove his own garments.

They undressed wordlessly, their gazes raking each other. She was finished before he was and as she watched him, the hunger in her expression so much like his own. At last, when they were both naked, he sat on the couch and pulled her down onto his lap. They kissed, tongues mating, teasing and tantalizing. Her hand touched his shaft and he let out a groan. He was already near bursting, and her provocative caresses threatened to send him over the edge. Grasping her wrist, he gently drew her hand away.

She gave a soft laugh and stood. Picking up her

purse, she removed a foil-wrapped condom. He was on the verge of suggesting they go into the bedroom when she tore open the package and approached the couch. He sat rigidly, gritting his teeth in an agony of arousal as she gently slid the condom over his heated, throbbing shaft.

All at once, something in him snapped. He could wait no longer. Grasping her arms, he pulled her down so she straddled him. As he held her, she arranged her body over his and slid her hips down until her tight, slippery sheathe surrounded him. He remained still, paralyzed by the nearly unendurable pleasure of their joining. She began to move, rocking her hips. With a groan he thrust his own hips upwards. She let out a wild cry.

She was impaled, helpless with the incredible sensation of his cock deep inside her. Her own rhythm forgotten, Allison let go and allowed him to take control. Each time he pushed up with his hips, he seemed to go deeper inside her. Touching her essence. Touching her soul.

Ecstasy, like fireworks before her closed eyes, exploded inside her as she peaked. A near-scream broke past her lips. And still he thrust inside her, pumping fast and hard. She hung on for dear life, the waves of bliss building and cresting inside her.

He let out a guttural moan and went still. She rested her head against his shoulder, feeling an incredible sense of completion and a moment of overwhelming tenderness. He was holding her as if he never wanted to let go. And she felt the same.

As if they belonged to each other. As if their souls had touched and merged.

For a moment, she reveled in the sensation. Then she slowly came back to the real world. The sense of connection between them faded and she slid off his lap, feeling a tiny bit embarrassed. As fantastic as the sex was, they'd been on a total of three dates. There was no way she could be in love with him. Lust at first sight, yeah, she could believe in that. But not love.

With that thought, she became self-conscious. Now that the sex was over, it felt a bit awkward to be sitting naked in his living room. If they were in bed, maybe it would feel more natural. They could lie around for a while, talk a bit and maybe even have sex again. He was young and virile, so hey, why not?

But they were on his couch, which made it more problematic. If she got dressed, would he think she wasn't interested in more sex? On the other hand, if she remained naked, he might feel she wasn't satisfied and was pressuring him to do her again.

The thought made her grab her clothes from beside the couch and head for the bathroom.

Chapter Ten

Connar repressed a sigh as he got up to dispose of the condom. For a brief time, they'd been so close. He'd felt the connection between their spirits, as strong as ever. But as soon as their bodies were no longer joined, the bond had seemingly vanished. She was back to being Allison, a woman he didn't truly know, whose actions he couldn't anticipate.

Returning to the living room, he reluctantly began to dress. Maybe he should have suggested they go to the bedroom. Maybe in that setting she'd have been more willing to cuddle. The wild, unrestrained nature of their lovemaking might have embarrassed her. She seemed very uninhibited, but maybe that wasn't how she thought of herself. Or maybe she still thought of him as a stranger.

The idea aroused an ache inside him. How long would it take to win this woman's heart? To make her understand she was the very reason for his existence? What if he told her they *weren't* strangers? Would that help or hinder things between them?

She was so skittish, so wary. He suspected it was because of the other man, Justin, the bastard who'd hurt her. If only he'd arrived in her life a little sooner. He could have spared her all that pain. Of course, Siobhan had warned him time travel was imperfect. And he'd needed those years to find his way in this era.

127

It hadn't been easy to learn a new language and find his way in the modern world. The gold he'd brought with him had helped, but it had taken a while to convert it into useable wealth. Most of the coin and precious metal shops hadn't wanted any part of it. Some of them seemed worried he'd stolen the jewelry from a museum, while others simply couldn't afford the purchase price. He'd been so desperate, he'd finally agreed to have the gold torc melted down and sold for scrap.

But he'd refused to do that with the bracelet and the dagger. They were works of art and it would have been wrong to destroy them. Thank heavens, he'd discovered the Renaissance Faire, where there were people who cared as much about the beautiful Celtic knot work design of the pieces as they did about the value of the gold and jewels they were made out of. Still, it had taken months to find a buyer wealthy enough to pay what the pieces were worth.

The sale had given him enough to buy a house and set up the shop. And the shop had done well, allowing him to keep the other jewelry he'd brought with him. Someday Allison would wear the woman's torc and bracelet. The thought of her decked out like a queen from his own era made his heart soar. Soon, he promised himself. Soon.

****

Once more clothed, Allison dared to examine herself in the bathroom mirror. Thankfully, nothing weird happened. Although she did notice how nice she looked. Her skin glowed. Her eyes were bright. Clearly, sex with Connar was good for her. *He* was good for her. That is, he seemed to be. It was hard to think clearly about their relationship. The sex was so fabulous it could easily make her lose her perspective.

No, that wasn't it. There was nothing negative about what she and Connar had. He treated her like a queen. He was tender and nurturing. And everyone who knew him seemed to think the world of him.

The only downside was the strange things she'd experienced since she'd met him including the terrifying hallucination she'd had in this very bathroom. The nightmare of people trying to kill her. The bizarre thing that had happened while he was sword fighting with Mark. No matter how she tried to tell herself otherwise, she remained convinced those experiences were linked to Connar.

Was it possible Megan was right and she was having a flashback of something from his past life, or maybe even her own?

What an unnerving thought, that sometime in the past she'd been chased down and threatened by an enraged mob. Why would they have wanted to do her in? Had she been a witch in another time?

She shuddered. This line of thinking was getting a little creepy. But it did make a weird kind of sense, especially given how uncomfortable she'd been with the whole Wicca thing. She'd assumed her unease had to do with her general aversion to group activities, but maybe there was more to it. All the women had been nice, but except for Megan, she had no desire to see any of them again. Somehow the whole experience gave her a bad vibe.

Strangely, she didn't feel that way about Connar, even though he was obviously involved in Wicca. With Connar she felt safe...cherished...adored. What more could a girl ask for?

Hot sex, maybe?

Facing herself in the mirror, she said firmly, "Don't be such a nympho. If you're ever going to find out if this relationship is real, you need to spend time doing other things with him beside mindless boinking."

Feeling suitably determined and motivated, she left the bathroom.

Connar was in the kitchen. He was fully dressed in jeans and a button-down shirt, but hadn't put on his belt or shoes. Hmmm. Did that mean he was keeping his options open? "Would you like some wine now?" he asked. "Or maybe some tea?"

If she had wine she probably shouldn't drive home, which could give her a good excuse to spend the night. Here she was, doing it again. It was only that he was so gorgeous, so lusciously male. He'd left his shirt unbuttoned enough that she could see the faint swirls of hair on his chest and imagine his glorious pecs.

And the black jeans... Yousa! They showed off his perfect butt and emphasized his long, lean build.

So many men wore baggy jeans and loose T-shirts these days. Of course, for some of them it was a way to camouflage their beer bellies and less than toned backsides. Few guys matched Connar's superb shape. Mark, too, had appeared amazingly buff. Must be the sword fighting.

Speaking of which... "I still feel bad about disrupting your workout," she said. "I guess Mark was pretty irritated with me."

"Don't worry about Mark. He has a bit of a temper. But he'll get over it soon enough. By the time we attend the Renaissance Faire this weekend, everything will be fine."

"I could drive you to the Faire instead of us going with him," she offered.

"I must arrive there quite early."

"I don't mind. In the summer it's easier to get up early than in the winter when it's dark in the morning."

"You have beautiful summers here," he said. "The sun shines nearly every day."

"It's not like that in Ireland? Even in the summer?"

He shook his head. "Maybe some years. But normally, we have a lot of cloudy days even in summer." He smiled. "That's why it's so green."

"I'd love to go there."

"I'd love to take you."

Here we go again! It was unbelievable, the way the sexual tension built between them. Over nothing. As his green eyes gazed into hers searchingly, longingly, the breathless, soaring hunger built inside her yet again.

She put down her glass of wine and approached him. A few inches away, she paused and waited.

He didn't disappoint. Putting his own glass on the counter, he reached out for her. She sighed as they embraced. Everything about him, the way he smelled, the feel of his body against hers, was sublime.

He kissed her with slow tenderness and mouthed her neck. His breath was hot upon her as he nibbled on her earlobe and licked the whorl of her ear.

She felt like swooning.

They kissed again. Long. Intoxicating. Their mouths a perfect match. Slow this time. No hurry.

Except she was trembling with desire. Near faint with the longing building inside her.

He finally broke away to say, "Maybe we should

go into the bedroom."

She nodded.

Their clothes were off in seconds, and they were on the bed. King-sized, to fit his tall frame. The brown velour comforter was soft beneath her. But now he wasn't kissing her lips but her body. Tenderly. Reverently. She felt as if he was worshiping her.

More delicious kissing. She gasped as he stuck his tongue in her navel. Shuddered with delight as his provocative mouth moved lower.

She slid her thighs apart, eager for more…so much more.

As he loved her with his lips—gently at first then with deeper pressure—a deep moan escaped her. Rivers of ecstasy flowed through her body, rising, surging… She tensed in expectation of her peak, then realized that despite the incredible pleasure he was giving her, she wanted more. She wanted him inside her!

"Connar, please…" she gasped. He raised his head, his lips glistening with wetness from her body and his green eyes dazed. "I want…you," she whispered.

He seemed to realize what she was asking for. His nostrils flared and his expression turned harsher, more masculine than ever. He looked as if he no longer wanted to worship her, but to conquer her.

He was on the verge of entering her when her brain kicked in. "Do you have another condom?" she whispered.

He nodded and rolled to the other side of the bed. As he took out a condom from the drawer and put it on, she suppressed a sigh.

I need to go back on the pill or something. This stopping to make sure we have protection sucks big-

time.

But then he rose over her and the magic resumed. She loved the way he looked at her, so fierce and intent, like a beautiful cat ready to pounce. Gazing deep into his green eyes, she surrendered utterly. He slid his cock deep inside her, and she let out a scream. "...oh...oh...oh...uhhhhh...!"

This was what she wanted

As he thrust, her cries rose in crescendo. Together they slid over the cliff, his deep groan of completion mingling with her own wild shriek.

Transformed. Shattered. She rode the swirling waterfall down, down, down, finally landing, gasping, in the deep pool below.

Breathless and wondering, she came to herself again. Her face was pressed against his sweat-slicked shoulder. Her heart pounded like a drum. "Oh my God," she murmured. "That was amazing."

He raised himself over her and smiled, and her sense of triumph intensified. Connar was always so serious. To make him laugh or smile felt incredible.

She touched his face, her heart swelling with tenderness.

When she looked at him like that... Connar felt a surge of intense satisfaction. He'd done everything to reach this moment. Her face glowed with happiness and her eyes shone with something that must surely be love.

He wanted to tell her what she meant to him, to finally reveal that she was his heart and soul, his very reason for existence. But something held him back, warning him not to risk breaking the spell, the magical closeness they shared at this moment.

This was Allison, not Aisling. Their spirits and

bodies were the same, and yet there were differences.

****

Allison woke. Eyes still closed, she stretched, feeling like a contented cat. Her body felt exquisitely, deliciously sore. She opened her eyes. The bed next to her was empty. Connar was already up. A vague disappointment pricked at her. Not that she wanted more sex. Hard to imagine they'd made love twice more over the course of the night. A record for her. Was it for Connar?

She sat up. Sounds drifted in through the open door. Mahon barked and Allison recalled the dog climbing up beside Connar late in the night. She wasn't sure she was ready to sleep with a giant, hairy dog, but at least Mahon had stayed on Connar's side of the bed. Mahon gave another short bark. A moment later, Connar entered the room, followed by the dog, tail wagging.

"Sleep well?" Connar asked with a smile.

"Yes. Very well."

"I'm glad you're awake. I thought I'd go purchase some groceries to make breakfast, and I didn't want you to wake up and wonder where I was."

"Breakfast? Mmmm, that sounds good."

"What would you like to eat?"

"I'd be happy with almost anything." She shrugged. "Get whatever sounds good to you."

He nodded. "I'll be back soon." To Mahon, he said, "Come on, boy. Let's go for a walk."

Ahh, that was what Mahon was so excited about.

After Connar left, Allison climbed languorously from the bed. Her dress lay on the floor, looking very much the worse for wear. Maybe she'd wear one of

Connar's shirts for now. She went to the closet and began looking for one of the beautiful cotton garments he wore. Finding a simple white shirt, she put it on and buttoned up the front. She swam in it—no surprise given Connar's very broad shoulders—but it would work.

She couldn't help taking a peek through his closet. More shirts, some fleece pullovers. Farther back, she saw a couple of the simple shirts without collars or buttons like the one Connar had worn while sword-fighting. She felt the fabric and realized they were made of linen. Boy, they must be a bitch to iron. He probably had to have them professionally laundered.

As she was about to quit her snooping, something in the back of the deep closet caught her eye. The glint of metal. There, half hidden, was a sword. It was mounted on the wall, most of the blade obscured by the hangers full of clothing. She drew back the clothing and stared at the huge and astonishingly beautiful weapon. The Celtic knotwork pattern on the hilt appeared to be of gold inlaid with genuine emeralds. Gazing at it, she felt a sense of awe and also a strange feeling of dread. Despite her unease, she reached up to examine the weapon. The next moment she heard the door to the apartment open. Connar was back.

She hurriedly left the closet and closed the door. Grabbing up her purse, she darted into the bathroom. As she took off the shirt and turned on the bathtub tap, her thoughts raced. If the gold and emeralds on the hilt of the sword were real, it was worth a fortune. And the workmanship was so detailed, so amazing, so obviously handmade. The sword looked as if it belonged in a museum. Where had Connar gotten it?

As she turned on the shower and got in, she wondered if she'd discovered the source of Connar's wealth. Maybe he was a dealer in ancient artifacts. Knowing he owned the Wicca shop and this beautifully decorated house, she'd assumed Connar had money. But believing he was comfortably well-off was one thing. Discovering he owned an ancient artifact that was probably worth hundreds of thousands of dollars was quite another. And if the sword was really what she thought it was, then it was probably illegal, or at least unethical, for him to have it in his possession.

And then there was the way her body had reacted to the sword, with a kind of instinctive fear. Why? Was it connected to the hallucination she had in Connar's bathroom the first time? Was she reliving events from Connar's past? Or her own? A shiver of foreboding rippled down her body.

As she shampooed her hair, she tried to quell her anxious thoughts. She told herself the sword must be an amazing reproduction, although she couldn't quite believe it. There was something about the sword that was so authentic. And then there was her instinctive reaction to the weapon. Finding a revolver in Connar's closet would have bothered her. But the way the sword made her feel was different. This response seemed to come from deep inside her, as if she'd somehow seen the sword before.

She finished her shower, dried off, put on the shirt, then combed out her hair and blew it partially dry. After putting on mascara, which she always carried in her purse, she tried to decide whether she should use her lipstick as blusher. She really didn't need it. Her cheeks were still rosy and glowing. Great sex could do that for a girl.

Great sex with a guy who had a huge, brutal-looking sword in his closet.

No, she wouldn't think about that.

She left the bathroom and found Connar in the kitchen making breakfast. "The food smells great," she said.

Connar turned to see Allison standing in the door of the kitchen and his heart seemed to turn over. With her hair still damp and disheveled and no make-up, she looked so much like the Aisling he remembered.

To hide the rush of emotion he felt, he turned back to the stove and lifted the lid on the pan. "I made an omelet. Mushrooms, green peppers and cheese. I hope you like all those things?"

"Sounds great." Despite her words, her tone seemed uncertain. When he looked at her, a shadow seemed to flash across her lovely features and she glanced away. "Anything I can do to help?" she asked.

"No, thank you. It's almost ready." He replaced the lid on the omelet and unwrapped a loaf of bread. As he cut several slices and put them in the toaster, Allison moved around the kitchen. There was no doubt about it. She was fidgety and nervous. Why?

He put portions of the omelet and slices of toast on plates.

"Do you want me to carry them into the dining room?" she asked.

"Aye. And what would you like to drink?"

"Milk if you have it."

"Would you like orange juice as well?"

"Sure."

A perfectly normal conversation, and yet

something, though subtle, seemed changed between them.

"Are you a breakfast person?" she asked as they sat down at the table.

He wasn't certain what she meant. "I'm sorry?"

"Do you usually eat a big breakfast, even when you don't have guests?"

He nodded. "A lot of days I only eat two meals, so they are often hearty."

"Two meals? Is that a special diet?"

"It's what I was used to growing up."

"An Irish tradition?"

"I suppose so." *Actually, it's a dark-age tradition,* he wanted to answer.

"Eating breakfast is supposed to be good for you," she said between bites. "But for me it's usually a bowl of cereal or a bagel. Then I eat a snack later in the morning. I guess I'm a 'grazer'. That's supposed to be healthy too—eating several small meals a day." She looked up from her food. "I should have asked you to get a newspaper. It's an old-fashioned habit of mine, reading the newspaper in the morning. I know most people get their news on-line, but I like print, at least for newspapers and magazines. I was an English major in college. I guess that's my excuse."

She *was* nervous. The way she kept talking, as if something was making her uncomfortable. She'd been like that in the beginning, but gradually relaxed as they'd spent more time together. *What had changed?*

As soon as she was finished eating, she got up and carried her dishes into the kitchen. When she started to run water in the sink, he stopped her. "Don't worry about the dishes. I can do them later."

She nodded. "I guess I should be going then. I have a lot to do today. I need to finish another article. Then I need to meet with the editor of the magazine."

She went into the bedroom and closed the door. Connar felt a twinge of alarm. Something was wrong.

He cleaned up the kitchen, struggling to figure out what had happened. A short while later, she came out, dressed in her own clothes and carrying her purse. His unease turned to distress. She was leaving, and some instinct told him it wasn't simply because she had things to do. When she kissed him lightly and then drew away, his worst fears seemed to be coming true. He tried to figure out a way to ask her what was wrong, but before he could come up with the words, she said, "I'll see you Saturday, for the Renaissance Faire. I....uh....I'm sure we'll talk before then."

Chapter Eleven

Allison walked swiftly to her car. She had to get away from Connar for a while and try to figure things out. If she could have asked him about the sword, he might have been able to reassure her. But how could she bring it up? The way she'd discovered the weapon made it look like she'd been snooping through his things. Which was exactly what she'd been doing. Besides, even if he gave her a perfectly reasonable explanation for where he'd gotten the sword, could she believe him? Coupled with her inability to find out anything about Connar's background on the internet, the sword set off all sorts of alarms.

Well, damn. All along, she'd thought Connar was too good to be true. Average, boring women like her didn't attract stunningly handsome wealthy men, men who then fell instantly in love with them. It was a fairy tale, and now it looked like her Cinderella story might be about to come to the end.

But if Connar was a criminal or a con man, why was he with *her*? She had nothing he could steal, no trust fund or jewelry or anything of real value. And if he was a sexual predator, he hadn't had to use much coercion to get what he wanted. Not to mention, she was certain sexual predators weren't so tender and loving with their victims.

She hadn't sensed anything kinky in all their bouts

of lovemaking. And that's what it had felt like—making love. Not hot sex. Not mindless getting-it-on. The real deal, the merging of their spirits as well as their souls.

"Sheesh, you are far gone, aren't you?" Here she was waxing poetic about their physical relationship when only a minute before she'd suspected him of all sorts of horrible things.

But it was impossible not to be affected by such a sublime sexual experience. It had been incredible, beyond anything she could imagine. Thinking about it, she let out a long sigh. All she had to do was think about making love with Connar, and all her doubts went away.

They eased even more when she talked on the phone with Megan after arriving home. When she told her friend about the sword, Megan was unconcerned. "Maybe it's an excellent reproduction. There are a handful of smiths in the country who do that kind of work. And the ornamentation is probably gold plate and green glass. And if even those are real emeralds, they're probably not jewelry quality."

"But what about the way it made me feel? I swear, I experienced this gut-punch of fear when I saw it."

"Well, you did say the people in your first vision were carrying weapons. If that's a memory of being attacked in another life, then your assailants were probably armed with swords. So swords are going to be a hot-button for you."

"I suppose so," Allison agreed. She wanted to believe what Megan was telling her. If she tried hard enough, and replaced her anxiety over the sword with memories of making love with Connar, she felt sure she could make the doubts go away.

"So, other than finding the sword, how are things between the two of you?" Megan asked.

"Great. Really great. I mean, we're so compatible it's crazy. In bed especially." Allison gave an embarrassed laugh.

Megan sighed. "Lucky duck. I'd give a lot to find someone like Connar."

"Well, who wouldn't? I mean, he's about perfect. Handsome, comfortably well-off, considerate and attentive. I could go on and on. And frankly, that's part of the problem, why I keep coming up with all these issues. Connar's too amazing to be real."

"Sounds like you're falling in love," Megan teased.

"Well, I certainly could fall for him, and fall hard. That's what scares me to death!"

"Relax. Maybe you're one of those lucky people who has found their soulmate."

"Do you believe in that sort of thing?"

"Well, why not? Somewhere out there in time and space, there must be someone for everyone."

"Time and space?" Allison laughed.

"Well, yeah. I mean, somewhere in some lifetime, I believe I'll find *the one*."

"Ah, the reincarnation theory. If things don't work out in this lifetime, you can always have hope for the next one, right?"

"Well, why not? It's a positive way of looking at things."

"I guess. If you can buy that New Age stuff."

"And you can't?"

"I don't know. Maybe I can. There is something about Connar. From the first time I met him I had this feeling...like I already knew him."

"See? There you go!"

"Okay. You've fulfilled your duty as a good friend and helped me get over my crazy worries. Obviously, you're right and I shouldn't worry so much. I need to stop analyzing everything."

"Good. Then I'll talk to you later. I have to get back to work."

"Bye. And thanks."

Allison clicked off her phone, smiling to herself. Yeah, that's what she'd do. Go with the flow and see what happened. At worst, she'd have experienced the best sex of her life. Maybe Megan was right and there was nothing sinister about Connar. If she just stopped agonizing and let things happen, their relationship might even become something permanent and lasting.

****

Connar stared at the cell phone in his hand and tried to decide what to do. Should he call Allison and try to explain? He was fairly certain he knew what was wrong. When he went into the bedroom to tidy up, there, lying on the bed, was the shirt she'd worn while eating breakfast. Since she'd obviously gotten the shirt from his closet, there was a good chance she'd seen the sword.

She'd probably guessed it wasn't a replica. While she couldn't know it had been made hundreds of years in the past and possessed magical qualities, she would obviously wonder where he'd gotten it. She might even think he'd stolen it. That could account for her strange behavior. If she thought he was a thief, she might worry he was dishonest in other ways.

How was he going to convince her the sword

belonged to him? He could tell her the whole story of who he was and how he'd come to be in this place and time. But he wasn't certain she was ready for that.

He put down the phone and began to pace. Why hadn't he thought to hide the sword before she came over? They'd made such progress. Finally started to get close. Then she saw the sword and grew wary. What if she refused to see him again? Then he'd have to tell her the truth.

Mahon padded over to him to see what was wrong. Connar leaned down and stroked the dog reassuringly. "Sorry, Mahon. I don't mean to upset you. It's Allison. I'm so worried I'll ruin things with her."

As Mahon gazed at him with his patient brown eyes, the cell phone rang. Connar let out a deep breath and checked to see who was calling. Allison. His heart seemed to be in his throat as he answered. "Hello."

"Hi." The mere sound of her voice sent an ache of longing through him. "I…uh…I wanted to apologize for leaving so abruptly this morning. I didn't want you to think I was…that I didn't enjoy…well, you know…" She laughed softly. It was the most beautiful sound he'd ever heard.

"Of course." He felt almost weak with relief. "It was…that is…I enjoyed it as well." What a foolish thing to say. But it was difficult to put what he felt into words. Not to mention, probably unwise. He'd didn't want to scare her off again.

"Well, anyway," she continued. "I was thinking…once I've taken care of the work things I need to do, I could pick you up and we could have dinner over here."

She wanted to see him! Thank the gods! "I could

take a cab," he said quickly. "Then you wouldn't have to bother picking me up. For that matter, I could have Mark drop me off. I'll probably take Mahon over to his place anyway. I don't like to leave him alone all nigh— that is...for too long." He was being presumptuous now, assuming she wanted him to spend the night.

"Of course. I'd have you bring him over here, but I'm not sure how Benjamin would cope. I guess they'll have to meet sometime, that is…"

The way she was talking implied they had a future together. At last, his dream seemed to be coming true!

"Well anyway, why don't you come by around six," she continued. "I should have everything done by then. I can't wait."

"I can't either."

After hanging up, Connar turned to Mahon. "I don't know what happened, but it looks like the gods have favored us." He let out a laugh. "Good thing, you can't talk, Mahon. Otherwise you'd probably tell me to stop grinning like a demented fool!"

****

Allison was working on her article when her phone rang. Not recognizing the number, she hesitated, thinking of everything she had to do before tonight. On the other hand, she was getting nowhere in her writing. Might as well take a break.

"Hello?" she answered.

"Hello, Allison? This is Sophia."

"Hi."

"I was calling to see how things are going for you. And to invite you to a ceremony this group I belong to will be holding in the mountains this weekend."

"I…uh…have plans for the weekend."

A pause. Then, "With Connar?"

She almost said it was none of Sophia's business. But that would be rude. What was it about Sophia that brought out the worst in her? The girl was nice enough, if a little pushy. "I'm sure I'll be seeing him some," she finally answered.

"I hope you'll be careful."

Sophia seemed to have some serious issues with guys. Or, maybe she was gay and was interested in Allison herself. An odd thought. She'd have to ask Megan. "We're taking it slow."

"I'm pleased to hear that." Sophia paused and then added, "And how is the article on Wicca going? Have you finished it? Do you need any more information?"

"Probably not anything you can help me with. Unless you know some other Wicca groups that aren't Celtic-based. I've heard some people worship Norse and Egyptian gods and goddesses."

"I can ask around. Maybe I can find out something, and we can meet for lunch next week."

"Maybe." *Or maybe not,* Allison thought as she hung up. Again, she wondered what it was about Sophia that bugged her. The woman seemed to give off weird vibes. Besides, she didn't like her attitude toward Connar. She'd never met him, so why did she always think the worst of him?

On the other hand, there were things about Connar that were very mysterious, like the amazing sword.

The next moment she thought about the other "sword" he'd wielded so expertly. The guy was built. And even more importantly, he knew how to make the best use of his *endowments*. Mmmm. She got hot merely thinking about it.

Sheesh. She had to banish him from her thoughts or she'd never get this article finished!

****

Connar arrived at six and the rest of the night went like a dream. They drank white wine and ate *coq au vin*—the fanciest dish Allison knew how to cook. Then Connar suggested they go for a walk. Allison decided to drive to the Cherry Creek Reservoir, and they strolled hand-in-hand along a pathway. Bathed in the warm golden light of the setting sun, with the deep purple silhouette of the Rockies in the distance, the setting was absolutely magical.

After a while, they stopped to watch the sunset. "I never get used to how big the sky is here," Connar said. "It seems as if you can see forever."

"I suppose Ireland's more like the Midwest. Even when it's fairly clear there, a haze seems to hover on the horizon."

Connar nodded. "Clear days like this one are fairly rare in Ireland, so we don't often get to see the sunset. Although I have seen a few over the cliffs that were amazing. But even then, it's different, more subtle. The waning sunlight shining through the mists coming up from the water creates rainbows everywhere you look."

At the mention of *cliffs* Allison felt a twinge of unease. She couldn't forget her hallucination of being chased to the edge of some massive outcropping over the ocean. Even now, thinking about it, she could almost see the enraged mob coming after her, while in the other direction was the sheer and terrifying drop-off. Despite the heat, she was instantly cold.

"What's wrong?" Connar asked.

She turned to look at him and went rigid. This

147

wasn't the Connar she knew, but another man. His hair was longer, his face younger, and he wore old-fashioned clothes. But what shocked her most of all was the sword in his hand. The very weapon she'd seen in his closet.

She blinked, waiting for him to transform back into *her* Connar. An expression of agony crossed his face, and he whispered, "Aisling."

Allison gasped. The next moment the image altered and she was looking at the Connar she knew. The expression on this version's face was puzzled and vaguely alarmed.

"Allison?"

She looked away from him, her heart pounding. Something was happening to her. Either she was losing her mind, or Megan's bizarre suggestion about past life memories had some merit.

"Allison?" he said again. "What's wrong?"

She shook her head, unable to answer. A moment later, the numbness seemed to leave her, replaced by panic. She had to get out of here! And most of all, she had to get away from Connar!

"We'd better go back," she said. "It will be dark soon." That wasn't exactly true, but it was the best excuse she could come up with.

"Of course." Connar took her hand, and she fought the urge to pull away. All at once, she was afraid of him, and she didn't know why.

The walk back to the car seemed to take forever. Neither of them spoke. About halfway there, Connar released her hand and let out a sigh. He clearly sensed how uncomfortable she was. A part of her felt bad about drawing away from him. But another part told her it was the right thing to do.

She's remembering. Not the things I'd hoped she'd recall, but the bad memories. Maybe even– Connar drew in his breath sharply. He'd feared this might happen. But he'd always told himself their love and all the special moments they'd shared were so intense and powerful they would make up for everything else. Clearly, he'd been wrong.

Don't look at me like that, Aisling...Allison! You have to understand, I thought I had no choice. I thought it was for the best!

They reached the car. She unlocked it and he climbed in the passenger's side, trying to decide what to do. He had to tell her. He had no choice. But how to begin? And what would he say when he told her about the end? How could he explain?

"Should I drop you off at Mark's?"

Her question startled him. "I...uh...aye, that would be fine."

"I just thought...Mahon's there, after all. And it *is* closer."

It was clear she wanted to get away from him as quickly as possible. Somehow, he had to restore the connection between them. As they drove through the traffic, it came to him. When she stopped to let him off, he would kiss her. As soon as he held her in his arms, she would understand.

He cursed himself for not thinking of this sooner. Instead of taking her hand after she drew away, he should have pulled her into his arms. He should have fought the terrible memory by replacing it with something good. By restoring the connection between them.

"I guess you and Mark will be leaving early for the Renaissance Faire tomorrow?"

He wanted to say they'd talked about going to the Faire together. But he'd better wait until he'd won her back. "Aye. Aye, we will."

"The traffic's terrible. I always wonder, what are all these people doing out on a Sunday night? Why aren't they home with their families, barbecuing or something?" She gave a nervous-sounding laugh. "Of course when you drive somewhere at two in the morning, it's not much different. The city that never sleeps. Or something like that." She laughed again.

She was trying to act normal. That meant her distress was ebbing and he had a chance. He would kiss her goodnight and hope for the best.

"It always amazes me how busy everyone is all the time," she went on. "Doesn't anyone ever relax and enjoy the simple pleasures of life? Like taking a walk at sunset, like we just did."

"That is true," he responded. "The simple things, being with the people you care about, that is what matters."

I love you, Allison. You are all that matters. He willed her to believe it. To feel what was in his heart. As soon as he kissed her, she would remember what they'd shared. Both in this life and in the past. At least he hoped so.

She turned down Mark's street. This was it. Everything depended on this.

Would he kiss her? Allison wondered. Should she let him?

Of course she should. She'd had a bit of a freak out, but it was over now. Whatever had happened at the reservoir wasn't real. Or anything to worry about. This was real. This man beside her. She'd made love with him a bunch of times already. Been as close to him as she'd ever been to anyone. During all those experiences, she'd never felt frightened or uneasy. Indeed, the opposite was true. Sex had never felt so right, so much like it was meant to be.

If she was having a past life experience, well then that was exactly what it was. A *past* life. It didn't have anything to do with the here and now.

She really didn't believe in reincarnation anyway. The way Connar had looked back at the reservoir was clearly her unconscious mind playing tricks on her. She'd always had a vivid imagination. That's why she'd become a writer, for heaven's sake. Maybe this was a new manifestation of her creativity. Or maybe Megan's witchy friends had put a spell on her, something that opened her mind and made her imagination run wild. Although the idea of a spell was even weirder than thinking she was remembering something from another life.

"This is it." Connar pointed to a modest older house.

Allison put the car into park, feeling a tiny twinge of anxiety. It was quickly overruled by a sense of expectation. Even if her mind fought it, her body remembered exactly how much pleasure this man had given her.

Connar gazed at her, looking as stunningly handsome as ever. Then he leaned near. His lips were as warm as sunshine and tasted as sweet as ripe fruit. His arms came around her, pulled her close.

Heaven. His hard chest against her breasts. His

strong arms cradling her. This was so right. This was meant to be. She dissolved. And with her body's surrender, all her doubts seemed to melt away. She floated in a haze of pleasure, not wanting it to end. But eventually, he drew back.

The expression in his eyes was hopeful, tender. "You will come to the Faire, won't you?" She nodded. Maybe she should ask him to stay at her place tonight.

But then he added, "The sword fighting starts at eleven." She immediately remembered the Connar she'd seen with the sword. The sword that looked exactly like the one in his closet.

"I'll be at the Faire," she responded. "Goodnight."

He kissed her again, a light, infinitely gentle kiss. Then he got out of the car.

Chapter Twelve

"It was good of you to come with me to the Faire on such short notice," Allison told Megan as they turned onto the interstate. "Although you are making me look bad with your great costume." She nodded toward her friend's low-cut medieval dress.

"Don't worry, we'll get there in time to buy something for you to wear," Megan answered. "And don't feel like you're putting me out, either. I usually go to the RenFest a couple of times over the summer. This year has been so busy I haven't gotten around to it, so this works for me, too."

"I'm probably being a baby, not wanting to go by myself."

"No, no, I understand. It isn't something you can really enjoy on your own."

"I'm mainly going to see Connar sword fight. I promised I would. If wasn't for that incident last night, we'd have gone there together."

"But like you said, you would have had to get up at the crack of dawn to leave. This is much more civilized."

Allison nodded. "And as poorly as I slept, I would have looked like hell if I got up at six. I swear, most of the night I was afraid to close my eyes for fear I'd see Connar with the sword, and that look on his face."

"I don't know why you're making such a big deal

over this. Even if what you saw was some memory of a past life, that's no reason for you to be afraid of Connar."

Allison shook her head. "I can't explain it, but seeing him with the sword scared me. It's like I have some bad memory associated with the sword...and with him."

"But the Connar you know in this life has never done anything to make you afraid. You don't feel afraid when you're around him, do you?"

"No. And even when I saw the old-fashioned apparition of Connar, I wasn't afraid at first. It was only when I saw the sword in his hand—the very sword in the modern-day Connar's closet—that's when I panicked."

"An apparition? Is that what you think it was?"

"I don't know. It wasn't the Connar I know. Not exactly."

"And this phantom version of Connar, did he look like he was going to attack you?"

Allison frowned, trying to remember what she'd seen. After trying for hours to forget the whole thing, it wasn't easy to recall. "I'd have to say his expression was more sad than murderous. He looked...haunted is a good word."

"So, there you go. There's no reason for you to be afraid of Connar, either in this life or a past one."

Allison glanced over at her friend. "You do know how crazy this whole conversation sounds."

Megan shrugged. "Concepts like the past and the present are a lot more fluid than most people realize."

"You're right. I mean, not necessarily about that, but about Connar. I shouldn't let all this strange paranormal stuff interfere with what we've had together. I'm telling you, he treats me like a queen, and the sex is incredible."

"Stop! Don't tell me things like that! I'm already green with jealousy. Here you've found the perfect guy, like your soulmate or something, and I haven't had a date in two months!"

"That's at least partly your own fault. You're always working, so when would you ever have a chance to meet anyone?"

"You met Connar through your work," Megan pointed out. "If you think I'm going to find Mr. Right cruising the bars...well you know that's not going to happen."

"Probably not," Allison agreed. "Still, you work an awful lot. That's why I'm glad you took today off to have fun."

"I am, too," Megan agreed. "Maybe I'll find a 'hot knight' during my 'day' at the Faire."

Allison rolled her eyes at Megan's wordplay and Megan laughed.

After following some twisty highways through the foothills, they reached the turnoff for the Faire.

"There are a lot of people here already," Allison noted as they followed the line of cars heading for the parking area.

"Everyone's probably trying to beat the heat. It's supposed to be another scorcher today. I'll probably wish I'd worn a less authentic dress. I don't know how women did it in the olden days. You'd think they would have expired of heat stroke in their long heavy gowns."

"They obviously didn't put much of a premium on comfort back then. They probably couldn't. I'm glad I live in the modern era. Can you imagine surviving without indoor plumbing and central heating?"

"Or antibiotics," Megan said. "Without them, about half the population wouldn't be alive."

As they walked from the parking lot to the Faire entrance, they saw people in costume everywhere: medieval wenches, fairies, pirates, knights and Renaissance ladies.

"I feel awfully boring in my normal clothes," said Allison.

"We'll remedy that soon enough."

After paying for their tickets, they picked up programs and entered the Faire.

"It's like a little medieval village," said Allison. "Cool."

They passed displays of cups and medallions, jewelry, hats, fantasy art and fairy headdresses.

"Here you go." Megan stopped and gestured to a shop selling medieval style clothing.

"I don't want to bake," Allison insisted. "We have to find something that's not too heavy."

Exploring the crowded shop, Megan picked up several pieces for Allison to try on. With some help from the clerk, she donned her costume.

"I look more like a pirate wench than a medieval lady," Allison said as she examined herself in the mirror. Megan had picked out a green skirt that hit just below her knees, a low-cut, cream-colored blouse and a red corset to cinch everything up.

"You look great. No way is Connar going to be able to resist you when you're wearing that."

"The corset does make the most of my 'assets', as they say. But it also makes it a little hard to breathe."

"You have to suffer for beauty, honey."

Allison nodded. There was no denying the constricting garment made her waist look tiny and her breasts much more voluptuous.

They shopped a while longer, visiting booths that sold shoes and hats, pottery and magic wands. "Maybe we should find out where Connar is performing," Allison suggested after a time. She glanced at her cell phone. "We'd better head over there. It's a quarter to eleven."

As they walked to the demonstration area at the other side of the Faire, Megan waved to a woman with short dark hair wearing jeans and a T-shirt. "There's Sophia."

"That's weird," said Allison. "She told me she was going to the mountains for some sort of retreat this weekend."

"I guess she changed her mind." As Sophia approached, Megan called out, "Hey Sophia, how's it going?"

"Very well. Thank you." To Allison she said, "Hello, Allison. My retreat was canceled, so I decided to come to the Faire instead."

"Hi."

"That's an interesting costume." Sophia motioned to Allison's attire.

Although she hadn't been embarrassed before, Sophia's keen gaze on her partially bared breasts made Allison say defensively, "I chose it for comfort more than anything. It's too hot to be covered up."

"Of course." Sophia's prim tone almost made Allison laugh. Who would have guessed a witch would be a prude!

"We're headed over to the performance area to see Connar sword fight," said Megan. "Want to come?"

"I don't think so. I don't care for that kind of thing."

"Just here to shop, are you?"

"I guess."

"Maybe you can join us for lunch later," Megan suggested.

Sophia nodded. "I'd like that. Why don't we meet by the food booths after the sword fighting is over?" She pointed to the stands selling everything from steak-on-a-stick to deep fried green beans.

"Yeah, let's do that," agreed Megan.

"I was going to ask you," Allison asked as soon as they were out earshot of Sophia, "Do you think she's gay?"

"It hadn't really crossed my mind. Why would you think that?"

Allison shrugged. "She's seems awfully interested in me."

"I think she's that way with everybody, or at least with women. I've seen her talking to Misty quite a bit, too. She probably sees herself as a mentor."

"She also seems kind of 'anti-men'. She's always warning me to be careful of Connar. Is that usual with female Wiccans?"

"Not that I know of. I mean some covens have a lot of male members. No pun intended," she added with a wry smile.

Allison laughed. "Cute!"

"Anyway," Megan continued, "If Sophia has issues with men, that's her deal. Maybe she'd been date-raped or something."

"I hadn't thought of that. If she's had a bad experience with a guy, that might be why she seems so concerned about me getting close to Connar so fast. She's worried I'll get hurt." Allison shook her head. "There are times I worry about that myself."

"Why? Are you still upset about your visions?"

"Well, yeah, it's partly that. But it's also, I feel like he's too good to be true. Especially the way he acts with me." She shrugged. "I mean it's one thing for me to feel like I'm falling in love after a few days, but what guy gets emotionally involved so quickly?"

"That's kind of sexist, isn't it? Implying that guys are only after one thing and don't have feelings like we do?"

"Hmmm. I guess you're right."

"Anyway, since you think Connar's falling for you, we'd better get a move on. You don't want to miss his performance and hurt his feelings."

Allison nodded and walked faster.

When they reached the demonstration area, Connar and Mark were already in the center of the arena. "Wow! Talk about hot knights!" Megan exclaimed.

Allison had to agree. With the mail vests emphasizing their broad chests and their muscular arms bare, the two men looked gloriously, impressively male.

"Although Connar's opponent looks more like a Viking than a medieval knight. OMG! Who *is* that guy?"

"Connar's friend Mark," Allison answered. She could see why Megan thought Mark looked like a Viking. With his blond hair worn loose, he looked even fiercer and more formidable than usual. "So, that's your type, then?" she asked Megan. "You like the murderous barbarian look?"

Megan nodded. "Works for me. Absolutely works for me."

"Mark is certainly striking. But frankly, I prefer Connar's more civilized demeanor. He looks like he could deal with pretty much anything, yet he doesn't seem quite so fierce."

"You probably think that because you know him. Someone looking at him right now would likely think he's one bad dude." Megan grabbed Allison's arm. "Come on. Introduce me to Connar's friend."

Allison held back. "Let's wait. It looks like they're about to start."

"I suppose you're right."

Connar and Mark had been talking casually, but now they moved away from each other and went to get their swords from where they were propped against a low barrier. Allison immediately looked to see if the sword Connar was using was the one from his closet. It wasn't, of course. There was no way he could use what was obviously a real weapon. It would be too dangerous.

A man who appeared to be the "referee" gestured, and Connar and Mark began to circle each other. Mark lunged first. Connar swiftly moved away. Then Connar attacked and Mark twisted out of reach of his sword.

Megan let out a soft sigh. "They're so graceful, like dancers."

"It probably wasn't quite so refined and civilized back in the day," said a delicate-looking woman wearing a fairy costume standing next to them. "Even if it was only a contest, they would have been absolutely determined to win. Winning would affect their whole status with the tribe. What they're doing now is mainly for show and entertainment."

That was true, Allison thought as she continued to watch the two men. She recalled the hallucination or "vision" she'd had at Mark's shop. Watching Connar sparring with the stocky man with the reddish blond hair, she'd felt as if Connar was fighting for his life. She clearly remembered the intent, almost desperate, look on his face. Today, he was focused, but his movements lacked the same urgency.

As she recalled the scene she'd experienced that day, she wondered again about the identity of Connar's opponent. Who was that brutal-faced man who seemed determined to kill Connar?

As if summoned by her thoughts, the world of the Renaissance Faire was replaced by another reality. She was in an open field. The air was damp and cool, and the sky cloudy. Once again, Connar's opponent was the stocky man with reddish gold hair rather than tall blond Mark.

Instantly, she felt the tension between the two men. She could sense the anger and hatred flowing between them as they sparred. They weren't merely fighting, but trying to kill each other!

She fought the panic rising up in her. *This is something happening in your mind. It isn't real.*

To her relief, the attempt to bring herself back to the real world seemed to work. In seconds, she was once again watching Connar and Mark in mock combat. She let out a deep breath.

"Are you all right?" asked the fairy woman, leaning near. "You went kind of pale all of a sudden."

"Allison?" Megan glanced at her, frowning. "Is it

happening again? Are you having a vision?"

"It's over, thank goodness."

"Vision? You have visions?" The fairy woman stared at her.

"Well...not exactly." Allison let out a nervous laugh.

"What does she mean?" the woman asked Megan, who'd turned away to watch Connar and Mark.

"It's hard to explain," Megan answered, her attention still on the two men. "One theory is that she's experiencing memories from a past life. If you believe that sort of thing."

From the way the woman was looking at Allison, it appeared she did. "That's amazing," the fairy woman said. "Although I get these glimpses now and then myself. I'm convinced I was a fairy in a past life. I remember being in this misty, magical forest. And I remember being able to fly."

Allison glanced at the woman's green voile wings. *Okay. This one was a real nut job.* To the woman she said, "Really?"

"Yeah. What were you in your previous life?"

The words seemed to form in Allison's mouth of their own accord. "I was an outcast, I think. I mean, I have this memory of people chasing me with flaming brands and weapons, as if they meant to kill me."

"Cool! Maybe you were a witch who was burned at the stake!"

"Why would that be cool?" Allison asked with a shudder.

"Well, not the burning at the stake part, but if you were a witch back then, you probably still have magical powers in this life."

"What if I was wrongly accused? What if I was someone who didn't fit in and that's why I was persecuted?"

"Well, that would suck," the woman agreed. "But you should investigate whether you have special abilities. Have you ever tried moving objects with your mind? Or leaving your body in astral travel?"

"Nope. Not into that." Allison motioned to their surroundings. "I'm here for the shopping and to see my boyfriend perform." She nodded to the two men, who were still engaged in pretend combat.

"If you're here to watch, then *watch*," Megan muttered over her shoulder. "If Connar glances over and sees you ignoring him, he's going to feel bad."

Allison nodded and turned her attention back to the two men. Megan was right. She shouldn't miss this—two gorgeous sexy guys squaring off. She could see why Megan was smitten with Mark. He was good looking. But she definitely preferred Connar. He seemed somehow more graceful than his opponent, the lines of his body more elegant. Like a cat, he was lithe and yet powerful.

And it was all due to the workout routine he was currently engaging in. Doing this a couple times a week appeared to be the equivalent of hours in the gym. Wielding the heavy sword had built up his shoulders, arms, and chest, while the rapid maneuvers he made to avoid his opponent's weapon had strengthened and shaped his legs and butt and sculpted his lean six-pack torso.

Watching his athletic movements reminded Allison of how powerful and skillful he was in bed. The man was obviously a natural, both at sword fighting and lovemaking. The only thing better than this would be if he was sparring naked.

A ridiculous idea with these massive swords swinging around. She wouldn't want him to get hurt.

At the thought, she remembered her vision. That had been real combat, and it had been terrifying to watch. This was like football. There was an element of risk to the participants, but the danger wasn't so great it distracted her from the pleasure of watching studly male bodies in action.

What stamina they had. She suspected she wouldn't have been able to wield one of those swords for a minute, and the two men had been at it for nearly ten. They must have to pace themselves to do this for so long. Although they were clearly tiring. A sheen of sweat glazed Connar's face, highlighting his fine strong features, and Mark was very flushed. Sooner or later, one of them would make a mistake and their opponent's sword would find its target.

Even as she had the thought, Mark drew back a moment too late and Connar's sword caught him in the chest. Mark stumbled backwards and Connar moved in and brought his sword up to Mark's throat. Mark gave a slight nod and went down on one knee.

A moment later, he was up. The two men stood side-by-side and held up their arms in a gesture of triumph. The crowd cheered, and the combatants turned to face the spectators on the other side of the arena. Then they turned back again and Connar met Allison's gaze. Gazing at his handsome manly face and the warm smile that seemed meant for her, she went all mushy inside.

As Connar started toward them, Megan said,

"Don't forget to have Connar introduce me to Mark."

Allison nodded. To Connar, she said, "That was great. I knew you would win."

Connar's smile broadened. "Knowing you were here watching gave me an advantage."

"Allison," Megan prompted, "Don't forget..."

"Oh, yeah. Megan wants to meet Mark. Can you bring him over here?"

"Aye. I'll be right back."

A moment later, Connar returned with Mark. "Mark, this is Megan. Megan, Mark."

Mark nodded politely. "Nice to meet you." His gaze moved past Megan. "And who is this?"

The fairy woman was still standing behind them. As Mark stared at her, she smiled and held out her hand. "I'm Tara. Nice to meet you."

"Mark," he said, his smile blinding.

Allison glanced at Connar, brows raised. *What's with your friend? Why did he ignore my friend and then make a fuss over this weird fairy girl?*

Connar frowned, looking confused.

"Are you from around here?" Mark asked the woman.

"Yeah. Highlands Ranch."

"Nice area. I live in Englewood, so not that far."

"No it's not." Tara laughed flirtatiously.

Allison couldn't believe it. After snubbing Megan, Mark was trying to pick up Tara! One glance at Megan told her the "snubee" couldn't believe it either.

Megan shook her head and came over to Allison. She shot Tara a dagger-like glare. Then she said, "I think we're supposed to meet Sophia for lunch. Maybe we should be going."

"Who's Sophia?" Connar asked.

"A woman from my Wicca group," Megan answered. "She's probably waiting for us."

While Allison wasn't terribly enthused about having lunch with Sophia, it was clear Megan hoped to get Mark away from Tara. "Yeah. We'd better go."

Connar nodded. "Mark? Are you coming?"

Mark didn't even glance at Connar. "Go on. I'll catch up with you later."

"Well, if that doesn't suck big-time," Megan fumed as she, Allison and Connar started walking.

"What's wrong?" Connar asked.

"I guess you didn't notice. Your friend Mark just dissed my friend, Megan," Allison responded.

"Dissed? What do you mean?"

"A verb meaning to blow off, rudely ignore," Megan answered in sharp tones.

"I still don't understand," said Connar.

"I know guys aren't great at verbal cues, Connar," Allison said. "But didn't you notice how Mark ignored Megan? You can't blame her for being a little bit put out."

"I'm not put out," responded Megan. "What can I say? I'm obviously not Mark's type."

Now Connar looked truly baffled. Allison sighed. "Never mind. I'll explain it all later."

Since she was secretly hoping Sophia had given up on them, Allison was heartened when she saw no sign of the dark-haired woman near the food booths. She was about to suggest they get in one of the lines when Megan called out, "Sophia! There you are!"

A woman with her face painted to resemble a cat's started walking toward them. It took Allison a moment to realize it was Sophia.

"Wow! Where did you get your face painted?" Megan asked. "It's really cool."

"There's a booth over there." Sophia pointed.

Allison was surprised. Sophia didn't seem like the kind of person to indulge in something whimsical like face painting, and especially to this extreme. The cat "mask" made her almost unrecognizable. Which prompted Allison to ask, "How did you know it was her, Megan? I swear, I never would have recognized her."

Megan motioned to Sophia's plain navy T-shirt and faded jeans. "Not many people around are dressed so normal. I knew it had to be her."

"That's funny," Allison said. "To think that looking normal would make you stand out. But I guess that's true here." Even the women at the Faire who weren't in costume tended to be wearing long skirts or boho dresses.

"Anyway," said Megan. "Sophia, this is Connar. I'm sure you've heard plenty about him from Allison." Megan winked.

"Pleased to meet you," said Sophia politely.

Connar smiled and inclined his head. "I'm happy to meet you, Sophia."

"So what sounds good to you guys?" asked Megan. "It appears we have to decide ahead of time what we want and get in the right line."

For the next few moments, they discussed the appeal of the different choices. Finally, they split up to wait in the appropriate queue. Although she'd hoped to end up in line next to Connar, at the last minute, Megan dragged him off to the steak-on-a-stick line, while

Sophia stepped in line behind Allison to wait for a turkey leg.

"What did you think of the sword fighting?" Sophia asked.

"It was incredible. I'd be hard put to swing one of those swords a couple of times, let alone wield it for a grueling match like that. Connar and Mark are both in amazing shape."

"Did watching them arouse any new memories for you?" asked Sophia.

"You mean from a past life?" Allison sought to keep her voice light. "No. I think I'm all finished with that." She didn't want to talk about it, and especially not with Sophia.

"Too bad. I was hoping you would remember something else."

"Why?"

"It sounds very intriguing. If I had a past life, I'd want to know about it."

"You might not feel that way if your past life involved being chased by a crazed mob." *And something else bad, something that involved Connar.* As hard as she tried to put the idea out of her mind, it wouldn't go away.

"Why do you think they were chasing you?"

"I don't know, and I really don't care." She gave Sophia a cold look. "Like I said, my goal is to forget the whole experience."

Sophia nodded, looking thoughtful. After a time, she said, "We're not moving very fast. And once we have our food, we'll have to wait in a different line to get our drinks. Why don't we split up? I'll get the drinks and you stay here and get the food. Here, I'll give you some money." She handed Allison a twenty. "What would you like to drink?"

"Some wine would be great." Allison breathed a sigh of relief as Sophia walked off.

A short while later, they both met up with Megan and Connar at a picnic table near the food area. They were all so hungry that no one talked for a few moments. Allison quickly finished her potato wedges and started on her turkey leg. It wasn't easy to be lady-like while gnawing on a big chunk of meat. She ate as much as she could without looking like a savage, and then washed it down with her wine.

As she was sitting there contemplating if she should be totally decadent and have a funnel cake, she was hit with a wave of dizziness. She shook her head, trying to clear it. Although the altitude here was higher than Denver, she didn't think it should affect her tolerance for alcohol this much. Maybe it was the heat.

She sat very still, but it didn't help. The world seemed to spin around her.

"Allison? Are you unwell?" Connar's voice seemed to come from far away and her limbs felt numb. The next thing she knew, she was sliding off the wooden bench. Then Connar's strong arms were around her. "Allison! What's wrong?"

Aisling. Grá mo chroí. She heard the words in her head, but they didn't match the movement of Connar's lips. Then she saw the sword in his hand and went rigid with shock.

From far away, she heard Megan calling her name.

Chapter Thirteen

She was lying on the ground. A dozen or more people including Connar, Megan and Sophia were gathered around her. "I'm all right," Allison murmured. She started to sit up.

"Hey, don't move too fast," Megan cautioned. She knelt down and slipped her arm around Allison's shoulders. Connar did the same on her other side. Despite what she'd experienced, having Connar next to her helping hold her up made her feel much better.

Between the two of them, they got her onto the bench. Allison took several deep breaths, seeking to clear her head.

"So, what happened, honey?" Megan asked, her voice gentle. "Was it the wine or...something else? Did you..." Her voice trailed off.

"I...it must be the heat. The wine. I don't know." She still felt dizzy and had a strong urge to lie down and sleep.

"We'd better get you back to the car. Can you walk?" asked Megan.

"I think so."

She got up and with Megan supporting her on one side and Connar on the other, they made their way through the Faire. It seemed to take all her concentration to stay upright and keep her feet moving. At the entrance to the Faire, they waited for a courtesy cart. When it arrived, Megan helped her get in, and then sat next to her, her arm around Allison's shoulders.

As they rode to the parking lot, Allison let herself zone out. Even when they arrived, she wasn't aware of much until she realized the car she was being helped into wasn't hers. "What about my car?" she mumbled.

Megan leaned near. "Sophia's going to take you home. I'll drive *your* car and take Connar home, then meet you at your place."

Connar leaned near and gently touched her cheek. "Feel better *mo chroí.*"

Allison nodded, wondering why the phrase sounded so familiar. Then she let herself slip into the darkness that beckoned.

It seemed only moments had passed and Sophia was shaking her. "Allison. Allison. We're here. Can you wake up enough to walk?"

Allison mumbled something, then opened her eyes and forced herself to get out of the car.

"Megan said it was apartment number 3B. Is that right?" asked Sophia.

She managed to nod.

A dozen steps up. A familiar hallway. The jingle of keys. As they entered the apartment, she heard Benjamin mewing and felt him rubbing against her legs.

"Hi, baby. Mommy's sick. But maybe Sophia can feed you." To Sophia she mumbled, "Cat food's in the upper shelf by the refrigerator. What he wants are some of the treats that come in a little pouch. Give him a handful or so."

"Of course," Sophia responded.

A few moments later Allison was in her bedroom

and then, blissfully, in her own bed. With a deep sigh, she gave in and let the unconsciousness wash over her.

****

When she woke, it was dark. She had a headache and her mouth felt like it was stuffed with cotton. When she sat up, a vague nausea kicked in.

"Allison?"

She gasped in surprise at the unfamiliar voice. Who was lying beside her?

"It's Sophia," the woman said, sitting up. "I helped you get home. Remember?"

Allison searched her mind and came up with very little. She was at the Renaissance Faire, watching Connar swordfight. A group of people. Something about eating. Then…nothing. Her mind was a blank.

"I don't remember much. What happened?"

"You got sick at the Renaissance Faire. Since you were too ill to drive, Megan took your car and drove Connar home. I brought you here in my car. Don't you remember arriving here?"

"Not really." She could recall feeling sick and dizzy, but that was probably because she still felt that way. And even if Sophia had brought her home, that didn't explain why she was lying beside her. And where was Benjamin? A vague panic overtook her. "Where's my cat? Where's Benjamin?"

"Don't you remember? You had me feed him when we got home."

"But where is he now? Why isn't he sleeping next to me?"

"I…he was restless. I was afraid he'd wake you."

That was why it was so dark. The bedroom door was closed. "You locked him out?"

"I didn't want him to wake you up."

She never locked Benjamin out. He must be frantic. *Oh, my poor baby.*

She started to get out of bed, then lay back with a moan when a wave of dizziness assaulted her.

Sophia got up on the other side of the bed. "What do you need? I'll get it for you."

"Benjamin. I need Benjamin. Open the door and let him in…please."

A few moments later, her baby was beside her, purring wildly. "Oh, my darling, it's all right." She stroked him until he settled down next to her.

"How are you feeling?" asked Sophia, standing by the bed. "Can I get you anything else?"

"I…uh… Nothing. I just need to lie here for a while."

If she didn't move, she didn't feel too bad. But what the hell had happened? Was it food poisoning? A sudden on-set virus? She'd never taken ill so rapidly in her life. Could it be related to her hallucinations? The one she'd experienced at Mark's shop had caused her to faint. After the other ones, she'd felt disoriented and a bit dizzy.

But always before, the feeling had passed quickly. And this was more than being dizzy. She'd been totally out of it. A whole chunk of time was missing. She had no clear memory of anything after watching Connar and Mark swordfight.

The vague sense of unease she'd felt since waking up intensified. Maybe she was truly losing her mind. So many weird things had happened to her in the past week. And it had all started on her first date with Connar.

Connar. Everything was connected to him.

She wanted to groan aloud. This must be some strange form of torture. She'd seemingly found the man of her dreams, but if she stayed with him, she'd probably lose her mind for good!

Damn! She really needed to talk to Megan. But it was the middle of the night, and it would be very inconsiderate to wake her. Poor Megan had already been forced to drive her car home from the Faire and then take Connar home.

She could talk to Sophia about her different theories. But somehow, that wasn't the same. Sophia seemed to have a strong opinion about everything, and had a bossy, "I know best" attitude. And she'd locked Benjamin out of the bedroom. People who didn't like cats were always a bit suspect. They might turn out to be all right, but it always made Allison wary.

Of course, Sophia might be allergic to cats. But if that was true, she'd never have been able to tolerate being in the bedroom in the first place. There had to be cat hair everywhere.

If Sophia didn't like cats, that was another strike against her. What kind of witch was she anyway, not liking cats? Allison almost laughed aloud.

She was finally feeling better, thank God. Maybe by morning she'd be herself again. And now that she had Benjamin beside her, she might even be able to go back to sleep.

That thought reminded her of sleeping with both Connar and Benjamin. Now that was nice. Obviously, Connar was the perfect man for her. He even got along with her cat.

Too bad he also seemed to turn her psychotic!

Chapter Fourteen

"Allison? Are you okay?"

At the sound of Megan's familiar voice, Allison sat up and looked around groggily.

Megan was beside the bed. "Hey, girlfriend, how are you?"

She did a quick evaluation of the condition of her stomach and head and answered, "Not too bad. I feel like I have a bit of a hangover, but that's all."

"What a relief. I was really worried yesterday. I was going to come over here after I dropped Connar off, but Sophia said she'd stay with you. She's in the kitchen now, making scones." Megan raised her eyebrows in an expression of disbelief.

"Yeah, she's been here the whole time," Allison answered.

"So, what do you think happened? I was worried about food poisoning, but I don't think you'd be over it today if that was it. Besides, if it was something like that, I figured you would have thrown up and uh…" Megan jerked her head toward the bathroom, "other stuff."

"No. It wasn't like that. I was just dizzy and completely out of it."

"I wonder if it could be related to your visions."

Allison nodded. "I've been thinking about that, too."

"Maybe you could find someone to hypnotize you and find out more about what happened in your past life."

"I still don't know if I buy that stuff."

"Well, what else could it be? Why are you seeing strange things? What's happening to you?"

Allison laughed weakly. "Maybe I'm losing my mind."

"I don't believe that. You seem fine most of the time. It's only when you're around Connar."

"Yeah. He is the common denominator in all of this."

"Have you asked him? I mean, have you discussed what's been happening to you and asked if he has any idea what it could be? Maybe he's experienced something similar. If you knew each other in a past life, maybe he remembers things that might help you solve this."

"I suppose I could talk to him. But if he hasn't had anything like this happen to him, he's going to think I'm nuts."

"No, he won't. He's genuinely concerned. You should have seen him yesterday. He was a wreck, worrying about you. In fact, I'm surprised he hasn't called to check on how you're doing."

"He may have. My phone's still in my purse. For that matter, I hope my purse is around here somewhere."

She started to get up. "Stay there. I'll go look for it," said Megan.

A few moments later Megan came back with her bag. Allison took out her phone from the side pocket and went to missed calls. "Yeah, he called all right.

Three times, it looks like. I must have been absolutely out of it, since I never heard it ring. Oh. The volume is turned all the way down. I suppose Sophia must have done that." She met Megan's gaze. "I know she's trying to help and all, but she's really controlling." Leaning near, she lowered her voice and added, "Sophia locked Benjamin out last night. I guess she thought she should stay with me, so she slept in here. I don't think she likes cats. What's up with that? How can she be a witch and not like cats?"

Megan laughed. "I guess the stereotype isn't always true. Anyway, you should check your messages from Connar."

"I should."

As she listened to Connar's deep voice, a warm feeling spread through Allison's body. "Poor guy. He does sound frantic. I can tell he's stressed because his accent seems a lot more pronounced."

The second and third messages were much the same. How sweet and tender he was. He ended up by telling her he was going to try to get some sleep but he would call in the morning. "Good night, *moi croi*."

Mo croi. The words seemed so familiar. Hadn't the version of Connar she'd seen while hallucinating said something like that? He'd also called her Aisling. Weird.

"Maybe you're right, Megan. Maybe I should talk to Connar."

"Good idea." Megan got up from the bed. "If you want, I'll go pick him up and bring him over here. Remember, I've still got your car."

"Then how will you get home?"

"Maybe Sophia can take me."

"Oh, yeah. I should probably get dressed and go out and thank her for everything she's done. And maybe eat some scones."

"But first you should call Connar. Put the poor guy out of his misery."

Megan nodded and pressed "call".

"Hello, Allison?"

"Yeah, it's me."

"Are you…is everything all right?"

"I'm fine. A little woozy maybe, but not too bad. If you want to see for yourself, Megan's offered to pick you up and bring you here."

She heard him let out his breath in a sigh of relief. "Oh, aye. I'd truly like to see you."

"All right. She'll be over in a little while."

****

Connar clicked off his phone and murmured, "Oh, Anu great queen, thank you."

Allison isn't ill and she wants to see me! There could hardly be better news.

He was so exhilarated he felt like shouting. Instead, he decided to take a shower, and as he washed, he went over what he would say to her. He'd decided to tell her everything. Explain who he was and who *she* was, and what had happened with Fergal and the rest of the tribe. Then he'd tell her Siobhan's plan to make it possible for him to follow her spirit to this time period. Then he'd somehow explain what he'd had to do to evoke the spell.

Thinking about it made him grimace. He'd wanted to wait until she was more comfortable with him. Until she'd fallen well and truly in love with him in this life. But he feared he dare not delay any longer. She was obviously starting to remember her life as Aisling. And it appeared the memories coming back to her were the awful ones. The dark and terrifying ones.

At the reservoir, for a few moments, she'd looked at him with fear in her eyes. And yesterday... He suspected she'd remembered what had happened at the end and the sheer terror of it had caused her to become ill. Her spirit was in conflict. Part of her recalled the love they had shared, while another part of her focused on the terrible things that had happened to her. Unless he explained everything, he feared for her physical and mental well-being.

There was also the risk she would remember the last few moments of her past life and know he was the one who had ended it. If that happened, she might refuse to see him again, and he'd never have a chance to explain.

The very thought made him ill, and spurred him to finish his shower. He toweled off quickly, pulled on his jeans, and went to the closet. As he started to grab a shirt, he froze in shock. The wall at the back of the closet was empty. The sword was gone!

For a moment, he stared in disbelief. Then he searched the floor of the closet. It wasn't there. It simply wasn't there.

He walked through the rest of the house, to see if anything else was missing. The TV, DVD player, stereo, laptop—everything was where it should be. Although when he went back to the bedroom and looked around, he had the sense that someone had been there, going through his possessions. They'd been hunting for the sword. It was the only thing they'd taken.

But how had they known it was there?

The only people in this time who knew about the sword were Mark, Allison, and Rowan. He used to keep it at the shop, in the storeroom. Rowan had come across it and asked him about it. He'd told her it was the first sword he'd ever purchased, so it had sentimental value and wasn't for sale. She'd seemed to accept his explanation.

Mark had seen the sword when he helped move Connar into this house. It was in a bag with some practice swords, and during the drive from the shop to the house, the blade had sliced through the canvas. When Mark tried to wrap up everything again to carry the weapons into the house, he'd seen the decorated hilt.

Connar had told Mark it was a very fine reproduction and worth quite a lot of money. That was months ago. Why, after all this time, would Mark decide to take the sword? It didn't make sense. But it was the only explanation. Although he felt certain Allison had seen the weapon, she would never have taken it. Given her history with the sword, she would likely be too terrified to handle it. So, that left Mark.

What should he do? He didn't want to offend his friend by implying he was a thief, especially when that seemed so unlikely. Still, he had to ask him. But not over the phone. He needed to see him in person.

He had to find the sword. Without it…by Anu, that didn't bear thinking about! A wave of panic washed over him.

And then the doorbell rang—Megan.

****

Allison moved restlessly around the apartment. As

soon as Sophia had left, she'd raced through showering and dressing and hurriedly put on make-up, which she'd needed today, pale as she was. Then she'd made an egg to go along with the scones Sophia had baked.

She'd done all that, and they still hadn't arrived. Megan had said she was going to get Connar and come right back. They must have run into bad traffic or something. Maybe there was an accident.

Allison paced across the room again and then laughed at herself. "I guess you're over being sick. Your sex drive has certainly recovered at any rate!"

She felt like she would burst into flames the minute Connar touched her. Of course, she'd have to control herself a little while. Before she and Connar could be alone, she'd have to drive Megan home. Speaking of which, where was she?

There was a knock at the door. Allison raced to open it. At the last second, she thought to check the peephole. Megan stood outside. Alone.

Allison let her in. "Hi. Where's Connar?"

"He's not coming."

"What?"

"I know. It's strange. I went over there and the first thing he asked is if I could take him to Mark's. I said, what about Allison, and he gave me all these ridiculous excuses, about how he left something in Mark's truck. Something he really needed. So, I took him to Mark's, who, by the way, has a very nice house. I assumed Connar would pick up whatever it was that he left and then we'd come here. But then he tells me he needs to talk to Mark about something, and I should just go without him and tell you he's going to be a while. He plans to take a cab over here later."

Mary Gillgannon

"You're kidding."

"Nope. That's what happened. Your devoted, can't wait-to-see-you lover bugged out on you for some reason, and I have no idea why."

"I don't believe it." Allison started to pace again. "He sounded so tender, so eager, so *desperate* to see me. What could have happened?"

"You got me. All I can think of is he's having second thoughts about how fast things are moving between the two of you. Guys panic about things like that, you know."

"Oh, and women don't?" Allison paced back the other way. "I can't stand it. All along I've been worried I was falling for him too fast, too soon. Now that I'm ready to dive in, *he* gets cold feet. I could scream!"

"It doesn't make sense. It seems more likely something else is going on. He seemed so distracted...and anxious. But I didn't feel like the anxiety was focused on you. Must be something else. Maybe there's a problem at the shop. Or with the sword fighting stuff he's involved in. He was determined to see Mark. Anyway, I know you're upset about this, but how about taking me to my car? We can speculate more about what's going on with Connar while you drive. And, by the way..." Megan glanced around. "What happened to Sophia? I thought she'd stay here until I came back."

"She left as soon as you did."

"Weird."

Allison nodded. "It's all weird. Let me grab my purse."

****

Connar sat on the couch, Mahon's head resting on

his knee as he stroked the dog's coarse fur and tried to calm himself. Mark had been his best hope. But when he'd gone to Mark's house and asked him about the sword, his friend had seemed genuinely confused. Mark was telling the truth, he would stake his life on it.

He sat back and tried to think things through. The sword was his only link to the past. Without it, he'd never be able to return there with Allison. But did that really matter? He doubted she would ever want to go back to her earlier life anyway. This incarnation of Aisling would never be happy in the ninth century. She was too independent and confident. If he was going to be with Allison, he had no choice but to remain in this era.

Staying in this time wouldn't be so distressing. There were many things about the modern world that were indescribably better than anything he'd known, the food, the cleanliness and comfort, the health care, the means of transport. It was amazing how much many aspects of life had improved, at least for people in this part of the world and in Europe.

Still, there were things about his old life he missed a great deal. But not enough to return there without Allison. Without her, he would never be happy in any time. She was his other half, an essential part of his being.

Aye, he could be content in this world if he had Allison. But he still wanted to get the sword back. The loss of the weapon haunted him. Not only was it his only real link to the past, but it also was magical. Who knew what powers it possessed? In the wrong hands, it might even be dangerous. He had to get it back.

Once again, he considered all the possible

explanations for its disappearance. He'd already called Rowan. She insisted she knew nothing about the sword. Since she'd always been a responsible, honest employee, he had to believe she was telling the truth.

Besides Rowan and Mark, who else knew about the sword? He recalled the metal smith, Niall, who'd purchased his other pieces when he first arrived in the modern era. Although he hadn't shown Niall the sword, he might have guessed he possessed other antique weapons. Maybe this summer when Niall came to Colorado, he'd decided to see what else Connar owned that might be worth stealing. He could have found out where Connar lived, slipped into the house, discovered the sword, and stolen it. He wasn't certain how Niall had gotten past Mahon, but maybe Mahon wasn't a good watchdog after all.

Connar shook his head. The metal smith hadn't seemed like a thief, but he'd only met with him briefly. Maybe Niall had fallen on hard times. Desperation could drive people to do terrible things.

Connar got up from the couch. As unlikely as it was that Niall had stolen the sword, he needed to talk to him about it. He'd go to the Faire and find Niall.

But how could he get there? He couldn't ask Allison. After what she'd experienced the day before, he doubted she'd want to return. Nor did he want to involve her in confronting a thief. There was no telling how the metal smith might react. Niall was a big man and dealt in weapons. He was definitely no one to underestimate.

Mark had said he had other plans today, but maybe he knew someone else who was going to the Faire. It was relatively early, only ten. With luck he'd find a ride with someone. Once he was on his way, he'd call Allison and apologize for not coming over as they'd planned.

****

Seeing Connar's number, Allison immediately clicked on the phone. "Hi."

"Hello, Allison."

"Hi Connar. So, where are you? Do you want me to pick you up?"

"I'm sorry. Something has happened…something related to the shop. I'm afraid I won't be able to see you until sometime later. Perhaps this evening…or tomorrow. I'll try to explain then."

Why was he doing business on a Sunday? "Okay." *I guess.*

"I care for you very much, Allison." *Care for you? Why not 'love'?*

"I care for you, too, Connar."

"I'll see you soon. Everything will be well."

"If you say so. Bye."

As she hung up the phone, Allison felt like a balloon with the air let out of it. "Damn! I finally get to the point where I'm ready to commit, and he decides to pull back."

As if sensing her distress, Benjamin came over and rubbed against her legs. She picked him up. "That's right, baby. Mama needs some comforting. At least she has one male in her life who won't let her down." Rubbing her face against his soft fur, she sought to take comfort from her beloved cat.

Her phone went off just as she'd headed into the kitchen to give Benjamin a handful of treats. She grabbed the phone, thinking maybe Connar had

185

changed his mind. But it was only Sophia. "Hi, Sophia," she said resignedly.

"How are you feeling?"

"Good enough. Once I ate, I seemed to be a lot better. Thanks for the scones, by the way. They were delish."

"You're welcome. I'm surprised to find you home. I thought you and Connar would go somewhere."

"Oh, he didn't come over after all. Guess he has some business to deal with or something." She hated to tell Sophia about Connar's defection and prove her right. But oh well.

"What sort of business?"

"He didn't say and I didn't ask." *Because we've just started seeing each other and I don't really have any right to pry, which sucks.*

"Perhaps it's for the best. You'll be able to rest up from your illness."

I don't want to rest up from my illness! I want to have hot sex with Connar! "You're probably right."

"Anyway, I wanted to see how you were feeling. I'll talk to you tomorrow."

What? You're not going to ask me to lunch or want to get together? Today, when I actually could use some company? "Well, yeah, okay."

"Goodbye."

"Bye." Allison clicked off the phone. "Well, wouldn't you know," she announced to Benjamin. "Here we are, a beautiful Sunday afternoon, and I'm all alone." Sighing, she added, "I guess there's no choice but to actually do some work."

She sat down at her desk and amazingly, after a bit of a struggle, ended up engrossed in her writing. A

186

couple of hours passed as she wrote and revised.

When the phone rang, she was almost irritated. She didn't want to talk to anyone...except Connar. With the thought that it might be him calling to say he was on his way, she grabbed her phone.

Although she didn't recognize the number, she answered anyway.

"Allison? It's Rowan. I work at Connar's shop."

"Yes?" Allison responded. Connar had mentioned Rowan, but just in passing.

"Would you...do you think you could come down here? I have to leave because of a family emergency, and I don't want to close the place down."

"But I...I don't know anything about the shop. I don't see how I can help."

"You wouldn't have to do anything much. Just run the cash register, and I can show you that."

"Well, I..." It seemed like a weird request, but maybe it was a ruse. Maybe Connar wanted to surprise her with something and had put Rowan up to this. "How long would I have to stay there?"

"Not long. The shop closes at five on Saturdays."

Allison glanced at the clock. It was nearly three now. By the time she got there, she'd have to hang out for an hour and a half at most. "I guess I could do that. But it will take me a little while to get there."

"Thanks so much. It will be a huge help!"

Allison hung up and started for the bedroom to change clothes. If she got to the shop and found Connar waiting, she wanted to look nice and be dressed to go out. She'd put on make-up earlier in expectation of him coming over, so it didn't take her long to get ready. In a few minutes, she was in her car. As she drove, she grew more and more excited by the idea that Connar wanted to surprise her. He was such a romantic guy!

Of course, she should be prepared to find out she was wrong and Rowan genuinely needed someone to relieve her.

Traffic wasn't too bad, and she got there fairly quickly. She parked on the street and walked briskly to the shop. There was no one at the counter when she arrived. Rowan must be in the back doing something.

She waited for a couple of minutes, looking around the shop. Then she realized that if it was a surprise, Connar might be expecting her to come looking for him in the stockroom.

She went behind the counter and walked through the kitschy hanging beads into the back. Halting, she gasped...and then gasped again. Her body seemed to freeze as shock and panic swept through her.

A young woman lay on a green velvet cape that had been spread out on the floor. Her throat had been cut and blood soaked her neck and flowed over the cape. Lying next to her was a sword...Connar's jewel-encrusted sword.

She felt herself sway. Her legs gave out and she went down.

When she opened her eyes, she could see a stormy gray sky above. In the distance, she heard the sounds of the ocean. She shifted her gaze and saw Connar. In his hand was the sword. He approached and knelt down next to her, his expression bleak and terrible.

She felt no fear, only enormous sadness. He leaned near and whispered, *"Logh dom mo ghra."* Then he brought the sword to her throat. As she felt the blade bite into her flesh, everything went black.

Chapter Fifteen

Hard floor beneath her. An unfamiliar ceiling above her. Allison sat up slowly, gradually remembering.

Rowan! Oh...my...God!

With a sense of horror, she looked across the storeroom. There was nothing there.

She got up, disbelieving, and walked over to where she had seen the body. No blood. Nothing. Rowan's corpse had vanished.

For a moment, she feared she would faint again. But then she realized someone had been there while she was unconscious and cold fear replaced her shock. She glanced around the storeroom warily, then crept to the doorway leading back to the shop. Seeing no one in sight, she rushed out of the shop.

By the time she reached her car, unlocked it, and got inside, she was shaking so badly she could hardly get her phone out of her purse. With trembling fingers, she called Megan. "Pick up. Pick up. Please!"

"Hello."

"Oh, Megan, thank heavens you answered!"

"What? What's wrong?"

"I...I went to Connar's shop and there was...I saw Rowan...her throat was cut!"

"What?"

"Yes. She is dead, I'm was sure of it. Murdered."

"Did you call 911?"

"No, thank heavens. Because you see…now the body has disappeared."

"Disappeared?"

"Yes. While I was passed out."

"You passed out?"

Allison took a shaky breath. "I had…another of my blackouts. When I came to, there was no body. It was gone. And yet, I know I saw it. That's why I blacked out and had the…the vision or whatever you want to call what happens to me. Although, I no longer think they're hallucinations. I think they're my unconscious mind trying to warn me."

"Warn you? Well, let's put that aside for now. What about the body? Start from the beginning."

Allison took a deep breath. This was why she'd called Megan. Megan would talk her through the situation and help her make sense of it. "I got a call from Rowan. About an hour ago, I think."

How long had she been unconscious? She glanced at the clock on the car dash. It read a quarter to five. "Rowan said she had to leave the shop and could I come and keep an eye on the place for an hour or so. I thought it was a little odd since I've never even met her, but I figured Connar had given her my name and number."

Her thoughts went back to the corpse. The young woman had looked a lot like Misty from the group, the same short dyed black hair and a nose ring. But that could be coincidence.

"So, anyway, I agreed to come. I thought maybe it was a ruse on the part of Connar to get me to the shop so he could surprise me, and we could go out." She gave a semi-hysterical laugh. "I arrived and there was nobody there, so I went into the back room. And there she was. Poor Rowan, lying on a long dark green cape with her throat cut and blood all around."

She took a deep, steadying breath before continuing. "If that wasn't bad enough, I had a vision. I was on that damned cliff again. Although this time I was lying on the ground and Connar was standing over me with a sword. Oh, the sword! I forgot to tell you that the sword I saw in Connar's closet was lying on the cape next to Rowan's body. But then, in my vision, the sword was in Connar's hand. He bent down and I knew…I knew he was going to cut my throat. I swear I felt the blade against my neck." She shuddered. "But then I woke up and I was back in the storeroom and the body was gone. No blood. Nothing. And yet I didn't imagine it. It was real, not like my visions at all." She took another deep breath. "So I ran. Just booked it out of there and came to my car."

"And that's where you are now?"

"Yeah. I'm sitting here, locked in, trying to calm down. I swear I can't stop shaking."

A long pause. Then Megan said, "Maybe you should go back to the shop and look around. Bodies don't simply vanish. Maybe whoever murdered Rowan came back and moved her corpse."

"Which means he might still be around! And you want me to go back there? Are you kidding?"

"Yeah, you're right. That's probably not a good idea. Maybe calling 911 would be better."

"Oh, sure. They'll come and find nothing, and I'll look like an idiot."

"Okay. What do you want to do? Do you want me

to meet you? We could go into the shop together."

"I…I really don't want to go back there." Just the thought of it made her start to hyperventilate.

"You should probably lock up at least. Can you do that?"

"I suppose so. But then I want to get out of here. And I don't want to go to my apartment, in case Connar shows up. Can't we just meet somewhere?"

"Absolutely. I'm at work right now, so somewhere close by. Maybe the coffee place we used to go to all the time when you worked here."

"Okay. I'll be right there."

"Sure you're good to drive?"

"As soon as I get out of here, I'll be a lot better!"

She tore back to the shop and found she was in luck. She could set the lock on the back of the door without even going in. There was also a deadbolt, but it needed a key, and she wasn't about to look for one!

Rushing back to her car, she started downtown. On the way, she tried not to think about anything but driving. She had to hunt for a parking place, which also helped distract her.

So did standing in line for a latte. But as soon as she sat down, the ghastly image of Rowan's body filled her mind. "Come on, Megan, come on," she muttered to herself. "I need to see you right now."

A few seconds later, Megan arrived. She waved and then got in line. Allison took her drink and went over to her.

"Are you all right? You look awfully pale."

Allison shook her head. "I can't stop thinking about the body. Then there's my constant fear I'll be sent back in time at any moment and have something horrible happen to me."

"So, which has you more freaked out? Seeing Rowan's body or your vision?"

"The body for sure. As intense as my visions are, now that I'm used to them, part of me knows it's a memory and not something happening now. But seeing Rowan with her throat cut, that was totally in the moment."

Megan reached the counter, ordered and paid. They moved back to wait for her drink. "Do you think enough time elapsed while you were unconscious that the killer could have moved the body?" Megan asked.

"Yeah. And since the body was laid out on a cloak, it would have been easy to move. But why, why would Connar do that? Why would he do any of it?"

Megan gasped. "You think Connar's the killer?"

"Who else could it be? It was his sword lying next to the body. The very same one I saw in his bedroom closet."

"I don't believe it. Connar's not a killer. Unless..."

"What?"

The clerk called Megan's name. "Tell you in a minute," she said and went to pick up her drink. When she came back, they sat down at one of the tables. After taking a few sips, Megan put down her drink and said, "Maybe Rowan wasn't really dead. Maybe it was staged. I mean, if Connar was the murderer, why would he leave his sword lying there like that? That would be totally stupid."

"But why would Connar *pretend* to kill Rowan? What could he possibly get out of it...besides scaring the bejesus out of me!"

"Unless he's trying to get you to remember. Maybe

he's someone from your past life and he's trying to make you recall events from that time period."

"But why would he want me to remember he killed me?"

"Is that what happened in your vision?"

Allison nodded. "I'm afraid so. It was so real. I could feel the sword blade slicing into my neck. And I swear it was the same sword that was lying beside Rowan."

"There, you see. That proves my point. Connar left the sword out, and when you saw Rowan lying there with her throat cut, you remembered him killing you."

"But why would he want me to remember *that*?"

Megan frowned and poked around in her iced coffee with her straw. "Maybe he's trying to warn you about something."

"Like what? That he's a homicidal maniac, and I shouldn't get too close? Or maybe he has a multiple personality disorder, and one of his personalities wants to kill me even as another one is falling in love!"

"It does sound pretty crazy."

"There's nothing sane about any of this!"

"Another possibility is that someone is trying to frame Connar. They used his sword and left the body where you'd find it, thinking you'd call the police and tell them the sword belongs to Connar."

"Then why did the murderer move the body while I was out? Without a body, there's no way to frame Connar."

"Maybe he got cold feet, or were worried the crime would be traced to him for some reason. If Connar had a good alibi for where he was today, then he wouldn't be a good suspect. Or…" Megan's face brightened.

"Maybe you were the target. The killer had Rowan call you and lure you to the shop. Then he killed Rowan to get her out of the way. The murderer might have been in the middle of moving the body when you arrived."

"Then why didn't he kill me while I was passed out? He had a perfect chance."

"You're right. That doesn't make sense either."

For a few moments, neither of them spoke. Then Allison said, "I'm so effin' confused. I don't know what to do or where to go. Frankly, I'm afraid to go back to my apartment."

"I can't really blame you. You could come to my place, although I do have to head back to work for a little while."

"Jeez, Megan. It's Sunday. Don't you ever take time off?"

"I took off all day yesterday, remember? Anyway, if you don't want to be alone, you could come to the agency with me and hang out while I finish up."

"I guess that would be better than being alone."

"Okay. Let's head over there so I can finish my work."

They left the coffee shop carrying their drinks and walked to the high rise building where the agency was located. As Megan was about to use her fob to let them in, Allison's phone chirped. She glanced at the number. "It's Sophia," she informed Megan. Megan shrugged.

"Hello," Allison answered.

"Hello. This is Sophia. I wanted to call and see how you are feeling."

"I'm fine." *Right.*

"I thought perhaps you might want to go out to dinner."

Allison fought the urge to instantly decline. Knowing Megan, she would be a while. Dinner with Sophia didn't sound like much fun, but it would be a good distraction. "I…uh…I might be able to do that."

Sophia jumped on it. "Did you want me to pick you up?"

"Actually I'm not at home right now."

"Do you want to meet me somewhere?"

"Well, I need to feed Benjamin, so I guess I should go home first." She did want to check on her cat. And if she knew Sophia was coming, she wouldn't be so panicked to be in her apartment alone. "Would you mind picking me up there, in say, an hour or so?"

"I would be happy to."

"All right. See you then."

Even as she hung up, the bell rang for the elevator. "I guess I'm not going up," she told Megan. "Sophia asked me to go to dinner and said she'd pick me up at my place."

"You must be desperate," Megan said wryly. Allison rolled her eyes. "But after that, do you still want to stay at my place tonight?"

"Yeah, that's why I'm going home now. I'll take care of Benjamin and pick up a few things. Then after dinner, Sophia can drop me off at your place. Surely you'll be done with work by nine or so."

"I hope so," Megan said, sighing. "Why don't you call me when you're leaving the restaurant?"

"Okay. And thanks for everything." She gave Megan a hug. "You've been great. I think I'd have lost my mind if hadn't been able to reach you after finding the body and all that."

"Are you going to tell Sophia about the 'corpse'?"

"I don't think so. I don't feel comfortable with her. I can't it explain it, you know. She'll say something perfectly innocent and I'll think, 'she's trying to control me'. Strange, huh?"

"She must remind you of someone from your past."

"Maybe. Anyway, I'd better let you get to work."

Megan nodded. "See you soon. And be careful."

"I will."

Allison walked briskly through the high-rise lobby. Exiting, she glanced up and down the street. Then she realized she wasn't sure what she was looking for. Did she really think some crazed killer was following her? Ridiculous. Or was it?

She couldn't shake her sense of dread. Talking about her experience with Megan had helped, but the nagging anxiety was still there. And she wasn't sure what freaked her out the most, finding a murdered woman in this era or the memory of her own death in the past.

She walked faster, in a hurry to get to her car. So far, she hadn't ever been transported to the past while she was driving. Thank God.

****

After climbing out of Charles's truck, Connar walked around to the driver's side. "Thanks for taking me to the Faire. I appreciate it."

"No prob, bro." Charles jerked his head up in a "see you later" gesture and drove off. Connar wondered again how a Charles, a "black dude" as he referred to himself, had gotten involved in the Renaissance Faire culture. Connar decided he'd have to ask him sometime. On the ride to the Faire and back, he'd been too preoccupied with his thoughts to feel like making conversation, so they'd listened to music, sixties' rock and roll mostly.

Connar walked into the house and sat down on the couch. Mahon immediately came in the pet door and sprawled out next to him. Connar shook his head as he stroked the dog's coarse fur. "What am I going to do? I didn't find the sword, and now I have no idea where to look."

As soon as they had arrived at the Faire, he discovered Niall didn't have a booth this year. In fact, Andre, who'd had a jewelry booth next to Niall's shop when Connar first went to the Faire, told him Niall had gone to another event in Washington State. That meant there was no way the metal smith could have stolen the sword.

Connar had spent the rest of the day helping Charles and the other re-enactors as they set up and performed a jousting demonstration. In between their performances, he'd had plenty of time to go over every possible explanation for the disappearance of the sword. Having eliminated Mark and Niall, he could only imagine that some random thief had entered his house and discovered the sword in their search for valuables. They then decided it was worth enough that they didn't need to steal anything else.

Connar sighed again. If a random thief had his sword, he'd probably never get it back. Somehow he had to go on without it. He had to remember the sword was merely a means to an end. He'd used its magic to come to this time and place so he could be united with Aisling. Being with her was what mattered.

Allison. He hadn't talked to her all day. She must feel as if he'd abandoned her. He went to the kitchen to retrieve his phone that he'd left charging on the counter. In his hurry to get to the Faire, he'd forgotten to take it.

As soon as he picked it up, he saw he had a text message. Thinking it must be from Allison, although she'd never texted him before, he saw the picture first. Registering the horrifying sight of Rowan with her throat cut, his gaze then moved down to read the words below.

The same thing will happen to Allison if you don't stay away from her.

Chapter Sixteen

Arriving home, Allison fed Benjamin, then changed clothes and packed some things in anticipation of staying overnight at Megan's. When Sophia still hadn't shown up, she sat down on the couch with Benjamin on her lap. Petting him, she started to relax. Maybe now she could consider her situation rationally.

She went over every detail of what had happened at the shop. Clearly, there were two issues here. But even though they were both connected to Connar, that didn't mean the events were linked.

One issue was Rowan's murder. It appeared to be a warning of some kind, although she wasn't certain of what. The only thing that might inspire someone to threaten her was the article she was currently writing about the dark side of the pagan scene in Denver. Was it possible someone was trying to keep the article from appearing? Maybe they'd used Connar's shop as a convenient place to stage a pretend murder. Connar might have nothing to do with it.

The more she thought about it, the more likely this scenario seemed. Of course, there was the other part of the experience. Her "memory" of Connar cutting her throat. Was it really a memory? It certainly seemed to be.

But even if he did kill her in a past life, that didn't mean he was a threat in this one. She recalled the expression on his face as he brought the sword to her throat. He'd appeared tormented, as if he didn't want to kill her but for some reason had no choice.

She shook her head, trying to clear it. This whole experience was enough to make her lose her mind, if she hadn't lost it already. What she needed was a break from thinking about these things. She hoped Sophia would get here soon.

Getting up, she started to pace. Part of her wanted to call Connar. If she could hear his voice, all her doubts would vanish. Another part of her was afraid. It seemed as if she was surrounded by a web of danger and much of it was connected to him.

Why hadn't he called her? Surely, he'd gotten his mysterious business taken care of by now. Maybe he *had* called, and she hadn't heard the phone ring. Sometimes that happened when she was in the car and had the music on loud, the way she had on the way home. She went to retrieve the phone from her purse. She'd just pulled it out when there was a knock at the door.

After checking through the peephole, she let Sophia in. "Hey. Good to see you."

"You look lovely." Sophia motioned to the dress Allison was wearing. The dress she'd put on back when she'd thought Connar meant to surprise her at the shop.

Allison shrugged. "I wasn't sure what you had in mind for dinner. Frankly, I'd like to go somewhere nice. I could use a relaxing meal and some pampering, unless you don't want to spend too much." She didn't have a clue about Sophia's financial situation. Maybe she wanted to go somewhere cheap.

"I'm happy to go wherever you'd like to eat,"

responded Sophia.

They finally settled on the Cheesecake Factory at the mall. It was close by and had a huge menu to choose from. Once there, to avoid thinking about her own situation, Allison decided to find out more about Sophia by asking her some probing questions.

It appeared she was independently wealthy and didn't have to work. She also didn't seem to have many interests other than Wicca and the occult. Several times, she referred to the other ceremonial group she belonged to and urged Allison to come to their meeting the following night.

Allison remained non-committal. Although the whole Wicca thing had begun to creep her out, she did need more information for the final article in the series, which was supposed to be about magic rituals performed by Wicca groups. Sophia said her group practiced "true craft", as opposed to the women who she had met at Andrea's. In fact, Sophia seemed disdainful of Andrea's group.

"So, why do you participate if you feel what they're doing is the equivalent of 'Wicca-light'?" Allison asked.

"It's an opportunity for me to meet other women interested in the craft," Sophia responded. "That's how I met Barbara and Rowan, both of whom have joined my group."

"Rowan is part of Andrea's group?" Allison asked in surprise.

Sophia frowned. "No…I mean…that is, she was at one time."

"But then she joined your group and left the other one?"

Sophia nodded. "She was much more serious than the others. She wanted to develop her skills, and that would never have happened there."

"What kind of skills?"

Sophia smiled. "If you come tomorrow night, you'll find out."

But I don't want to come. Why can't you just tell me?

Allison felt her familiar exasperation with Sophia returning. Why did the woman have to be so secretive and at the same time, somehow condescending?

"So, what do you, work spells to turn men into toads?" she asked snarkily. "Fly around on broomsticks?" She knew she was being rude and ridiculous, but she didn't care.

Sophia glared at her. "No, we do *real* magic. If you set aside your foolish fears and prejudices and come, I think you'll be very surprised."

"You think I'm afraid?" Allison asked defensively. It might be true, but it was irritating to hear Sophia call her on it. "What is there to be afraid of? Do you practice black magic or some kind of satanic stuff or something?"

"Satan is a concept the Christians came up with," Sophia responded with dignity. "As for black magic, what does that mean? If we call upon the powerful spiritual forces surrounding us to do our will, how is that wrong?"

"What if 'doing your will' causes someone else harm?"

Sophia appeared on the verge of a sharp retort, but seemed to catch herself. When she spoke, her tone was gentle and conciliatory, "Of course we don't work magic that would hurt anyone. That's one of the precepts of the craft: 'do no ill'."

"I'm glad of it," Allison responded, not wanting to fight either. "I don't mean to criticize, or suggest you're working magic to hurt people. But I have heard there are people who practice the darker arts, and my editor wanted me to find out if there were groups like that in Denver. You don't know about anything like that, do you? Maybe they drink blood or practice ritual sacrifice—the sensational stuff?"

Sophia seemed to be mulling over her answer. Waiting for her to respond, Allison realized that while the journalist in her hoped Sophia could give her some useful information, on a personal level, she'd much prefer if Sophia told her there were no black magic sects in Denver. This conversation was already veering too close to the one thing she did not want to think about. Rowan's bloody corpse lying in the back room of Connar's shop.

Finally, Sophia answered. "There may be groups like that in Denver, but I've never encountered them. It seems like something men involved with Wicca might pursue, and all the people I know in the craft are female."

It was on the tip of Allison's tongue to mention Connar. But then, Sophia had met Connar for the first time at the Faire. And for all that Connar owned a Wiccan shop and knew a great deal about pagan belief, he'd never once mentioned being part of a group, or practicing any rituals.

Could it be because he didn't think she'd approve of such things? Was it possible he and some of his guy friends had their own group? It was difficult to imagine

Connar and Mark—the only one of his friends she'd met—holding hands in a circle and calling down the gods under the full moon. They were too practical and straightforward. And definitely too masculine.

A shaft of loss went through Allison. She ached for Connar, longed for him with her whole being. No matter how hard she tried to tell herself she should keep things cool with him until she figured out what happened to Rowan, a part of her wanted to call him up and beg him to come get her, take her home, and make love to her until she forgot everything else. She sighed.

"What's wrong?" Sophia asked.

"Nothing. I…maybe we should change the subject. Our current topic is kind of a downer."

But it wasn't so easy. She and Sophia didn't have any other connection besides Wicca. It was clear from looking at her that Sophia had no interest in fashion and girly stuff, and when Allison tried to bring up the music scene in Denver, Sophia had stared at her blankly. What *were* they going to talk about for the rest of dinner?

They ended up falling back on small talk—the food they were eating, the hassle of driving in Denver, and other bland generalities. As soon as she finished her chocolate mousse, Allison glanced at the time on her cell phone and inwardly sighed with relief when she saw it was after eight. Surely by now Megan had finished with work, and she could have Sophia drop her off at her friend's apartment.

****

Connar took a deep breath before punching in the numbers for Megan's cell phone. Megan was Allison's best friend, and smart and level-headed besides. She was the only person he could think of who might be able to help him protect Allison

He'd tried several women in the Wicca group Megan belonged to before reaching Andrea, who had agreed to give him Megan's number. Now as the phone rang, he tried to think how to begin. He'd decided to tell Megan everything, but he worried she wouldn't believe him.

"Hello?"

"Megan. This is Connar, Allison's—"

"Connar. Of course. What's up?"

"I have something I wish to discuss with you, but I'd rather not do it by phone. Would it be possible to meet me somewhere?"

He held her breath as he waited for her answer.

"Well. I...Frankly, I'm shot, Connar. I've been at work all day. The advertising world never sleeps, you know, and I'm about brain-dead at this point."

"Brain-dead?" He wasn't sure what she meant.

"Uh, tired and not thinking clearly. Yeah, that's how you could describe it."

"I'm very sorry to have to ask for this favor, but it's important."

"I see. Does it involve Allison?"

"Very much, I'm afraid."

"You're afraid?" She sounded alarmed.

"Aye. It's...very complex. That's why I'd like to meet with you face-to-face."

"Where?"

Now she sounded wary. He hadn't thought she'd be so reluctant. He was going to have to be more direct. "Allison's safety...her very life might be involved."

"Okay. But you still haven't told me where you want to meet. How about a restaurant downtown? I haven't eaten dinner yet."

He didn't want to tell her the whole story in a public place. There was always the possibility that whoever was behind the threat might follow him to the restaurant. But it appeared he had no choice. Either Megan was truly hungry, or she didn't want to be alone with him. Or both. "Wherever you'd like to go will be fine. But I would prefer somewhere quiet."

"All right. How about the Hard Rock?"

"I'll take a cab and be there in half an hour."

"OK. That will give me time to finish up and walk over there. See you then."

****

"Finally," Allison said when she got through to Megan. "Did you have your phone turned off, or what?"

"I was on another call."

"Oh, right. So, are you about to head home? I've got all my stuff, and I thought Sophia could drop me off at your place."

"Something's come up and I won't be home for a while, I'm afraid."

"What? More work? It's Sunday night for heaven's sake!"

"Well, I haven't had supper yet and I thought I'd get a bite before going home."

"Where are you going? I could meet you there. Have a glass of wine while you're eating."

"Actually, I'm meeting someone. A man. So it would be better if we got together later."

She couldn't believe Megan was letting her down like this. Here she was, potentially being stalked by a murderer and Megan was ditching her to go out on a date! "Megan…" She knew she was whining, but she didn't care. "You know I'm afraid to be in my apartment alone."

"I thought you were with Sophia."

"I am but…" She could hardly explain how uncomfortable Sophia made her with Sophia sitting right there. She could kick herself for not excusing herself before calling Megan.

"Oh, all right. What time do you think you'll be done with dinner…or are you anticipating that dinner is going to lead to something more?"

"No, of course not. I'll still come get you."

"Okay. Call me, I guess."

As she hung up, she tried to hide her distress.

"Is something wrong?" asked Sophia.

"No. But Megan has a date or something. So we can't hook up until later."

"Would you like to come to my apartment in the meantime?"

"I guess so," Allison answered. It was either that or be alone, which she definitely didn't want to do.

****

"…and then I got the text, warning me to stay away from Allison, along with the picture of Rowan with her throat cut."

As Connar finished, he glanced at Megan. Her eyes were wide, stunned-looking, and her complexion ashen.

"Well," she said. "I kept telling Allison she was experiencing things from a past life. But even so, I never imagined…" She shook her head.

"Does Allison remember her life as Aisling? What has she told you about it?" The prospect both excited and terrified him.

"Most of it was the scary stuff. People chasing her with staves and burning brands. Watching you fight some fair-haired guy and getting wounded." Megan paused. "She also recently had a memory where you used a sword to cut her throat. It came right after she discovered Rowan's body."

"What? She saw Rowan dead?"

Megan nodded. "I didn't really believe her at the time. Especially since when she woke up from the vision, Rowan's body was no longer there. I couldn't figure out why anyone would kill Rowan and leave the body for Allison to find, and then take the body away. I still don't get that part."

"When did this happen? And where?"

"Today. This afternoon. At your shop." When Connar exhaled sharply, Megan nodded. "First, Allison got a call from Rowan, asking if she could come to the shop and cover for an hour or so, since Rowan had to leave. Allison thought it was strange since she'd never met Rowan, but she wanted to help out, so she agreed. When she got there, there was no one in the main part of the shop, so she went in the back. That's where she found Rowan."

Rowan was dead. Poor Rowan. And it was his fault. Whoever had killed her was obviously targeting him.

"Anyway," Megan continued, "right after she found Rowan, she had this vision...or memory or whatever it was. She said she was lying on a cliff by the sea and you were there with a sword in your hand. The same sword she saw lying next to Rowan's body. The same sword she saw in your closet." Megan's eyes were accusing, vaguely hostile. "You were standing over her.

She said you knelt down and brought the sword to her neck, and she knew you were going to kill her. Then the shock and terror she felt caused her to black out. When she came to, she was back in the shop and Rowan's body was gone."

Connar let out a deep breath. "By the gods, I'd hoped she wouldn't remember that part of it."

"So, it's true? You're the one who killed her?" Megan looked horrified.

"It is," Connar answered. "But you have to understand, it was the only way we could remained connected." He gestured desperately. "It was the only way I would be able to follow her spirit through time. Besides, if I hadn't cut her throat, she was going to be burned to death. My father had decreed it. I wanted to tell her why I was doing it, but Siobhan wouldn't let me. She said Aisling's fear of me would make the connection between us even stronger. But that meant she died thinking I…" He gritted his teeth as he remembered the terror in her eyes.

"Who's Siobhan?"

"Aisling's sister. One of the Nine Sisters, the sect that Aisling belonged to. They healed my foster brother Fergal, which is when everything started."

"Everything?"

He told Megan about Fergal's injury, going to the cave, meeting Aisling and all the rest. Speaking of it brought so many feelings back. As he explained Fergal's anger at learning the Sisters had healed him and the awful things his foster brother had done because of it, an aching chill filled Connar. When he'd finished his explanation, he faced Megan grimly and said, "It's almost if the rage and hatred of that time have somehow followed me here and are again threatening everything I care about."

"But how is that possible?"

"I don't know. There's no way Fergal followed me here. He would never involve himself in magic. And I can't imagine Siobhan would agree to aid him, no matter how he might threaten her. Besides Fergal, there's no one who hates Aisling enough to go to the extreme of traveling to another time."

"Unless it's you they're after. Maybe you're the target and not Allison. Is there anyone you could have upset enough since you've been in this time, that they might seek revenge against you? Someone you've humiliated or embarrassed? What about Mark? He seems like the tough, he-man sort. Could he hold a grudge against you for beating him at sword fighting and making him look bad?"

"We're so well matched we each win about half the time. I don't think there is any anger or resentment between us."

Megan nodded. A moment later, she frowned. "Allison mentioned her editor wanted her to explore the dark side of the pagan movement and see if she could find any groups that did the sinister, creepy stuff that witches always get accused of doing. Animal sacrifice, drinking blood, that sort of thing. Maybe while doing her research, she inadvertently upset someone, made them feel threatened in some way."

"But if they're after Allison, why involve me?" Connar insisted. "I'm the one who received the threatening text. If someone was afraid of what Allison might write, why wouldn't they direct the threat at her?"

"That's true," Megan agreed. "But it's all I can come up with."

"It's such a maddening puzzle," Connar said. "And the most terrifying thing is that since I don't know who is doing this, I can't protect her. I'm so afraid for her. I want to be with her to protect her. But if I do that..." He clenched his jaw in helpless anguish, and then added, "What if I fail? What if I lose her again in this lifetime?"

Megan appeared to mull that over. Finally she said, "Until we know for certain who the real target is, I think it might be better if you stayed away from Allison."

"You don't think I should go to her and warn her?"

"If you're the target it might put her in even greater danger. And right now, that's what seems most likely. If someone was after Allison, why bother killing Rowan, who Allison has never even met?" Megan shook her head. "No, I think someone's after you, and killing Rowan was an attempt to frame you for her murder. I don't know why the body was moved, though. That doesn't make any sense. Maybe the killer plans to leave other clues, so when the police find Rowan's body somewhere else, they'll follow the trail back to you. Maybe we should go to the shop and look around. We might find clues to help figure this out."

Connar nodded. "If you think I'm the person they want to hurt, and you're confident Allison is safe with Sophia..."

"I am." Megan got up from the table. "Let's go."

"Perhaps you should call Allison first," Connar suggested. "To make certain she's safe."

Megan got out her phone and called. Connar

listened as she asked Allison how she was doing. Apparently satisfied with her answer, Megan explained she was still at dinner and suggested Allison stay at Sophia's.

"Uh, uh. Yeah. No, of course not." The conversation continued for a while, and then Megan hung up. "She's not thrilled about staying at Sophia's. I think she's worried she'll be bored to death. Sophia's apparently a real snooze. But at least with her she'll be safe, and this way we can take as much time as we need to investigate."

"Let's go," said Connar.

****

As she hung up the phone, Allison told herself it was unfair of her to expect Megan to interrupt her date to come get her. Megan appeared to be having a good time, so it was her duty as a good friend to suck it up and stay here so Megan could see where things went with this guy. Besides, it was already nine thirty. In a little while, she'd claim fatigue and go to bed. Sophia's couch looked comfortable enough, probably better than Megan's rock-hard futon.

Although she told herself these things, she couldn't quite quell her sense of gloom. Why did Sophia get on her nerves so much? Oh, well. She would put on her big girl panties and get through this. It was only one night.

Sophia came out of the kitchen. "Would you like some hot chocolate?" She held out a mug. "I make it with real cocoa."

"Sounds fabulous," Allison said, faking a smile.

She took a sip. It was kind of bitter. But then she hadn't had real hot chocolate in years. And it was certainly creamier and more chocolaty than the stuff in packets.

Sophia went back into the kitchen to clean up, and Allison drank steadily.

About halfway through the hot chocolate, she started to feel strange. She put down the cup, and opened and shut her eyes, trying to clear her vision. Everything seemed fuzzy. Fuzzy turned to dizziness and she had no choice but to lie down on the couch. Just before consciousness swam away, she realized Sophia had drugged her.

Chapter Seventeen

"Nothing seems out of place." Connar walked around the cluttered stockroom at the back of the shop, looking for anything amiss. When he turned around, Megan was leaning over, examining the floor.

"I wish we had some luminal," she said. "It's this stuff you spray on surfaces to detect blood. Even if someone has cleaned up, if there's any trace of blood, it will glow under a black light." She straightened. "I watch a lot of crime shows on TV."

"Do you think Allison could have imagined seeing Rowan dead?"

"I don't think so. All of Allison's visions seem to represent real events in the past. As far as I know, she's never seen anything in this time period that wasn't actually there. But I do wonder if what she saw wasn't real."

"But you said—"

"She may have seen something that looked like Rowan with her throat cut, but it could have been staged." She gestured. "You know. Fake blood, the whole deal."

"But why?"

"To frighten Allison and convince her to stay away from you. If she discovers a corpse in your shop, what's she's going to think? That you're a murderer. She may be falling in love with you, but she's bound to reconsider the relationship if she thinks you're a crazed sociopath."

"Is she...falling in love with me? Do you believe that?" Connar's heart swelled with hope.

"Well, yeah. I mean, it's not my place to tell you, but yes, I do think she's smitten."

As Megan's words warmed him, Connar told himself not to be a fool. Even if Allison loved him, there were still many obstacles between them and a happy ending. He still had to tell her about the past...about what he did to her. And now there were other problems.

"If someone was trying to frame you, it seems to me they would have left more trace evidence here." Megan walked around the storeroom, her expression thoughtful. "I mean, Rowan was...maybe still is...your employee, not your girlfriend. So if she disappears, you're not going to be the most obvious suspect. Unless Allison tells the authorities what she's seen. Then you would be. I just wish I knew for certain who the real target is here. Is it you? Or is it Allison?"

As Megan faced him questioningly, Connar shook his head. "I don't know anyone who truly wishes me ill...at least not in this time period. In the past, there were several people I considered enemies."

"Hmmm. Well, I'm ready to give up for tonight. How about you?"

Connar nodded. "Perhaps we will think more clearly tomorrow. But there is one thing I'd like to do before retiring for the night."

"What?"

"Call Allison. If I could at least hear her voice, I would feel better. The text warned me to stay away from her, but a phone call…surely that would cause no harm." He gave Megan a pleading look.

"Sure. Call her. But use my phone. Just in case whoever is threatening her has your phone hacked."

Connar took Megan's phone, found Allison's name and pressed call. It rang once. Twice. Three times. He was about to give up when another woman answered.

"Hello."

"Is Allison there?"

"I'm afraid she's gone to bed."

"Very well. I'll call her later." Connar hung up.

"What happened? Did it go to voicemail?"

"No. Someone answered. Sophia perhaps. Said that Allison had gone to bed."

"Boy, she must be stressed. It's not like Allison to turn in this early. Maybe she went to bed to get away from Sophia. I do feel kind of bad about ditching her tonight. But it seemed more important to try to figure out what's going on. Not that we've made any progress. Maybe if we get together early in the morning and give it all a fresh look, we'll come up with something."

Connar nodded, although he wondered how fresh he would be, given he didn't think he could sleep at all.

****

But he did sleep, dozing off on the couch soon after Megan dropped him off. He woke early in the morning in the middle of a dream where he was making love to Allison. As he realized the warm body next to him belonged to Mahon rather than his love, he felt a keen disappointment. It was followed quickly by anxiety as he recalled the events of the day before.

Although it wasn't yet dawn, he decided to get up and make something to eat. As he was preparing eggs and toast, he went over everything Megan and he had discussed. His thoughts focused more and more on the sword. It could hardly be coincidence that it was stolen only a day before Allison saw it next to Rowan's body. But the sword was only meaningful to people from the past. Even if someone from this time period wanted to frame him, as Megan said, it was unlikely they would have stolen the sword to do so. It would have been much easier to leave one of his practice weapons by the body.

But if an enemy from the ninth century had followed him to this era, who were they, and how had they gotten close to him without him realizing it? How could they travel to this time period without Siobhan's assistance? And why would she help them threaten Allison? Siobhan loved her sister and would do anything to get her back. *Anything.*

Connar gasped aloud and let the spatula slip to the floor. *Siobhan!* What if she had come to this time period to bring Aisling back herself?

The idea stunned him. Siobhan had only helped him because she believed he would return her sister to their own time. What if she suspected he no longer intended to do so, but instead meant to remain with her in this time?

How could she know this? She could not see into his mind despite her magic. Unless she had guessed this might happen and followed him here. But how? And once she got to this time period, how had she survived?

The same way I did.

He hadn't found it easy to learn modern English, to adapt to the contemporary world and find a way to survive, but he had done it because he had no choice.

Siobhan would also have no choice, and she was a very strong, determined person.

If she was here, why hadn't he recognized her?

Unless he'd never met her. Siobhan's goal would be to get close to Allison, but she would obviously avoid him. He'd only had contact with Allison for a little more than a week. Not enough time to meet everyone around her.

Connar shifted the now-ruined eggs off the burner and went to get his cell phone.

He called Megan, but it went to voice mail. The second time, she answered. "Connar? What is it? What's wrong?"

"I think I know who threatened me…who is responsible for everything."

"Who?"

"Siobhan."

"Allison's sister? But she's still in the ninth century."

"Perhaps not. She's the one who sent me here. She may have found a way to follow."

"But you said the only way you could meet up with Aisling in the future was to kill her with the magic sword. Once that was done, Siobhan wouldn't have any way of traveling to this time herself."

"That's what *Siobhan* said. But perhaps she was lying. Perhaps there was another way to travel to the future and she used it."

"So, you think she might be here in Denver? That she's the one who killed Rowan and who stole your sword?"

"Aye."

"Well, in one way that's a relief. Allison is

obviously not in any danger. You're the one Siobhan's after."

"I believe that to be true. And it is a relief. But it still makes things difficult. Siobhan must intend to punish me. To make it look as if I murdered Rowan. How will I fight that? And how will I convince Allison I didn't do it."

He took a deep, wrenching breath. "I must see her now. I don't care if she's asleep. I have to talk to her. I have to explain!"

"Okay. Okay. I'll come pick you up. We'll go to Sophia's together."

After hanging up, Connar showered, dressed, and cleaned up the kitchen. Every moment made his impatience burn more intensely.

Once Megan picked him up, it was no better. He clenched his hands into fists as they drove to Sophia's. When Megan got lost, he struggled not to snap at her.

"I'm sorry. My sense of direction is terrible," Megan apologized. "But don't worry. The longer we take to get there, the better mood Allison will be in when we arrive. She's not exactly a morning person."

Connar nodded. Everything she said made sense. But it didn't stop his growing panic. It was illogical, but some part of him insisted that something was wrong, and he needed to see Allison *now*!

Finally, they arrived at the apartment building and found the right one. Megan knocked and they waited. She knocked again and they waited longer.

Unable to bear it, Connar began to pound on the door. "Allison! Allison! Please answer!"

"You're going to wake up the whole floor," warned Megan.

"What else can I do? Something's wrong. I know it. I've felt this way the whole journey here."

"Maybe they're listening to music and can't hear the door. Or, maybe they went out to breakfast."

"Do you think Allison would do either of those things this early?"

"No," Megan agreed. "That doesn't sound like her. It really doesn't." She let out a frustrated-sounding sigh. "Okay, what are we going to do? We can hardly break the door down. The neighbors—who are probably awake by now—will obviously call the cops if we try something like that."

"I don't know. I don't know." Connar felt paralyzed with dread. How could he lose Allison all over again?

Nay. He would not accept that. He had to find her.

"Maybe Sophia took Allison back to her apartment. I'll bet that's it. Come on." Megan grabbed his arm.

Connar followed her down the stairs, his mind racing. Megan's explanation made perfect sense. So, why did he feel like this? Where did this feeling of terror and despair come from?

At the car, he halted. "I want to believe you, Megan. I want to. But I can't. I feel in the deepest part of myself, the part that's connected to Allison. Something is wrong. Allison is in danger."

"From Sophia? But why…"

Sophia. Siobhan. They sounded very similar. Was it possible? Connar took a sudden, panicked breath. He'd met Sophia at the Faire. They'd all eaten lunch together before Allison got sick. Sophia had this strange paint on her face to make her look like a cat, and he hadn't been able to tell what she looked like. Her hair was short, and she was wearing modern clothes. But she was the right height and size. And her hair was dark like Siobhan's.

"By the gods," he murmured. "I should have known. I should have been able to tell it was her."

"What? *What?*"

"It's Sophia. I think she's actually Siobhan."

"You're kidding. But she's...oh!" Megan stared at him. "I guess it makes sense. Sophia has this strange accent. Not like yours, but unusual, nevertheless. I thought she was Eastern European or something. And she's definitely different. Kind of a *nouveau* hippie, I thought. The drab clothing, no make-up, her obsession with Wicca." She shrugged. "Well, don't look so panicked. You said yourself Siobhan would never hurt Allison. I'm sure she's fine."

"But what if she takes Allison back to the past?"

"Relax. Allison isn't going to agree to that. I told you, she's in love with you. Once you explain everything to her—"

"What if Siobhan takes Allison back to the ninth century against her will?"

"Could she do that? But how?"

"If Siobhan has the sword, she could kill Allison and take her back to the past."

Megan's eyes grew wide. "You think that's possible?"

Connar nodded. "If it worked once to bring me to this time, it might work to go the other way. Even if it doesn't, it will be too late. Allison will be dead in this era. You and I will never see her alive again!"

Megan sucked in her breath. "We have to find them. We have to find them now! But where would

Sophia take her?"

Connar tried to keep the panic from his voice. "I don't know. I barely know Sophia."

Megan grabbed his arm. "But you know Siobhan…and they're the same person."

"Aye." Connar nodded and began to pace. "She would want the ritual to be proper. They would have to go somewhere private, somewhere she could feel the gods." He whirled to face Megan. "Is there some place your group holds rituals? Somewhere outside?"

"Well, Andrea's back yard, but she'd never allow something like this. But Sophia belongs to another group, and I heard her tell Allison they meet in the mountains. But I don't know where." Megan frowned in concentration, and then said, "I think Misty and Stacy are part of the group. I'll call them."

****

Allison woke feeling disoriented and sick to her stomach. She was in a car and they were moving. More distressing, her hands were bound.

She fought back panic and tried to remember how she'd gotten here. Sophia had given her hot chocolate that tasted strange. She'd started to feel woozy, exactly the way she'd felt at the Faire after the wine.

She remembered starting to come around. Lying on the couch. Sophia's face looming near. She'd offered her something to drink. Had she drunk it? She feared so.

Drugged! Sophia had drugged her! She was a prisoner, and Sophia was taking here somewhere. To do what? Kill her like Rowan had been killed?

She must have a made a sound of some kind, for the person on the passenger's side of the car turned and looked back between seats. It was Misty. *No, it was Rowan!* When she'd seen Rowan with her throat cut, she'd thought she looked like Misty. Now she realized they were one and the same.

Which meant Rowan wasn't dead after all. The knowledge should have relieved her, but it didn't. She was too disturbed by the excited, expectant expression on Rowan's face. And when Rowan turned to the driver and said, "She's coming around. What should we do?" Allison felt the choking dread return.

They were going to kill her, she knew it!

All her visions and dreams of being murdered were coming true. But the killer wasn't Connar, it was Sophia.

But Sophia wasn't Sophia, she was...

Allison struggled to sit up and get into a position where she could see the driver of the car. The person at the wheel glanced back at her. Perhaps it was her keen, searching expression, or the way her disheveled hair framed her face, but all at once Allison knew her. Siobhan.

The name seemed to emerge from some dark, hazy part of her brain. Connar had once mentioned a Siobhan. As soon as he'd said the name, an expression of alarm had crossed his face. But the name had meant nothing to her then. Now she was certain Siobhan was someone she'd known in another life. And now she was here.

And she intends to kill me!

Why? If only she could remember.

Allison searched her mind. Tiny glimpses came back to her, but then slipped away before she could make sense of them.

But her instincts didn't lie. All along, her instincts had told her that Connar represented safety, love, and happiness, even as they'd made her uncomfortable with Sophia.

I should have trusted my feelings. I should have known Connar would never hurt me. I should have trusted him and asked for his help. Instead I thought the worst of him and ran. And in fleeing him, put myself in the hands of the real villain!

For little while she indulged in self-pity, beating herself up for being so stupid. She'd found the perfect man, her soulmate. Then she screwed up and lost him. She was going to die without ever getting a chance to tell Connar how much she loved him!

Stop it! You aren't dead yet!

She clung to that awareness and used it to pull herself out of despair.

In fact, she was fortunate. She wasn't in the clutches of some crazed serial killer, but the captive of two women. Two fairly small, unathletic women.

Unfortunately, that description also applied to her. Not to mention, her hands were tied. And she was still muddle-headed and weak from the drug. And they probably had a weapon.

The sword! It had been lying next to the dead Rowan, who wasn't really dead at all. Which meant it was now in their possession.

A huge, very sharp, sword. The one she'd seen in her vision when Connar cut her throat. Except he hadn't, had he?

She couldn't think about that. She had to forget Connar and concentrate on her present circumstances.

A sword was a deadly, very scary weapon. But it

wasn't a gun. You had to be right next to a person to use it. If she attempted to run, they wouldn't be able to shoot her.

Now would be the time to try to get away. Before they got wherever they were going. Before they realized she had recovered enough to escape.

But the car was going fast. They must be on the freeway. Probably I-70, heading west. Sophia had mentioned the ceremony was in the mountains.

It would be suicide to throw herself out of car going sixty or more. With the usual traffic on I-70, she'd probably get hit by another car if she didn't die in the fall.

Scratch that idea. But when they stopped, she must be ready. At least they hadn't tied her ankles together. Maybe she could wriggle out of the rope binding her wrists. True to her "natural" lifestyle, Sophia hadn't used plastic to bind her victim, but plain old rope.

After some furtive wriggling, Allison decided plain old rope worked pretty well. She gave up on getting her hands free.

But she didn't need her hands free to run. The key was surprise. Too bad they now knew she was awake. Maybe she could convince them she'd only come to briefly and was once more comatose.

It was hard to lie still with the adrenaline coursing through her. Hard to wait for her chance to escape.

Run, run, run. She envisioned herself as fleet as a deer. She'd been fast as kid, but hadn't done much with it since then.

This is my chance to prove I haven't lost it. My chance to save myself.

She thought about her first vision, or whatever it

was. The people chasing her as she ran out onto a cliff. At least there was no sheer drop-off into the sea here. But there were a lot of sheer drop-offs in the mountains.

Damn!! She hated heights!

Chapter Eighteen

"Stacy, it's Megan. Thank God I reached you. Listen, do you know where Sophia's group meets? I think it's somewhere in the mountains. Really? That's the only place?"

Connar held his breath as he listened to Megan's conversation. What if no one knew where Siobhan had taken Allison? What if by the time they figured it out, it was too late?

He closed his eyes and fought for control. Nay, he couldn't lose her. The gods would not be so cruel.

Megan called someone else. Someone named Ginny. The conversation didn't last long before Megan hung up and sighed.

"I'm getting nowhere. I can't find anyone who knows anything about this other group. I wish I could reach Misty. I feel like she's the one most likely to know, since she's pretty tight with Sophia. But she isn't answering her phone."

"What can we do?" Connar asked. "Isn't there someone else you can call?"

"There are five other women in the group. But I don't have their numbers. I'll have to call Andrea to get them."

Connar waited impatiently while Megan called Andrea. But Andrea was at work and didn't have her list of phone numbers with her. "I guess she has them written down in an old-fashioned address book instead of in her phone," Megan said when she hung up. "She promised to call me when she goes home at lunch."

"How long will that be?" Connar asked desperately. *He couldn't endure this. To wait by helplessly while Allison was in danger.*

"Andrea goes to lunch in an hour, so it could be worse. In the meantime, maybe we should try to eat something, too."

"I can't," said Connar.

Megan nodded. "I feel the same." She put her hand on Connar's arm. "Look at it this way, Sophia's unlikely to get very many members of the group together until this evening. People have jobs, and even once they're off work, they'll still have to drive up to the mountains. Unless you think Sophia isn't going to wait for a formal ceremony. That she'd try to do this on her own?" Megan's gaze was questioning.

"When we performed the ritual last time, it was only Siobhan, Aisling and me." He shuddered as he remembered that awful day. "We have to do something now. We can't wait much longer."

"What should we do?"

"We could start driving toward the mountains."

"But we don't know where they are headed. What if we choose the wrong route? We could end up having to backtrack."

Connar nodded, feeling as if he would burst with frustration. "Very well. We'll wait until Andrea calls. In the meantime, we should go to my house so I can check on Mahon."

****

The car was stopping. This was her chance!

229

Allison could hear Sophia and Rowan talking in low voices. She strained to listen, while at the same time she tried to decide which of the back doors of the car they would open first. As soon as they opened one, she'd have to scramble out the other side. In the meantime, she'd lie still and pretend to be unconscious.

They were getting out. Only a few more seconds…

They must be walking away from the car. But which direction?

She raised her head, trying to see. She still couldn't tell. Pushing herself up with her bound hands, she scanned the area around the car.

There they were, to the left! She took a deep breath, then scooted over and clumsily opened the door on the other side. A wave of dizziness assaulted her, but she shook it off and climbed out. Merely staying on her feet was an effort. How was she ever going to run? She had to try.

She staggered forward, feeling like a wobbly colt taking its first steps. Her head was spinning. Her vision blurry. So hard to see where she was going.

She heard a shout and tried to go faster. Then she tripped and went down.

Stabbing pain shot through her arms.

Get up! Get up!

She climbed to her knees, despite the pain that made her nauseous.

Voices behind her. Sophia calling out the name, Aisling. Then they were on either side of her. As they took hold of her arms, she squeezed her eyes shut, despairing, and slumped forward.

Rowan's grip was like iron around her left arm. Sophia held her right one much more gently. Sophia's voice was coaxing, urging her to stand up.

No! I won't make it easy for you.

Rowan muttered a curse and then released her. "I'm going to the car! I'm getting the drug."

"No!" Sophia shouted. She sounded panicked. "No! She has to be awake! She has to see me! The spell won't work if she can't see me!"

"All right, then we'll drag her!"

"I don't want to hurt her!"

"What difference does it make if you're going to cut her throat?"

Cut her throat. The way Rowan's throat had been cut. Except it hadn't. Rowan was very much alive. And very angry.

"Rowan, please..." Sophie sound frantic.

"Please what? You know we have no choice. The others won't be here for hours. It will be better this way."

Sophia made a sound of assent. Rowan left, presumably to go back to the car.

This was her chance! She had to get away now!

But how? She could barely stand, let alone run.

Reason with Sophia. Talk her out of this.

"Sophia, don't do this, please. It's not worth it. No spell or ceremony can be worth what you're about to do. It's...it's murder. And you'll never get away with it. Megan knows I'm with you. If you kill me, they'll know you were involved. Even if they don't find my body, all the clues will point to you. They'll come after you. You can try to hide but you'll never be free. Never!"

"That's not true," Sophia said. "Where I'm going, where *we're* going, there's no way anyone can follow.

Only Connar knows the way, and without the sword, he can't come after us. Which is as it should be. He had no right to take you from us, from your sisters."

Sophia was mad, or at least severely delusional. Allison could see that now. If only she'd realized it sooner. If only she'd listened to her nagging sense that this was someone she should avoid. Now it was too late. She was in the clutches of a crazy woman.

But Rowan? What was her story? Why was she doing this? Maybe she was the one Allison should try reasoning with.

As soon she heard Rowan coming back, Allison raised her head and called out, "You'll never get away with this. Megan knows I'm with Sophia. The police will trace my disappearance back to her, and they'll start digging around, searching for her accomplice. They'll figure out it was you. They'll find you out and put you in jail. Megan will see to it, and so will Connar. They'll find a way to make you pay!"

"Oh, just shut up, Allison," Rowan responded. "You don't know anything about it. If they're going to put us in jail, they'll have to travel back to the ninth century. We don't have a thing to worry about."

A prickling dread spread over Allison's body. Maybe Sophia wasn't deranged. Maybe there was something to their bizarre plan. "You're right. I don't know anything about it. So tell me, Rowan. Explain why you're doing this."

Rowan crouched down on the ground next to her. "It's simple. Sophia cuts your throat with the magic sword. As you die, the energy released will transport Sophia and me back to the past, to the time period that Sophia—and you—originally lived in."

"You're killing me so you can travel to the past?" Allison said incredulously.

"No!" Sophia broke in. "We're not killing you! We're freeing you from this time period, this life that isn't truly yours! You'll be in the world where your spirit truly belongs!"

Allison thought of all her strange experiences. They must be memories from her life in the past that Sophia was talking about.

"No," she said. "I don't want to go back there. I wasn't happy in that time. Awful things happened to me." To Sophia, she added imploringly, "Don't make me go back there, please! If you care for me at all, don't make me go back!"

"It won't be like that this time." Sophia touched her arm soothingly. "This time I will protect you. I won't let Connar get near you."

"But Connar is the only good thing I remember. He's the only reason I would consider going back."

"You're wrong," Sophia insisted. "Connar is the one who brought about your death. He's the reason everything went awry."

"This is a waste of time," interjected Rowan. "It doesn't matter what she wants. Everything is already in motion. You promised, Sophia." Rowan grabbed Allison's arm and gestured to Sophia to grab her other one. "Come on. We have to get her to the circle."

"No! I won't go!" Allison shouted. If they were going to take her some place where they intended to kill her, they'd have to drag her there.

It quickly became clear Rowan was willing to do exactly that. When Allison refused to stand up and walk, Rowan jerked her forward. Allison fell onto her hands. She cried out as pain stabbed down her arms once more.

"Stop!" cried Sophia.

"No," Rowan insisted. "I won't. If she won't walk, I'm going to drag her there, by myself if I have to."

"All right. I'll walk," said Allison. It seemed better to give in and avoid getting hurt, if she hadn't already injured herself. Her right arm hurt like hell.

Sophia helped Allison to her feet. Rowan held onto Allison's left arm and propelled her forward. They were climbing up a hill. Allison turned to look back and caught a glimpse of a big fancy house in the valley below. This was obviously private land. Which meant it was unlikely anyone who wasn't in on the plot would come along to rescue her. Damn!

When they got to the top of the hill, Allison saw what Rowan meant by the circle. Tall stones had been arranged in a mini Stonehenge-like formation with a large flat stone in the very center.

Oh, crap! That must be the altar, where they made their sacrifices, and she was the intended victim. The prickling dread moved down her spine once more. She'd thought all this Wicca stuff was harmless. Now she was about to end up being put to death in the middle of a stone circle.

As they came to a halt, Allison turned to Rowan accusingly. "I thought one of the precepts of Wicca was 'do no harm'? Yet you're going to cut my throat."

"I told you, you aren't going to die. We're actually helping you."

"We're freeing you from this life, this time that you don't belong to." Sophia touched Allison's shoulder gently. "At last we'll be together again, which is the way it should be."

"Who are you?" Allison asked. "I mean in my other life."

Sophia's eyes were sorrowful. "I'm your sister. Don't you remember?"

"No, I don't. The only one I remember is Connar." That wasn't quite true. From the beginning, she'd had a vague sense of having known Sophia. But her reaction hadn't been affection and warmth, but irritation. "Are you going to send Connar back, too?" she demanded. "Because if you aren't, then I don't want to go."

Sophia's expression grew hard. "You don't know what you're saying. Connar destroyed your life. He ruined everything. I knew he would, as soon as I sensed him coming to the cave. I knew he would destroy the Nine Sisters. And I was right."

"Who are the Nine Sisters?"

"Your family." Sophia responded. "You grew up with them. They were always there for you."

"I don't remember. I don't want to remember."

"It doesn't matter," said Rowan. "You'll find out soon enough."

Allison turned to Rowan. "Are you from the past, too? 'Cause I have absolutely no memory of you either."

Rowan glared at her. "I'm sure I'm from the past, although I wasn't one of Nine Sisters Siobhan is referring to. But I'm certain I was a priestess of some kind in the past. I belong there. I can feel it calling to my soul."

"That's the way I feel about Connar!" Allison exclaimed. "I belong with Connar. He's my soulmate."

"Nay!" Sophia exclaimed. Her voice rose in

hysteria. "You belong to me! *I'm* your soulmate!"

Allison wanted to protest, but she knew it wouldn't do any good. Rather than arguing with these women, she needed to let them think she'd given in. Then when they let down their guard, she'd have a better chance of escaping.

She said, "You mentioned other people coming. Who else is going to be around when you...send me back?"

"You don't know most of them," said Rowan. "But a few of them belong to Andrea's group, Stacy, Rose and Barbara."

That Stacy was involved made sense. She was young and impressionable. But Allison was surprised Rose and Barbara had agreed to be part of this. Rose was old enough to know better. And Barbara? A spoiled trophy wife like her seemed an unlikely member of a crazy, "out-there" group like this one.

"Why are they doing this?" she asked. "What do they get out of this ceremony?"

"They get a chance to do real magic. To realize their own powers." Rowan answered.

Allison whirled to face Sophia. "What if you're wrong? What if the magic doesn't work? What if, when you cut my throat, I just die, rather than traveling to the past? Are you willing to take that chance? Can you risk it?"

"It will work," Sophia said stubbornly. "I know it will. It worked for Connar, and he's male and has much less power."

"But the connection between Connar and me is stronger than the one you and I have. Maybe that's the magic ingredient that made it work."

"That's not true!" Sophia shouted. "That's a lie!"

Shut up, Allison, shut up! Didn't you just tell yourself not to provoke them?

"Okay. You're right. It will work. But I warn you, I won't be happy in the past. I'll be miserable, and then I'll make you miserable."

"I'm tired of this arguing," Rowan said. "We need to prepare." She reached into her pocket and took out an old-fashioned brown medicine bottle. "And we can't do that if we have to watch Allison every minute."

Allison eyed the bottle with horror. They were going to drug her again! No! She clamped her mouth shut, determined not even a drop would go down her throat.

But she wasn't prepared for how strong Rowan was. And there were two of them, and maybe she'd made Sophia mad by talking about Connar.

But for whatever reason, Sophia didn't argue when Rowan shouted, "Hold her still!"

She gripped Allison in a bear hug while Rowan pried her mouth open. Allison tried to fight them, but some of the drug trickled down her throat.

Rather than risking aspirating, she swallowed.

"I think that's enough," Rowan pronounced after releasing her. "Just a little to knock her out for a few hours. By the time the others get here, we should be able to wake her up again."

Allison observed the satisfied expression on the faces of the two women and felt a wave of despair.

****

Megan clicked off her phone and glanced at her handwritten list. "Besides Misty, who still won't answer, Barbara's the only one left. And it's seems unlikely she'd be a member of Sophia's group. I'm not sure how she'd fit it in between her manicures and shopping." She made a cynical face.

Connar felt the familiar panic. If they couldn't find anyone who knew where Sophia had taken Allison, they'd never reach her in time. Could the gods be so cruel as to make him lose Aisling twice?

"Call her," he said. "Call Barbara. We have to believe she'll be able to help us. If she doesn't know where the ceremony will be held, then we'll call everyone again. Someone must have some knowledge of where they are."

Megan nodded and punched in the number. When Barbara answered, she said, "Hey, Barbara, it's Megan. Sorry to bother you, but I'm trying to find Sophia. She's having a ceremony up in the mountains. I'm supposed to go, but I've lost the directions and Sophia won't answer her phone. Do you have any idea where this place is?" Megan's expression darkened. "Well, uh, Sophia just asked me yesterday. Yeah. Why wouldn't she? You're going to call her? Well, good luck, 'cause I haven't been able to reach her. Sure. Fine."

Megan hung up. "Houston, we have a problem." She met Connar's gaze. "She clearly suspects Sophia doesn't want me around for this ceremony, and she's going to call Sophia and check for sure. So now we're really screwed. If she gets in touch with Sophia, then Sophia will know we're trying to find her."

"She must realize that already," said Connar.

"I suppose you're right. And it doesn't matter if Sophia knows we're on to her because we have no way of finding out where she's taken Allison. Barbara was my last hope." Meagan shook her head. "Sophia had this all planned out. For all I know, the rest of the group is involved and that's why they've all been putting me off and pretending not to know anything about this ceremony."

Connar felt it all slipping away. But he wouldn't give up. "If Barbara is involved, then she should be leaving soon to go to the ceremony. Why can't we follow her?"

"That's a good idea. The only problem is, I don't know where Barbara lives. Somewhere in Highlands Ranch, but where?" Megan frowned. "I could call Andrea back, but what am I going to tell her? Besides, what if she's in on this whole thing, too?"

"I think we must try. We must keep trying."

"You're right." Megan rapidly called Andrea back.

"Hey, sorry to bother you again. I finally got in touch with Barbara, and she told me to meet her at her place so we could head up to the ceremony together. But I realized after I hung up I don't know where she lives and now I can't reach her. Do you have her address by any chance?"

Megan grimaced as if expecting the worst. Then her face relaxed. "You do? That's great. Sure, I'll hold on." Covering the phone, she mouthed "Yes!" A few moments later, she was writing rapidly. "Gee, thanks so much Andrea. I owe you for all of this. We'll have to get together when this is over and I'll tell you all about it…Yeah, I know…I was okay with what we were doing in your group, too. But Sophia's so intense and all. Uh, huh. I agree."

Connar made a panicked gesture, to remind Megan they needed to hurry to Barbara's house before she left.

At last, Megan hung up. "Andrea sounds like she's

been suspicious of Sophia all along. I wish she'd said something sooner. Oh, well. We'd better get going. Except…" She gazed at Connar questioningly. "Shouldn't we take weapons…just in case?"

Connar nodded. "I have another sword. It's not magical, but it would be an effective weapon." He headed for the cupboard in the hall to fetch it.

"What about me?" Megan asked, following him. "I mean, I probably wouldn't be much good with a sword, but don't you have a dagger or something?"

"Aye. I'll find you a weapon." He opened the cupboard and took out the handmade sword in its leather scabbard. After giving it to Megan to hold, he removed the wooden box behind the sword and took out the dagger stored inside. "They're both replicas, but the blades are true."

He took the sword from her and gave her the dagger. She touched her finger along the blade. "Jeez, you weren't kidding. This could do some real damage."

"Do you think you can use it if necessary?" he asked.

She grimaced. "Yeah, if I had to, I suppose I could. Although I'd rather have a gun. You don't have to get close to your opponent with a gun."

"I'm afraid I don't have any guns."

"You're probably the only macho guy in Colorado who can say that, more is the pity." She gestured. "Okay, cowboy, let's go get them."

They scarcely talked as Megan drove to where Barbara lived. They exited the interstate and followed the busy street to a neighborhood of giant houses. As she turned into the housing development, Megan let out a low whistle.

"Your little house would fit into one of these places about a dozen times. And the crazy thing is, I'll bet most of them only have a handful of people living there. Barbara doesn't have children, so it's only her and her husband."

Connar nodded while looking for the street number. When they finally found the right house, Megan parked down the street within sight of the driveway.

"I don't think Barbara has any idea what kind of car I drive, but just in case, we need to stay back."

Time passed with excruciating slowness as they waited. Finally, Connar said, "What if she's left already? She might have driven away as soon as she hung up from talking to you."

"I don't think so. I don't believe they'll hold the ceremony until at least sunset. It doesn't sound like the sort of thing you'd want to do in broad daylight." Megan turned to face him. "I still can't quite wrap my head around this. You're telling me Sophia is going to cut Allison's throat and somehow in doing that, it will send the two of them back to the ninth century?"

"It's because of the sword," Connar responded. "It possesses magic that makes all this possible."

"And you really did that...cut Allison's throat back in the time you're from?"

Connar nodded. "It sounds terrible...and it was. But you have to remember, I knew if I didn't kill her, my tribe would have. My foster brother Fergal was convinced she had cursed him and ruined his life. He believed the only way to break the curse was to have her put to death. He had convinced my father, the tribe chieftain, there was no other way. Only by promising I would kill Aisling myself, was I able to protect her."

"And Allison believed the magic would work? When you cut her throat, did she think the two of you would be reunited in another lifetime?"

Connar shook his head. "Siobhan insisted I couldn't tell her. She said the spell wouldn't work if Aisling knew what was going to happen. But I think Siobhan was lying. I think Siobhan wanted Aisling to remember me killing her so that when we met again in this lifetime, the terrifying memory of how she died would keep Aisling from falling in love with me."

"But her plan failed," Megan said thoughtfully. "Although Allison eventually remembered you cutting her throat, by then she'd already fallen in love with you."

"I hope that's true. I hope so."

Megan patted his shoulder. "It is. I know it."

"But none of that will matter if Siobhan kills Allison. She'll go back to the past and I won't be able to follow her."

"True. If Siobhan gets her way, then it will suck for all of us. You and I will lose Allison, and she'll be stuck in the past and be totally miserable. But we aren't going to let that happen, are we?"

Connar met Megan's gaze. "We will not. I vow it." The next moment he glimpsed a car backing out of Barbara's driveway. "Look. It's time."

Megan waited until the car was headed down the street then started her own vehicle and pulled out.

They followed Barbara out of the housing development and as she turned west toward the mountains. They drove in silence as Megan concentrated on keeping close behind Barbara, but not too close.

When they finally got through most of the traffic and reached a main highway, Megan's posture relaxed a bit and she said, "So, presuming Barbara leads us to this place where Sophia took Allison, it seems like we should have a plan when we get there."

Connar nodded. "How many women do you think will be there?"

"Our regular group has nine, give or take."

"Nine, like the Nine Sisters," Connar mused.

"And we know Sophia/Siobhan will have the sword," Megan continued. "Some of the other women may have ceremonial knives. Misty carries one, I know for certain."

In his own time, Connar would have been confident he could best a group of women. But the females of this era were much fiercer than the ones of the past. And in the upcoming confrontation, Siobhan would have *the* sword. If the weapon could enable someone wielding it to travel across time, what other magical powers might the sword possess? And did Siobhan know of them?

She was the one who had brought him the sword and explained how to use it to free Aisling's spirit so they could be reunited in another life. Where had she gotten the weapon? Was the power of the weapon innate, or caused by a spell the Sisters had worked over it? He'd never thought about these things before, so intent had he been on reclaiming Aisling. But now the questions loomed ominously.

Should he discuss his concerns about the sword with Megan? Doing so might distress her and make her less effective in rescuing Allison. For that matter, was he doing the right thing in involving Megan at all? While he needed her to drive him to where Allison was being held, once they arrived he should probably insist Megan stay in the car. His connection to Rowan had cost the young woman her life. He didn't want Megan to be killed as well.

But if Megan wanted to help him, what then? If he'd learned one thing in this time, it was that women of this era didn't always want to be protected and cared for. They often sought to pursue their own destinies, whatever the consequences. Some of them even became soldiers, fighting wars like the men.

That thought decided him. He would warn Megan of the possible risks and then leave it up to her if she wanted to help him.

He turned to look at Megan. "About the sword," he began. "There is no certainty I can prevail against someone wielding it. My own sword is an ordinary weapon, while the one Siobhan possesses is magical. I'm willing to take the risk that I will lose the battle and die in this life, and perhaps forever. But you, you must understand the danger you face. You might well suffer the same fate as Rowan."

Megan glanced at him. "Allison's my best friend. I'm willing to do whatever I have to do to help her, even if it means risking death."

"I'm very grateful for your help," Connar responded. "And if you are willing, I have a plan."

"Okay. Spit it out."

"I think you should confront Siobhan. Perhaps you can reason with her. I will wait somewhere nearby, so I can hear what's happening. If I sense you are in danger, or it appears we must overpower Siobhan to save

Allison, then I will come to your aid."

"That's a good idea. I think seeing you might set Siobhan off. If she thinks it's just me, she might not be so defensive. But I worry what the other women are going to do. That's where I may need you. Brandishing a sword, you're damned intimidating. Seeing you and knowing how determined you are might be enough to get them to back off."

"We can hope so," Connar agreed.

He closed his eyes, willing himself to reach the state of calm and concentration that would allow him to do battle most effectively.

Chapter Nineteen

Someone was calling her name. The sound came to Allison from a distance. Then someone was shaking her. Even that didn't really rouse her. It was only when she realized she couldn't move that she forced herself to climb out of the smothering darkness. The more aware she became, the more the anxiety built inside her. Something was wrong. Terribly wrong.

"Allison, Aisling. Wake up. Wake up." The voice, coaxing and tender. And yet it did the opposite of soothing her. She hated that voice, hated it. She tried to move away and realized why she could not. Her wrists and ankles were bound.

Panic swept her, forcing her eyes open. As she gazed up at Sophia, it all came back to her with a rush of horror. The ceremony. The sword. They were going kill her. *Oh, God!*

She was lying on the huge flat rock in the center of the circle of standing stones. The angle of the light and the long shadows told her it was late in the day, almost evening. She raised her head and saw she was surrounded by women. Sophia and Rowan, and several others, all wearing long dresses.

Her terror increased. "No," she whispered. "Don't kill me."

"I told you," Sophia answered. "You'll only die in this life. Your spirit will go back where you belong."

"No, no! I don't want to!" She raised her body so she could see the faces of the other women. "Help me! Please! I don't want to go to the past! I don't want to leave this world, this time period! Don't let her do this! It's not right! Please!"

The women stared back at her, their expressions stoic and calm. They clearly expected this. Of course. They could see she was bound. They already knew she was unwilling. Her pleas meant nothing to them.

Allison lay back. She could feel tears forming. They oozed out and trailed down the sides of her face. Her situation was hopeless. She was going to die, and there was nothing she could do about it.

She lay there, waiting for the feel of the sword cutting into her flesh. But nothing happened. She could hear Sophia and Rowan moving away. They were talking casually.

Gradually the pounding of Allison's heart eased. They weren't going to kill her, yet. They were waiting for something. For sunset. Nighttime. Something. For now, she had a reprieve.

Gradually, she figured out what had happened. They had been testing to make certain they could rouse her. Now that they knew she was alert and aware, they were content to wait until when they felt the time was right.

It seemed incredibly cruel. To make her wait like this, anticipating her death. But they didn't care. They were all heartless bitches intent on their ceremony, the stupid ritual that was supposed to send her back to the past.

Of course, it might well work. If what Sophia said was true, that was how she came to the twenty-first century. Both she and Connar.

Connar, oh, Connar!

Another round of tears flowed down her cheeks. If she went back to the past, she'd never see him again. It was heartbreaking. She'd found the man she belonged with. Her soulmate. And now she was going to lose him, again. And all because of this selfish, manipulative bitch who supposedly was her sister.

Anger replaced her despair. If it was true that they were both going back to the past, then Sophia would be very sorry when they got there. She'd make her life miserable! She'd make certain Sophia never found happiness! She'd never speak to her. Never!

It was an utterly hopeless, hollow plan. There would be little satisfaction in ruining Sophia's life when her own was over.

She let out her breath in a long drawn-out sigh. How sick and weary she felt. Downright hopeless. Maybe that was the answer, to lie back and let it happen and not care. When Sophia decided it was time, she would lie there like a corpse.

But then another thought came to her, filling her with excitement. They wanted to her to be awake! According to what Sophia had said, she needed to be aware for the magic to work. What if she refused to open her eyes? They couldn't make her. There was no way.

Relief flooded her. She had a plan. A way of fighting them. There was hope she could delay the ceremony. Maybe if she could delay it long enough, Megan would figure out she was missing. She'd contact Connar and the two of them would start searching for her. Maybe if she dragged things out long enough, someone would come and save her. A frail, desperate hope, but she had nothing else.

****

"Barbara's turning," Megan announced. "Now, to stay close without her realizing she's being followed. I'm going to have to drop back. I hope I don't end up losing her."

They followed Barbara up a winding road into the foothills. Gold and purple wildflowers swayed above the tawny-green grass and they passed stands of aspen, silvery green leaves shivering in the breeze. Ahead of them, steep blue gray mountains rose dramatically, silhouetted against the vast sky, slowly darkening as the sun sank toward the horizon.

"Crap!" Megan slowed the car as they reached a fork in the road. "I can't tell which way she went."

"Which direction seems to lead to higher ground?" asked Connar. When Megan turned to look at him, he said, "I think Siobhan is planning to do this somewhere high up, perhaps with a sheer drop-off on the other side."

"You think she'd seek out a location like the cliffs by the sea where you did this in the past?"

"Aye. I do."

"Okay. Then it looks to me like we should go this way." Megan steered the car onto the left branch of the roadway.

The road climbed upwards, winding its way up a steep hillside. When they reached the top, Megan slowed the car once more. Tucked away at one end of the long sloping valley below them was a huge stonework house surrounded by pine trees.

"Wow. That's quite the mountain hideaway," said

249

Megan. "It must belong to Barbara. Well, so much for the element of surprise. They'll be able to see us coming as soon as we start down the hill."

"But did she go to the house? I don't see her car."

"Good point," said Megan. "Oh, yeah, you're right. I see a cloud of dust over there. Must be another road. We'll let her get a head start and then follow."

"Perhaps we should park the car and follow on foot," Connar suggested.

"You're probably right. That would be more discreet. Although tramping across the countryside is not my thing. Hope there aren't any rattlesnakes around here."

They drove a little farther, then parked the car and set off, following the road as it wound up the hill. Connar tried not to walk too fast so Megan could keep up. "I need to get in shape," she muttered from behind him. "I've been spending too much time sitting at a desk lately."

The sun was almost behind the mountains, casting the landscape into shadow. But about two thirds of the way up the hill, Connar saw several vehicles parked along the road.

When Megan reached him, he motioned to the vehicles. She nodded and they continued on, moving more slowly. They encountered a compact car that Connar recognized as Sophia's, then another vehicle and finally two SUV's, one of which was Barbara's.

Connar felt his heart begin to drum wildly. They were close, very close.

Just beyond the SUV's, the road ended. Leading off it was a footpath that continued up the hill. Connar turned to Megan. "What do you think? Should we split up here?"

She nodded. "I'll follow the path, while you see if there's another way up." She patted her back pocket where she'd put the dagger he'd given her and started up.

Connar angled around in an attempt to reach the top of the hill from the other side. But it soon grew very steep. With his leather-soled shoes and the sword in the scabbard on his hip, he wasn't equipped for climbing.

He returned to the path and followed it until he saw a boulder near the top of the hill. As he angled toward it, he heard voices. Hurrying to the boulder, he pressed himself against it.

Women's voices. Shrill and intent. But there was enough wind to make it impossible to tell what was being said. He had a new dilemma. When should he intervene? Should he wait for Megan to call out? Would he hear her if she shouted for help?

He decided to wait a little longer. If they were arguing, that meant nothing had happened yet.

A moment later, he heard a scream. He dragged the sword from the scabbard, rushed past the boulder and up the hill.

The sight that met his eyes horrified him. A dozen huge stones formed a large stone circle on the hilltop. In the center of the circle was a giant flat rock with a naked woman lying on the top of it. She appeared to be unconscious and her hands and feet were bound.

Allison!

The women were gathered around the rock, with Siobhan nearest to Allison. Beside her was Rowan, who was clearly alive. Between Connar and the rock were Megan and a woman Connar had never seen before.

The woman was beautiful, with long pale hair and a haughty, elegant face. She smiled as she saw him, a smile of malevolence and scorn.

"This must be Connar. Our hero…come to rescue his beloved." In her right hand was the sword—the ancient magical sword.

She raised the sword and started toward Connar. He prepared to do battle. But even as he tensed to lunge at the woman, Megan crashed into her from behind. The two women fell to the ground and the sword went flying. Connar went after the sword, but Siobhan reached it first and snatched it up. She wielded the sword wildly, her expression frantic.

Connar tried to decide how best to disarm her. As he hesitated, he was struck from behind. He went down, still gripping his sword.

He raised himself but was immediately pushed down again. Two women were on top of him, using their weight to keep him from getting up. With a roar, he rose to his hands and knees. He shoved them away and struggled to his feet.

The blond woman—Barbara—was trying to wrest the magical sword from Siobhan. Behind them, Allison screamed. Connar raised his own sword and tried to decide which woman represented the worst threat. Something crashed into him from behind and he went down again.

His two tormenters were back. He fought them off, but before he could get away, he heard an inhuman cry, followed by a scream.

Lunging upwards with all his strength, he threw off the two women and got to his feet.

The altar stone was empty.

He stared at it, the terrible awareness washing over him. *Allison was gone! He'd lost her!*

The sword fell from his nerveless fingers and he sank to the ground and brought his hands to his face. The despair drowned him like an enormous wave. *Too late. He was too late!*

Even as he let out a moan of grief, he heard someone else sobbing. Near him, his two attackers were moaning and making soft sounds of dismay. *How dare they show their distress? They were the ones who caused this!*

Enraged, he confronted the two women. "What are you weeping for?" he screamed. "You wanted this! You made it happen! I tried to stop it, but you wouldn't let me!"

His rage was terrible. He wanted to kill them. To pick up his sword and murder the whole lot of them!

Nay. Allison wouldn't want that. She wouldn't want more people to die. More people to suffer. The anger drained out of him, replaced by suffocating grief.

And then he heard it again. Sobbing coming from behind the altar stone. Soft. Plaintive. And yet, somehow familiar. It sounded like...

He approached the stone. The blond woman—Barbara—lay next to it. Her eyes were wide and staring. In her midsection was a gaping wound. The kind of wound a sword made.

A faint hope stirred inside him. If Barbara was dead and Siobhan had vanished, then that meant....

Even as he made his way around the stone, he told himself not to hope...

The blood seemed to drain from his body. Allison lay next to the stone. She was curled up, her eyes closed, her face contorted with weeping.

"Allison," he whispered. She stiffened and then looked up at him. Her eyes went wide. "Connar? Oh, Connar!"

She raised her bound hands as if to reach out to him. Her eyes shone with love, longing, and something else...grief. Terrible grief.

"Oh, Connar," she whispered. "I'm so glad you're safe. So glad. But, oh...oh!" She closed her eyes, once more overcome with grief. "She's gone. She's gone!"

He bent down to stroke her cheek, struggling to make his voice tender, even though the awareness that she was weeping for Siobhan infuriated him. "It's all right. It's what she wanted."

"No. No!" Allison shook her head wildly. "She never would have wanted *that*! What will she do? How will she survive? Oh, no!" She started sobbing again.

Connar was confused, and suddenly afraid. He'd thought the bond between himself and Allison was stronger than what she shared with Siobhan. But what if he was wrong? What if he'd broken her heart by preventing Siobhan from taking her back to the past?

He drew away from Allison, feeling more distraught than ever. He had to find Megan. She would know what to do. She would reassure him, tell him that Allison would get over this, that she loved him.

Megan? She was nowhere to be seen. What had happened? Had she been killed in the fight with Barbara? No wonder Allison was weeping.

But where was the body? Maybe Allison was wrong. Maybe Megan was badly wounded instead of dead.

"Megan?" he called out. "Megan?"

"It won't do any good." Allison's voice was choked. "She's gone. I saw her vanish. Siobhan took her!"

"Vanish? What are you talking about?" He couldn't make sense of it. Barbara had died, killed by the sword. And the magic had transported her spirit and Siobhan back to the past. But Megan...Megan couldn't be gone.

Allison let out a deep sigh. "I know. I can't believe it either. Maybe it's because Megan was touching Barbara when Siobhan killed her. Somehow the sword made Siobhan and Megan both disappear. Megan was trying to save me, and somehow ended up being affected by the spell. And Barbara, she knew how the magic worked, and she wanted to go back to the past. When she realized she wasn't going to be the one who killed me, she forced Siobhan to kill *her*." She let out another gasp of misery. "If only Megan hadn't gotten in the way. She was trying to protect me...and now she's gone!"

Connar didn't know what to say. As his shock faded, grief and loss welled up inside him. Megan had been his companion and partner over the last day. She had worked with him tirelessly to save Allison. He'd truly liked her. Nay, *loved* her. Like a sister. A dear, sweet sister.

Now she was gone. Just like that. Vanished to another time. His time.

He wanted to rescue her. To go back and save her, as he'd sought to do with Aisling in this time. But without the sword, it was impossible.

"Oh, Allison," he said. "I'm so sorry. Megan was so brave. So fearless. I've never known a warrior as valiant and bold." Crouching next to Allison, he began to loosen her bonds. "Megan isn't dead. And I believe she will survive and even thrive in the past. She's very strong and that will aid her. She will not let being in another time period defeat her."

Allison gave a hiccupping sob and then nodded. "You're right. No one is braver. Or stronger. Or a better friend. But that's why I'm crying. She was my best friend and now I'm never going to see her again!"

She broke down once more. And Connar struggling with the knots in the rope, let a few of his own tears fall.

Chapter Twenty

"Does being here bring back bad memories?" Connar asked.

Allison shook her head, but even as she did so, she couldn't help taking a tiny step back from the wildly churning waves below the cliff-face. "No. It doesn't bother me because you're here with me. Besides, there's no enraged mob chasing after me."

"I'm glad. I worried that coming here, to the site of the worst moments of your past life, would upset you."

"It's weird, but I actually haven't had any flashbacks at all since I've been in Ireland. It's almost like, now that I know who you are and who I am, my subconscious is content and all the memories, good and bad, have vanished." She turned to face him. "Does that bother you? That I don't recall what things were like between us back then?"

"As long as you love me in this time, I don't care if you remember anything about the past."

They shared a kiss, then Allison turned back to admire the view. The faint rays of the setting sun created subtle rainbows in the mist rising up from the sea and surrounded everything with a soft, pearlescent light. "This place is spectacular. I can see why you wanted to come here."

"The mountains of Colorado are beautiful, but there's nothing like Ireland. And yet..." He touched her arm so she turned to meet his gaze. His green eyes shone with warmth as he said. "The most important thing is being with you. Wherever you are, that's where my spirit feels content."

"I feel the same way," Allison whispered.

He leaned down to kiss her again.

A few moments later, she broke it off, laughing. "If we keep this up, we're going to have to go back to the bed-and-breakfast. It's a little damp to engage in love play here. I don't know how people managed in your era."

"Back then, cloaks and outer garments were woven with wool that still contained lanolin, so they were almost waterproof."

"But lying down on them must have been terribly uncomfortable. I can't even wear modern-day wool without anything under it. It's simply too scratchy!" She gave a mock shudder. "As much as I love you, Connar, I'm very glad we ended up in my time period rather than returning to yours."

He nodded. "The way things happened was definitely for the best."

"For us at least. But for Megan..."

He nodded, looking solemn.

Allison felt tears spring to her eyes. It had been almost a week since Connar had rescued her in the mountains, but she still felt a gnawing grief when she thought about what had happened to Megan.

"I have to believe Megan will make the best of things and find happiness," said Connar. "She's a very strong person."

"That's true. She always had such an upbeat, positive attitude. That will take you far in any era. But I can't imagine the challenges she'll face. She won't know the language, for one thing. Hopefully Siobhan will help her, but still, I don't know how you ever managed to learn modern English."

"It took me over two years, and even now I've been known to lapse into Irish at times. But it wasn't as difficult as it might have been. That surprised me in the beginning. Now I think I know the reason for it." Connar hesitated, then continued, "I think I was able to learn modern English so easily because I spoke it in another life…a life that I lived somewhere between the past I remember and this time period."

"Another life? How many lives do you think you've lived?"

"I don't know. Several, perhaps. But I don't want you to think that means we're not what they call soul mates. I followed you to this time because I knew we were meant to be together. Yet, I also believe I've lived other lives…lives where I was lonely and searching and never found you."

"It makes sense to me," Allison agreed. "Even before I met you there were times in my life when I experienced the sensation of having done something before. And not all of those experiences were necessarily connected to my past life with you."

Connar nodded. "When I arrived in Denver in this century, it wasn't as jarring as it should have been. There were things that came rather easily, such as the language. While I don't think I lived in America in a past life, there was definitely English spoken in the time I lived in. A lot of words weren't completely unfamiliar to me."

"Do you think Megan might have lived in Ireland

sometime in another life and that will help her adjust?"

"It seems likely, doesn't it, especially with her coloring."

"I hope you're right. And if nothing else, maybe in the past she'll find *her* soul mate. She does love the barbarian/he-man type. The minute she saw Mark, she was smitten. Of course, he looks more like a Viking than an Irish warrior."

"There *were* Vikings in Ireland."

"But not in your time, right?"

"It would have been a hundred years or so later. I do hope Megan gets some benefit out of being sent back to the past."

"If not, maybe she can get Siobhan to send her back to this time period," Allison mused. "After all, Siobhan has the magic sword."

The next moment she felt a surge of panic. She stared open-mouthed at Connar. "I've been trying so hard not to worry about these things. But now, mentioning Siobhan, I've just thought of something awful. What if she uses the sword to return to this time period and tries again to kill me so I'll go back to her era?"

Connar touched her arm soothingly. "I don't think that's possible. Her link to you is gone. She can't kill you in the past to travel to this era."

"But she could kill *Megan* and use her spirit to travel here. While it would be great to have Megan back, I hate the thought of Siobhan coming after me again. I know you'd do your best to protect me, and now that I know what Siobhan looks like, I wouldn't be such an easy target. But still…" Allison shuddered as she thought about how close she'd been to losing her life in this time, and losing Connar as well.

"I don't think killing Megan would work," Connar responded. "Even if Siobhan used Megan's spirit to travel to another era, there's no way Siobhan could be certain they'd end up in this century. Megan's spirit may have lived in several other times, and they could end up in any one of them. For that matter, since Barbara is the person whose death actually sent them back to the past, all three women might have ended up in a time connected to one of *her* lives."

"Oh, wow! That's right. Barbara is the one who was stabbed with the sword. It was her spirit they connected with. So, they could end up anywhere in time that Barbara has ever lived!"

"I don't know how the magic works," said Connar. "The only one who might know is Siobhan. She clearly understood the power of the sword much better than she ever revealed to me."

"I wonder how much she told Barbara," Allison said thoughtfully. "It still makes no sense to me that Barbara wanted to go back to the past so much that she let herself be killed."

"Perhaps Barbara remembered happy, positive things from another life and that was why she was willing to risk death here to return to the past."

"I suppose that must be it. Maybe she'd even used the magic before, and that's why she was willing to do it again. The whole thing is so unimaginable. If I hadn't seen for myself how Siobhan and Megan vanished as Siobhan drove the sword into Barbara's body, I would never believe it happened."

"Even more extraordinary is the way Barbara's body disappeared."

Allison nodded. Almost immediately after the three women had vanished, Rowan had taken charge. She'd insisted Allison and Connar drive Megan's car back to her apartment building. Meanwhile, one of the other women took Barbara's SUV to the mountains and someone else returned Sophia's car to her apartment complex in Denver. Once that was done, Rowan, Ginny, Rose and Stacy planned to meet back at the hilltop and perform a cleansing ceremony before burying Barbara's body somewhere nearby.

But when Connar called Rowan the next day to discuss what they were going to tell the authorities, Rowan insisted there was no need to worry. When she and the other women went back to the stone circle, Barbara's body had vanished, and there was no evidence—blood or anything else—it had ever been there.

Recalling Rowan's stunning news, Allison asked Connar, "Do you think we did the right thing, trusting Rowan's story rather than going to the stone circle to see for ourselves if Barbara's body was gone?"

"Rowan has no reason to make something like that up. If Barbara's body was still on the hillside somewhere, Rowan would be much more at risk of being charged with her murder than the rest of us. She was the one closest to Barbara, so the police would suspect her first."

"It seems so incredible her body would simply vanish."

"That might be part of the magic. Perhaps when Barbara's spirit reached the time and place of her new life and she no longer needed her body here, that's when it disappeared."

"If that's true, it means soon after you killed me when I was Aisling, my body must have vanished."

"Aye."

"In that time period, everyone would probably attribute my body's disappearance to my being a witch, or sorceress, or whatever they thought I was. But I don't think in the present day the authorities are going to buy that. They'll keep investigating, even if there are no bodies. I mean, for three women to vanish. It's bizarre. A lot of people are going to be very suspicious. Which makes me wonder if our traveling to Ireland was such a good idea."

"Why does that concern you?"

"It might look like we're running away because we're guilty."

"But guilty of what? If there are no bodies, how can they accuse us of murder without evidence someone has died?"

"They probably can't. But still…"

"Do you want to go back?"

She knew Connar was asking if she wanted to cut short their visit, rather than asking if she would be willing to live with him in Ireland. But over the past few days since they'd been here, she'd begun to wonder if she ever wanted to return to her life in Denver. Other than Benjamin—and there must surely be a way to bring him here—there was nothing she truly missed. All she'd left behind in Denver was the beginning of a writing career and a few friends, none of them nearly as dear as Megan.

"No. I don't want to go back. But I will tell you what I'd like to do, I'd like to see the valley where we met and the cave of the Nine Sisters."

Connar frowned. "Are you certain? I thought you wanted nothing to do with that part of your past life."

Allison shrugged. "I'm curious. Maybe seeing it will trigger some memory that will help me understand Siobhan and our relationship back then."

He still looked uncertain. "Although the valley was where I first met you, I can't help associating it with Fergal and all the suffering he caused." He shook his head. "My memories of my foster brother continue to haunt me. At one time we were close, and then he turned against me."

Allison nodded. "In one of my visions, I saw the two of you fighting. It was when you were practicing with Mark and I fainted. In the battle I saw, it looked like the other man, Fergal, was going to kill you. "

Connar nodded. "He could have, if it had been a battle to the death. I'd let him prevail, thinking it would prove the Sisters hadn't put a spell on him. But my plan didn't work. Even when he bested me in combat, Fergal wasn't satisfied. He insisted you had bewitched me, and that was why I lost the battle. He convinced my father, and my father insisted I must prove I wasn't under your spell by killing you. I refused, of course. But then Siobhan came to me with her plan. I was desperate. I didn't know what else to do." Connar gazed at her pleadingly. "I knew Siobhan loved you. I couldn't believe she would have me kill you unless she was very certain the magic would work."

"It turned out all right in the end," Allison soothed. "Siobhan's plan worked. You were able to follow my spirit to the future and reunite with me."

"Aye. But I still regret the pain I caused you in the past."

"It wasn't your fault." She took his arm. "Come on. It's time to face the past, all of it. That way we will banish its power to cause us distress."

He nodded slowly, and they headed back to the car.

"Perhaps here in Ireland, I'll learn to drive," he said as she started the rental vehicle.

"I'm actually doing okay with it, don't you think? I still struggle with all the roundabouts, but I'm getting there."

"Aye, you're doing very well."

"I guess now you're here, the word 'yes' is gone for good from your vocabulary," she teased.

"Do you mind?"

"Not at all. I've always loved the archaic, formal way you talk. It's part of what makes you unique."

For the next few minutes, Allison concentrated on driving. Connar directed her to take a side road leading away from the coast. After a few minutes, he said, "Stop here. We'll have to walk the rest of the way."

"Do you think we'll get in trouble for trespassing?"

"I hadn't really thought of that. I guess I assumed…" He shook his head. "In my era, everyone avoided this valley."

"Because they didn't want to encounter the Nine Sisters?"

"I suppose. Although there was a mist guarding the cave where they lived. I believe I only found it because they allowed me to."

They left the car and started walking. It was mostly pastureland, divided into smaller sections by ancient-looking stone fences. "Were there fences here in your time?" she asked.

"It was all common land. Most of the cattle

belonged to my father. The sheep belonged his clients, who paid tribute in wool."

Gazing at the landscape, Allison tried to imagine how it must have looked in Connar's day, an unbroken mass of vivid green.

He stopped for a moment, squinting into the distance. "Everything is so different. I wonder if I'll be able to find the valley." A few seconds later, he started walking again. "I think it's farther over."

They walked in silence. Allison inhaled the sweet scent of grass and wildflowers, glorying in the extravagant vegetation. There was something about this place, something distinctly familiar. All at once, she knew where she was. She called out to Connor, a few steps ahead of her. "It's this way."

He turned around, looking startled. "You know where we're going?"

"It's coming back to me." Seeing how worried he looked, she added. "It's all right. I don't feel scared or anxious. In fact, I'm kind of excited."

She started walking, feeling the steady pull of... What was it, this sense of having been here before? The sensation grew as they climbed uphill.

****

Connar followed Allison, feeling the tension build inside him. Despite her enthusiasm, he worried what she would remember and how it might affect her. What if returning to the cave awakened her memories of the Nine Sisters? They might still have a hold on her. What if their spirits were calling out to her, and that was why she wanted to go to the cave?

As if to match his uneasy mood, the sun vanished behind a cloud and the day turned gray and gloomy.

Although he was used to the fickle Irish weather, the rapid change struck Connar as ominous. When they reached the top of the hill and looked down to see a dense mist obscuring the landscape below, his anxiety turned to dread. Did the magic of the Nine Sisters still guard this valley after all these centuries? What if they meant to reclaim Allison's spirit?

"I don't think we should go down there," he said.

She turned, looking puzzled. "Why not?"

He gestured helplessly. What could he say? He had no right to keep her from them.

She smiled. "It's all right. Nothing's going to happen. I just need to see, to know..." Her eyes were pleading.

He nodded, although his insides felt as if they had turned to stone. When she started down the hill, he followed.

The first time he'd come here and encountered the mist, he'd refused to be afraid. His determination to save Fergal, lying senseless in the cart behind him, had driven him on. As he'd made his way into the valley, the mist had thinned and he'd seen Aisling and Siobhan waiting for him.

But this time, the mist didn't thin. It grew denser, until he could barely see Allison walking a few feet ahead of him. How did she know where she was going?

Abruptly, she halted.

He pulled up behind her and put his hands on her waist. "Allison, what is it?"

"Don't you see them?" She pointed. "They're in a circle. One...two...three...four..." She paused. "Nine, I think. It must be them. It must be the Nine Sisters."

He couldn't see anything. A cloud of mist, as thick

and tangible as a stone wall, blocked his view.

As she started forward, he let go of her waist. If she wanted to go to them, he would not stop her. He had no right to interfere.

Nor could he follow. Fear froze him where he stood. *Nay, Aisling...Allison...don't leave me. They may love you, but not the way I do. And I need you. I can't bear the thought of living without you!*

The sound of her laughter came to him, exultant and magically lovely. "Connar," she called. "Come look! You won't believe it."

He moved forward, his feet heavy. His flesh seemed to turn to ice, even as his heart froze in grief.

Slowly, the dark figures emerged out of the pale mist. Nine of them, aye, there were nine. *Nine standing stones.*

Connar halted, unable to believe what he was seeing. Nine standing stones arranged in a circle. They were of varying heights and shapes. Looking at them, seeing the slight differences between them, he could almost imagine them as the various Sisters. Was not that short, rounded stone Nuala? The majestic pale one, their leader, Maebbina?

The others he wasn't certain of. He wondered, was there any way to tell? Was it possible one of the stones was Siobhan?

Allison came to stand beside him. "I don't suppose these stones were here in your time period?"

He shook his head. A part of him was still afraid that at any moment, the standing stones would turn into the Sisters and they would take Allison away from him.

"For that matter," he said, "there aren't supposed to be any standing stones here in this era either. When I looked on the map when I was trying to find how to get to the cliffs, there was no marker indicating a stone circle here."

"Maybe when the Sisters died...they turned to stone."

"Perhaps."

"I wonder. Do you think Siobhan is one of them? Do you think when she went back in time, she ended up here?"

"I don't know."

"And who's the ninth one? If I'm still alive, in fleshly form, then how can there be nine stones here? Unless I exist in both forms as once."

The thought of Allison, even only an incarnation of her in the past, turned to stone, horrified Connar. But then he considered something else. "There were actually ten women who lived in the cave, counting you. When they performed the ceremony to heal Fergal, you didn't take part, as you weren't yet one of the Sisters. I think you were in training and meant to take the place of the oldest, frailest woman. When she died, you would finally become one of the Sisters."

"But that never happened. Because you killed me and sent me to the future."

He nodded.

"It's all pretty crazy, isn't it?"

"Aye."

"But it turned out all right in the end. Because our spirits found each other in this lifetime. And now we know nothing can keep us apart."

"Aye. Not even death."

She drew near, smiling, and kissed him.

Even as he savored the sweet magic of her lips

against his and the feel of her slender body in his arms, the swirling mist around them vanished and golden sunshine poured over them. And finally, he knew the spell of the past was broken and there was only the future ahead of them.

A word from the author...

I am fascinated by history, as well as by Celtic myth and legend. These interests inspire and enrich my books, both romance and fantasy. Raised in the Midwest, I currently live in Wyoming with my husband and four very spoiled cats and a somewhat spoiled dog. I also have two grown children and have worked at the local public library for over twenty years. In my spare time, I enjoy gardening, travel, and reading, of course!

Thank you for purchasing
this publication of The Wild Rose Press, Inc.

If you enjoyed the story, we would appreciate your
letting others know by leaving a review.

For other wonderful stories,
please visit our on-line bookstore at
www.thewildrosepress.com.

For questions or more information
contact us at
info@thewildrosepress.com.

The Wild Rose Press, Inc.
www.thewildrosepress.com

Stay current with The Wild Rose Press, Inc.

Like us on Facebook

https://www.facebook.com/TheWildRosePress

And Follow us on Twitter
https://twitter.com/WildRosePress